THE BOOK LOVER'S EUROPEAN BUCKET LIST

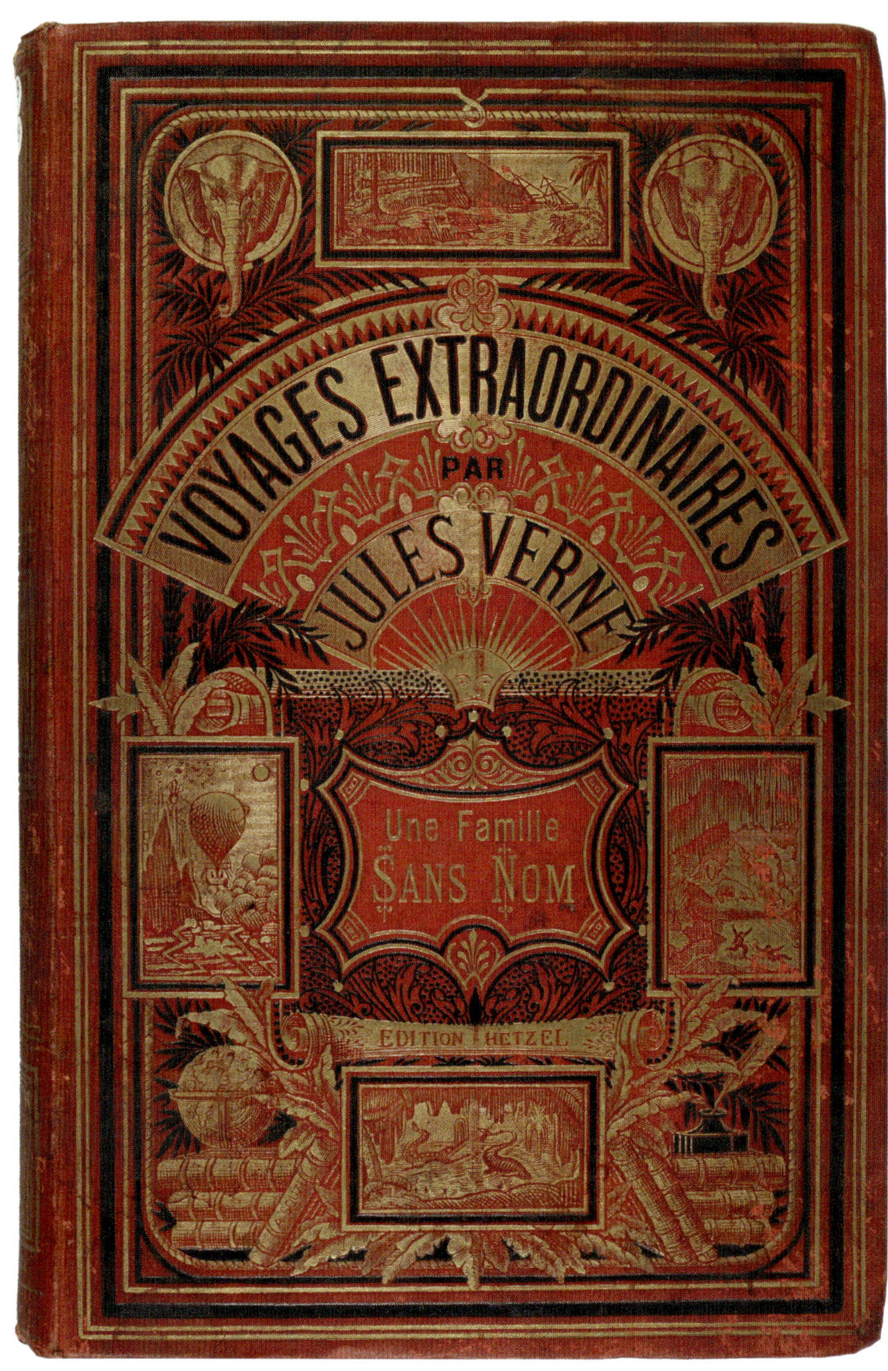
VOYAGES EXTRAORDINAIRES
PAR
JULES VERNE
Une Famille
SANS NOM
EDITION HETZEL

CAROLINE TAGGART

THE BOOK LOVER'S EUROPEAN BUCKET LIST

A LITERARY GRAND TOUR

BRITISH LIBRARY

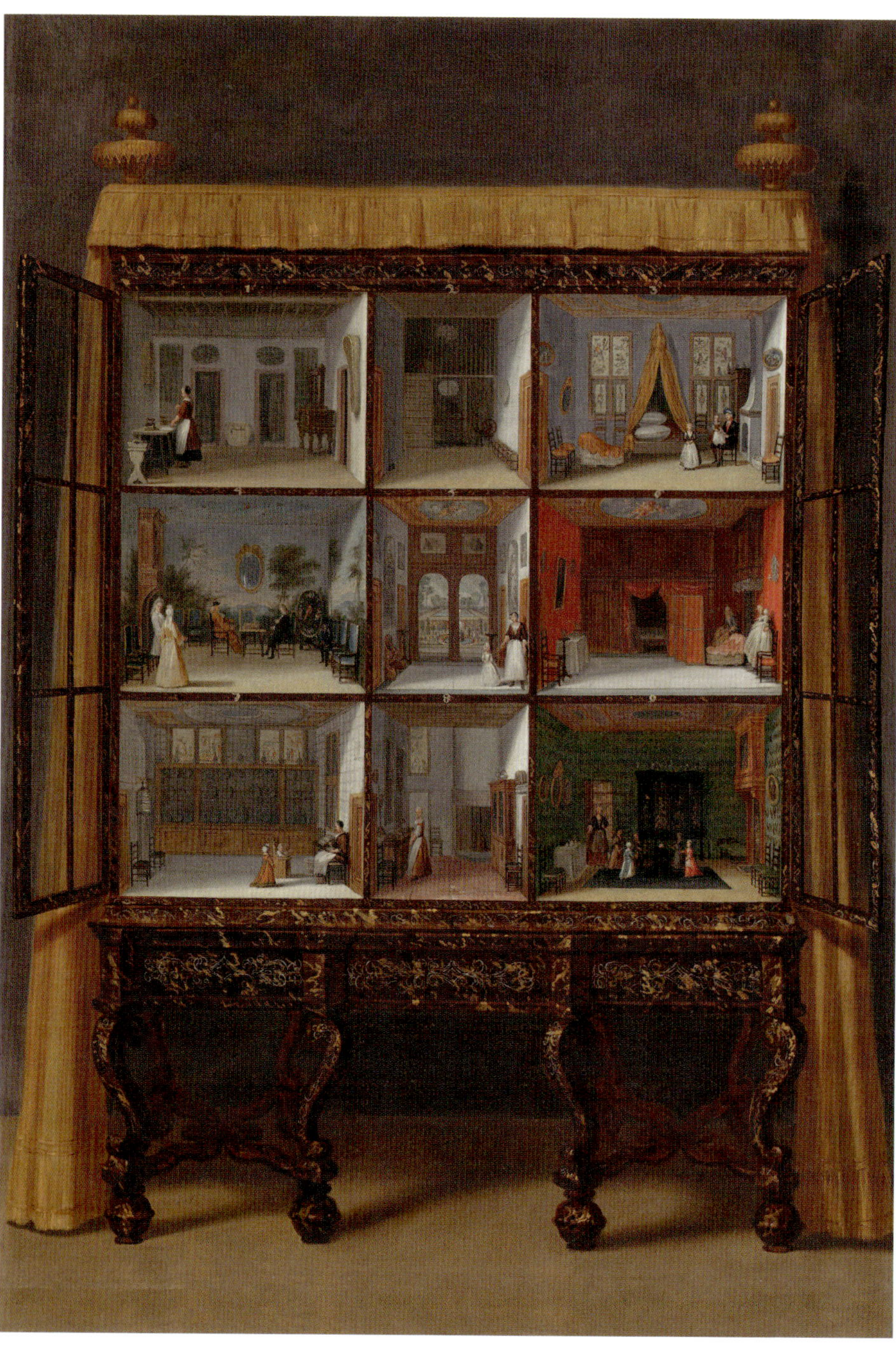

CONTENTS

BELGIUM & THE NETHERLANDS

GERMANY & POLAND

SCANDINAVIA

AUSTRIA, SWITZERLAND & THE CZECH REPUBLIC

ITALY

SPAIN & PORTUGAL

INTRODUCTION

A comprehensive literary guide to Europe would be a very large volume indeed, and anyone setting out to produce such a thing would be bound to provoke carping responses from readers annoyed at the omission of such and such a place in Liechtenstein or Albania or San Marino. So this book makes no such claims. It confines itself largely to Western Europe – with a few nods further east, to people who cried out to be included: Tove Jansson in Finland, Joseph Conrad in Poland, Franz Kafka in the Czech Republic. And it concentrates on places, urban or rural, that are closely associated with writers and/or their works.

Even so: from so many, which writers to choose? Well, there are those whose works have survived for so many centuries and been translated into so many languages that – no matter where we come from or what language we speak – they have crossed our path. We think we must have read them, or at least feel a bit guilty if we haven't: Shakespeare, Dante, Cervantes, all that crowd. If those names feel a bit daunting, though, the list of 'most translated books' contains some surprisingly approachable ones: children's favourites *The Adventures of Pinocchio*, *Alice's Adventures in Wonderland* and the tales of Hans Christian Andersen and the Brothers Grimm all feature in Wikipedia's Top Ten, and the 'father of science fiction', Jules Verne, is the third most translated author of all time (beaten only by those who contributed to the Bible, and by Agatha Christie).

Some writers evoke their settings so vividly that just to visit those settings is to immerse yourself in their work: think Venice as conjured in Donna Leon's Commissario Brunetti novels, the Naples of Elena Ferrante's *My Brilliant Friend*, Harry Hole's Oslo in Jo Nesbø's dark thrillers. Many great cities – Dublin, Edinburgh, Berlin, Kraków – have inspired such a vast range of authors that simply to wander their streets is to follow in sets upon sets of literary footsteps.

The attraction of Europe's various cultures, liberal attitudes and (to British writers drawn to Italy in particular) salubrious climate means that many places with literary associations are connected with expatriate authors: the Shakespeare and Company bookshop in Paris with the Irish James Joyce and the American Ernest Hemingway; Rome with the English poets Keats and Shelley; and the Reichenbach Falls in Switzerland with the Scottish-born creator of Sherlock Holmes, Sir Arthur Conan Doyle. The Frenchman Alexandre Dumas travelled in Belgium, Russia and Italy; and the Russian Ivan Turgenev spent time in Dresden, which was then part of the Kingdom of Saxony, though it had previously been the home of the Polish monarchs and would shortly afterwards join the newly formed Germany.

So the purpose of this book is two-fold: to encourage you, if you've read a book, to visit the place where it is set; and to inspire you, if you've visited a place, to read the book or see the play that is associated with it. Although I've included plenty of museums and historic birthplaces, there are also the wild western shores of Ireland that inspired John Millington Synge, and the Swiss Alps where you can follow the Heidi adventure trail; cemeteries in which to pay your respects to Oscar Wilde, Émile Zola or Wilfred Owen; cafés where you can linger over a coffee or a cognac and imagine you are waiting for Simone de Beauvoir or the great Portuguese *flâneur* Fernando Pessoa. Just remember to take a book with you, in case they don't turn up.

A Note on Visiting

The opening times given at the start of entries are intended as a guide only. Many sites keep shorter hours from October to March than they do the rest of the year; some open late one evening a week; some are largely closed during the winter, but put on special events at Christmas. There may be a *fermeture exceptionnelle* at short notice, because of the weather or because someone suddenly needs a wedding venue. Many – even those that don't charge an entrance fee – require or advise you to book a timed slot. It's always a good idea to check in advance.

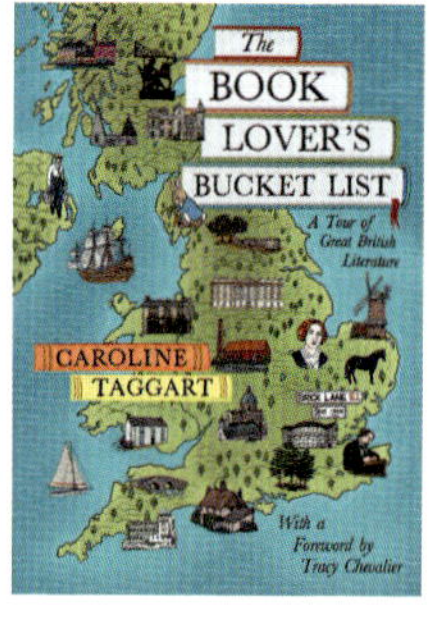

The Book Lover's Bucket List
A Tour of Great British Literature
ISBN: 987 0 7123 5324 3

The first book in Caroline's best-selling literary bucket list series, based on the UK and Ireland, was published by the British Library in 2021.

FRANCE

NOTRE-DAME
DE PARIS.
ΑΝΑΓΚΗ

Notre-Dame de Paris
Victor Hugo

notredamedeparis.fr

The original, French, title of what the English-speaking world calls *The Hunchback of Notre-Dame* is simply *Notre-Dame de Paris*, the name of Paris's iconic cathedral, where much of the novel is set. Yes, the hunchback Quasimodo's doomed love for the beautiful gypsy Esmeralda is in there – that isn't entirely a Disney fantasy – but in Victor Hugo's novel it's Notre-Dame itself that is the star.

Hugo (1802–1885), politician and activist as well as poet, playwright and novelist, was a passionate champion of the unfashionable French Gothic style of architecture embodied in Notre-Dame (and in the cathedrals of Chartres, Reims and others). To him it was a symbol of much that was valuable in French culture, which he saw as being under threat. The six-hundred-year-old Notre-Dame had been badly damaged during the French Revolution and, at the time Hugo was writing forty years later, was desperately in need of restoration. Still in his twenties when *The Hunchback of Notre-Dame* was published in 1831, he was already a leading literary figure, and what he wrote carried weight. It isn't so much that he wrote a novel about an iconic building: rather that by making that neglected building the centrepiece of his novel, he turned it into an icon.

A huge fire in 2019 all but destroyed Notre-Dame; if the vast programme of repair runs to schedule (which, incredibly, it seems to be doing at the time of writing) it will have been completed by the time you read this. You can already go down into the crypt – the most important archaeological crypt in Europe, belonging to an earlier church that occupied the square in front – and see the impressive remains of the various buildings that have been constructed there since Roman times. The new spire is intended to be an exact replica of the old one; although the one that burned down dated only from 1859, it was itself a fairly accurate copy of the original, so the twenty-first-century replacement will be recognisable to a time-travelling visitor from the thirteenth century, or indeed from the fifteenth, when the novel is set. The towers – and the post-Revolution replacements of Quasimodo's beloved bells – survived the fire, but whether you will ever again be able to climb up to visit them remains to be seen. You can still hear them, though, and in so doing you can share in the love Quasimodo felt for them, even though he couldn't hear them himself:

What he loved above all else in the maternal edifice ... that which sometimes rendered him even happy, was the bells. He loved them, fondled them, talked to them, understood them. From the chime in the spire, over the intersection of the aisles and nave, to the great bell of the front, he cherished a tenderness for them all. The central spire and the two towers were to him as three great cages, whose birds, reared by himself, sang for him alone. Yet it was these very bells which had made him deaf; but mothers often love best that child which has caused them the most suffering.

It isn't just the bells: the entire cathedral looms large over all the events of the novel. First, it nurtures the child Quasimodo:

Notre-Dame had been to him successively, as he grew up and developed, the egg, the nest, the house, the country, the universe.

Later, it is the place of sanctuary where Quasimodo can keep Esmeralda safe when he has rescued her from the gallows. Then, when Esmeralda has been arrested again (betrayed by Archdeacon Frollo because she has rejected his advances), the action moves to the north tower – the one from which public executions in the Place de l'Hôtel de Ville can be seen. Quasimodo, unaware that Esmeralda is to be hanged that day, discovers Frollo in the tower, gloating over her imminent death. In a burst of fury, the hunchback tips the priest over the balustrade. In this climactic moment, the architecture really takes centre stage:

The abyss was there below him. A fall of more than two hundred feet and the pavement.

In this terrible situation, the archdeacon said not a word, uttered not a groan. He merely writhed upon the spout, with incredible efforts to climb up again; but his hands had no hold on the granite, his feet slid along the blackened wall without catching fast. People who have ascended the towers of Notre-Dame know that there is a swell of the stone immediately beneath the balustrade. It was on this retreating angle that the miserable archdeacon exhausted himself. He had not to deal with a perpendicular wall, but with one which sloped away beneath him.

Nurturing mother, sanctuary for the persecuted and now executioner, righter of wrongs. No one who read Hugo's novel looked at the cathedral in the same way again.

Victor Hugo's Homes, Guernsey and Paris
Victor Hugo

maisonsvictorhugo.paris.fr/en/museum-collections/place-des-vosges-apartment-visit
victorhugo.visitguernsey.com/hauteville
Open April to September; closed Wednesdays

If you find yourself in Guernsey on a wet day, you may well choose to visit Victor Hugo's house there: it's one of the island's principal indoor attractions. As a politician as well as an author in his early years in Paris, Hugo championed the rights of the poor and advocated universal suffrage and free education. He wasn't the sort of man to support (or keep quiet under) a dictatorship, so when a coup in 1851 gave the former president Louis Napoleon absolute power as the Emperor Napoleon III, Hugo found himself banished from France. He subsequently lived in Hauteville, on the outskirts of St Peter Port, for fifteen years. It was the only house he owned, rather than rented, in the course of his long life, and he designed every tile and hanging himself. His son Charles Hugo described the house as 'an autograph on three floors and a poem in several rooms'.

The guides who take you around speak reverently of the great man's achievements and of the attention to detail that he paid to the decoration of his home, but you may find yourself distracted by the sheer over-the-topness of the place. Hugo may have loved sitting in his belvedere overlooking the town, but the densely patterned hangings and upholstery won't be to everyone's taste. Downstairs, the fireplace bedecked with staggered rows of tiles is reminiscent of a Mesopotamian ziggurat, while the Chinese salon with its intricately carved ornaments, and crimson damask even on the ceiling, is perhaps just a touch claustrophobic. Be grateful that Hugo did much of his thinking in the small and unpretentious garden: it gives you an excuse to go out and get a breath of air. Here, the centrepiece is the so-called 'United States of Europe oak', planted by Hugo himself in the hope that it would live to see a united and peaceful Europe; you can also see his 'contemplation bench' and take in a lovely view over the harbour.

If you don't happen to be in Guernsey, or it's too fine to be indoors, never fear. You can get a feel for Hugo's home there if you visit the apartment he rented in Paris for sixteen years before his Hauteville days, in the upmarket Place des Vosges. Now a museum, it's divided into three phases – pre-exile, exile and post-exile – and guides you through the story of his life and work.

By the time Hugo moved to Place des Vosges in 1832 he had established himself as a poet and playwright, and had published the hugely successful *Hunchback of Notre-Dame* (see page 13) the previous year. Firmly at the centre of the French Romantic movement, he entertained other notable literary figures such as Alexandre Dumas (see page 47), the poet Alphonse de Lamartine and the author and critic Théophile Gautier in a salon hung with red damask, which today also displays various family portraits and a marble bust of Hugo himself. If you look closely at the décor, you'll see numerous instances of the monograms VH and JD, the latter referring to the actress Juliette Drouet, who was Hugo's mistress, secretary and constant companion for fifty years until her death in 1883.

The 'exile' section of the museum is the most striking of the three, because it has recreated two of the Hauteville rooms with furniture brought from there: the lounge featuring Chinese panels on the walls, to complement the author's collection of porcelain; and the dining room furnished in the Gothic and Renaissance styles. Much of the furniture for this room, which Hugo sought out himself, was dismantled from its original form and reassembled by skilled carpenters under his direction – the table-top is a converted door, spools of thread have been reconfigured as candleholders, chests have been turned into sideboards or benches. Like the house in Guernsey, it shows an attention to detail that borders intriguingly on the obsessive.

Hugo returned from exile in 1870, after Napoleon III had been overthrown and the republic re-established. By this time he was a national hero; there was a period when he was a serious candidate for head of state. Although he didn't go back to the Place des Vosges, the museum has replicated his study from his last years; its chief attractions are the portrait by Léon Bonnat and the bust by Auguste Rodin, both of them showing him as a revered elder-statesmanlike figure. Finally, you see a recreation of his last bedroom, including the Sèvres vase presented to him by the government on the occasion of his eightieth birthday – further evidence of Hugo's importance, as gifts of that style and value were usually reserved for royalty. That same birthday was marked by a parade that took six hours to pass Hugo's house, where he watched from a window. A painting by Jean-François Raffaëlli – in the museum's collection but not always on display – shows crowds, including very small children, waving hats and flags at the old man on the balcony above their heads. When he died two years later his funeral took place under the Arc de Triomphe, where, according to the *New York Times*, six funeral orations were delivered 'in the presence of nearly all the illustrious men in and of France'. His coffin was then carried to the Panthéon – a burial place reserved for the greatest of the great and good – in a procession joined by two million people. You can see his tomb there, in a vault he shares with Alexandre Dumas and Émile Zola (see page 34).

Say what you like about all that crimson damask, this was a man who had made his mark.

Paris Opera House
Gaston Leroux

operadeparis.fr

Guided tours every day unless there's a matinee performance

Something was very wrong. Instead of producing her usual bell-like notes, the soprano was croaking like a toad:

> *The house broke into a wild tumult. The two managers collapsed in their chairs and dared not even turn round; they had not the strength; the ghost was chuckling behind their backs! And, at last, they distinctly heard his voice in their right ears, the impossible voice, the mouthless voice, saying:*
>
> *'SHE IS SINGING TO NIGHT TO BRING THE CHANDELIER DOWN!'*
>
> *With one accord, they raised their eyes to the ceiling and uttered a terrible cry. The chandelier, the immense mass of the chandelier was slipping down,*

coming toward them, at the call of that fiendish voice. Released from its hook, it plunged from the ceiling and came smashing into the middle of the stalls, amid a thousand shouts of terror. A wild rush for the doors followed.

That fiendish, mouthless voice may have been a figment of Gaston Leroux's imagination, but the basic incident was true enough. On 20 May 1896, one of the weights holding a chandelier in place above the auditorium of the Paris Opera House came loose and fell into the audience, killing a woman sitting beneath it. Leroux (1868–1927), then a budding journalist, reported on the incident for his newspaper and later incorporated it into his most famous novel.

The Phantom of the Opera (1910) has, of course, reached a wider audience in various guises since its initial publication. But whether you know the story from the book, the numerous films or the musical version, you can trace its source to the Paris Opera House, also known as Opéra Garnier, after its architect, or Palais Garnier, because of its opulence. The building was commissioned during the reign of Emperor Napoleon III (1852–70) and built in the Second-Empire style named after his reign: part Baroque, part Gothic Revival, part Renaissance, no surface inside or out left unadorned. Grand Guignol isn't a style of architecture, but if it were, the Opéra Garnier would be its crowning glory: sensational, extravagant, designed to make an audience gasp.

You can do a tour any day that there isn't a matinee, and even without a fiendish voice in your ear you are likely to be struck dumb. Having admired the facade, with its many columns, arches, gilded statues and a frieze bearing the initials NE for Napoléon Empereur, you enter a much-carved lobby from which a double-sided staircase in various colours of marble curves around a statue of Pythia, High Priestess of Apollo, god of the arts.

Before climbing the stairs to the auditorium, see if you can peek through the grating that covers the underground 'lake'. This is hardly the place for the romantic boat ride you may have seen on stage; more a giant basin than a natural water feature, it came into being as a practical solution to a serious problem. Back in the 1860s, workers digging the foundations for the building hit an arm of the Seine and found it impossible to pump all the water out; the only alternative to moving site altogether was to contain the water in a sort of cistern. Like the tragedy with the chandelier, it was a real-life event that Leroux could adapt to good effect.

Upstairs, the auditorium itself is everything that the staircase may have led you to expect. The seats and hangings are a rich red and practically everything else is gilded: the three tiers of boxes and the columns separating them, all intricately carved with theatrical masks, leaves, curlicues – you name it, it's golden. Only the ceiling 65 feet (20 metres) above your head strikes a slightly

discordant note. When Leroux describes the scene as the two managers make their way to box five on the grand tier (the box that they have been instructed to place at the disposal of the Opera ghost for every performance), he mentions figures 'lost in M. Lenepveu's copper ceiling, [that] grinned and grimaced, laughed and jeered at MM. Richard and Moncharmin's distress'.

It must have been the Phantom's malign influence that made the figures grimace: in fact, they were perfectly friendly-looking Muses floating through the heavens. But Jules-Eugène Lenepveu's ceiling is no longer visible: his style fell out of fashion in the mid-twentieth century and was replaced in the 1960s by the painting you see today. Created by pioneering modernist/surrealist Marc Chagall, the new ceiling depicts scenes from the works of great composers through the ages, including Tchaikovsky's *Swan Lake*, Bizet's *Carmen*, Wagner's *Tristan and Isolde* and Mozart's *The Magic Flute*, each on its own panel and forming a circle some 55 feet (17 metres) in diameter. Every panel has its own dominant colour (*Swan Lake* is golden yellow, *Carmen* bold red) and sixty years on, opinion remains divided as to whether the result is a great work of art or an abomination at complete variance with Garnier's original concept. The nay-sayers may yet win out: Chagall's work is on canvas and is glued to panels rather than directly on to the ceiling, so if one day fashions change again we may be able to have another look at Lenepveu's Muses. There's something pleasingly *Grand Guignol*, pleasingly Phantomesque, about the idea of one ceiling lurking behind another, ready to re-emerge when the moment is right.

And what about box five on the grand tier? Well, it isn't the greatest seat in the house: it's too side-on to the stage. On the other hand, it has an excellent view of the auditorium. If you had arranged to have a chandelier fall on some unsuspecting member of the audience and wanted to watch it happen, you couldn't ask for a better spot.

Shakespeare and Company, Paris
James Joyce, Ernest Hemingway and others

shakespeareandcompany.com

In those days there was no money to buy books. I borrowed books from the rental library of Shakespeare and Company, which was the library and bookstore of Sylvia Beach at 12 rue de l'Odéon. On a cold windswept street, this was a warm, cheerful place with a big stove in winter, tables and shelves of books, new books in the window, and photographs on the wall of famous writers both dead and living ...

I was very shy when I first went into the bookshop and I did not have enough money on me to join the rental library. [Beach] told me I could pay the deposit any time I had the money and made me out a card and said I could take as many books as I wished.

There was no reason for her to trust me. She did not know me and the address I had given her, 74 rue Cardinal Lemoine, could not have been a poorer one. But she was delightful and charming and welcoming and behind her, as high as the wall and stretching out into the back room which gave onto the inner court of the building, were shelves and shelves of the wealth of the library.

This is a young, unknown and impoverished Ernest Hemingway (1899–1961), in his memoir *A Moveable Feast* (published posthumously in 1964). He's in Paris in the early 1920s and has found American Sylvia Beach (1887–1962), who moved to Paris towards the end of the First World War and opened an English-language bookshop and library, Shakespeare and Company, on the arty Left Bank in 1919. Its aim was to promote and encourage innovative writing, an aim which reached its apotheosis in 1922, when the company published James Joyce's *Ulysses* (see page 204). In an interview Beach gave towards the end of her life, she expressed the opinion that Americans had flocked to Paris because of two serious causes of discontent in their homeland: 'They couldn't get drink – it was Prohibition – and they couldn't get *Ulysses*.' She had met Joyce at a party and told him about her bookshop; he soon became a regular and told her about *Ulysses* being suppressed in the United States. According to her version of the story, she – completely inexperienced as a publisher – asked him, 'Would you like me to publish it?' It really was as simple as that.

French, British, Irish and American writers and readers all frequented 12 rue de l'Odéon: French poet Louis Aragon (1897–1982) would come in and recite his poems; Hemingway, whose day job was as a sports reporter, taught Beach about boxing and cycling; she stocked the works of Samuel Beckett (1906–1989) 'when no one was reading him in English'. Up-and-coming Americans F. Scott Fitzgerald (1896–1940), Thornton Wilder (1897–1975) and John Dos Passos (1896–1970) were also 'part of the crowd': 'We knew all the young American writers at that time, because they were all abroad.'

Shakespeare and Company was forced to close after the Nazi invasion of 1940, and the current bookshop of that name honours Sylvia Beach's memory. Founded in 1951, not far away on rue de la Bûcherie, in a seventeenth-century building that used to be a monastery, it was originally called Le Mistral, but changed its name in 1964, the four-hundredth anniversary of William Shakespeare's birth. From the first, founder George Whitman (1913–2011, another American) sought to carry on the spirit of Beach's shop, inviting aspiring writers not only to browse but in times of need to sleep there. His list

of early visitors includes James Baldwin and Richard Wright (see next entry below), Lawrence Durrell (1912–1990) and Allen Ginsberg (1926–1997): the new incarnation of Shakespeare and Company became as much a hub of literary Paris in the 1950s and 1960s as the original had been in the 1920s and 1930s. The shop, now run by George's daughter, Sylvia Whitman (named in honour of her illustrious predecessor), continues to encourage new writers. Jeanette Winterson (born 1959), in her introduction to a 2016 history of the two stores (the wonderfully subtitled *Shakespeare and Company: A History of the Rag & Bone Shop of the Heart*), likened the modern incarnation to a Tardis, 'modest enough on the outside, a labyrinth on the inside':

> *A rickety staircase carries you like a fairy-tale hero to a warren of rooms on the first floor where you will find treasure. There's a piano, a typewriter in a booth, a few armchairs, a couple of cats, a big reading room looking out onto Notre-Dame ...*

Shakespeare and Company, she tells us, 'is a reminder that business and pleasure can go together'.

If that is no bad accolade, here are two more: Hemingway wrote of Sylvia Beach, 'No one that I ever knew was nicer to me', while George Whitman displayed a sign in his shop that perfectly summed up Beach's ethos: 'Be not inhospitable to strangers, lest they be angels in disguise.'

Bohemian Paris
Simone de Beauvoir, James Baldwin, Ernest Hemingway and others

lesdeuxmagots.fr
cafedeflore.fr
lacoupole-paris.com
larotonde-montparnasse.fr
restaurant-ledome.com

James Baldwin (1924–1987), black and gay in a time when it wasn't easy to be either in the United States, escaped to Paris at the age of twenty-four; it was a move that enabled him to write and be recognised not as a black writer, but simply as a writer. One of his early essays included a criticism of the work of fellow Afro-American expatriate Richard Wright (1908–1960), whom Baldwin accused of stereotyping the black situation. The two men had a major falling out, but Paris was clearly big enough to house them both: Baldwin remained

for ten years and produced his best-known work, while Wright, who had moved there two years earlier, used it as his base for the rest of his life.

Paris in the first half of the twentieth century didn't attract only black American authors. Its many cafés – often glamorous, lavishly decorated Art Deco establishments – were full of aspiring writers and artists from all over France as well as Britain and the United States, most of them impoverished intellectuals who drank, danced and never seemed to go to bed – at least, not to sleep. In addition to Wright and Baldwin, James Joyce (see page 204), Henry Miller (1891–1980), Ernest Hemingway (1899–1961), Jean-Paul Sartre (1905–1980), Simone de Beauvoir (1908–1986), Albert Camus (1913–1960) and many others could generally be found in one or other of these cafés, mostly in the Montparnasse and Saint-Germain areas of the Left Bank, making a single cup of coffee last as long as they decently could before having to buy another, debating politics or philosophy with others of their circle, or working on their latest novel in surroundings that were warmer than their own lodgings.

If you begin at Saint-Germain-des-Prés métro station, you'll find Les Deux Magots facing you, with Café de Flore a few doors to the west. Magots are mandarins or Chinese businessmen, and the two statues that give the café its name still adorn the dining room, as they have done since the place opened in 1884. Choose your table carefully and you'll also find a photograph of Pablo Picasso and his lover and muse, the photographer Dora Maar, gazing out at you.

Simone de Beauvoir was a regular at Café de Flore during the Second World War and her description of it – in her memoir, *The Prime of Life* (published in 1960, but covering the years 1929–44) – paints a vivid picture that

Market Stalls and Smoky Bistros

One place you can't visit as you could in the 1950s is Les Halles, once Paris's central market for fresh food, and a useful breakfast venue if you had been up all night. In James Baldwin's *Giovanni's Room* (1956), it is the destination on the morning after the naive American narrator David has met the irresistible Italian Giovanni. There, 'on the sidewalks, in the streets, before great metal sheds', they find vast gleaming mounds of all sorts of fruits and vegetables, trucked in and out from every corner of France. Giovanni obviously loves it, but David remarks that 'Nothing here reminded me of home'.

Les Halles is a modern shopping centre now, so – sadly – you won't find walls and corners 'combed with *pissoirs*, dull-burning, makeshift braziers, cafés, restaurants, and smoky yellow bistros', as David and Giovanni did.

Life Lessons in Paris

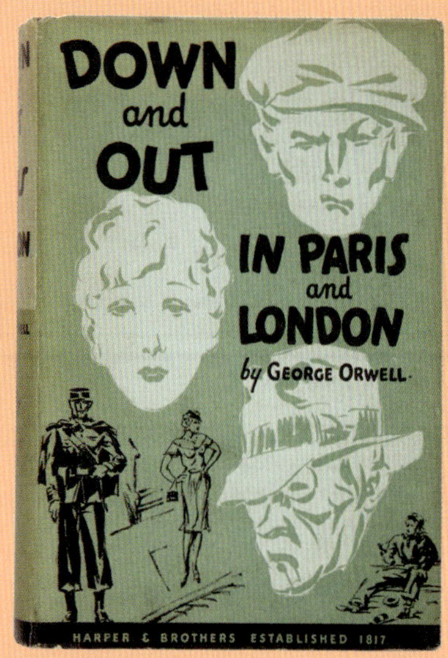

There's a big difference, of course, between being bohemian and being down and out. George Orwell (1903–1950) has to survive on a very few francs a day during the time he describes in *Down and Out in Paris and London* (1933), and he doesn't frequent cafés. Instead, he does a lot of walking, often in the company of his Russian refugee friend Boris, looking for work. On their first day of job hunting they cover about nine miles/fourteen kilometres on pavement and are so tired that they waste precious funds to get the métro home; on another fruitless day they cross the Seine eleven times. Orwell is soon reduced to patronising a pawnshop with 'grandiose stone portals (marked, of course, "*Liberté, Egalité, Fraternité*" – they write that even over the police stations in France)'. Here he receives seventy francs for a bundle of clothes he had valued at two to three hundred and acquires a useful life lesson:

> *Afterwards, when it was too late, I learned that it was wiser to go to a pawnshop in the afternoon. The clerks are French, and, like most French people, are in a bad temper till they have eaten their lunch.*

could have applied equally well to a dozen other cafés in the *quartier*, filling up in the course of the day:

> *...till by aperitif time it was packed. You would see Picasso there, smiling at Dora Maar, who had her big dog on the lead ... a noisy discussion would always be going on at the cinéastes' table – they had been meeting there almost daily since 1939.*

She goes on to describe two elderly locals who were also regulars: one was afflicted by a disease of the prostate and had 'some kind of apparatus' bulging under his trouser leg; the other, obviously a social cut above the rest, used to play dominoes with two young women, both rumoured to be 'kept' by him.

These particular attractions may not be on offer today, but the Flore was lucky enough to escape war damage, so that what you see is the original Art Deco interior. It also maintains its literary traditions: the Prix de Flore, awarded annually to a promising young French-language author, is named after it and the presentation takes place here.

From the Flore, turn south towards Boulevard du Montparnasse and you'll find a cluster of three more cafés: La Coupole, La Rotonde and Le Dôme. La Coupole is another that still boasts its original interiors. At La Rotonde, which opened in 1903, the walls were once adorned by works by promising young artists such as Picasso and Modigliani. The original owner would take a painting in lieu of cash from those who couldn't afford to pay for their meal, on the basis that the artist could buy it back when he was in funds. In the meantime, the restaurant served as a makeshift art gallery and attracted wealthy connoisseurs as well as penniless creatives.

One Dôme regular was Ernest Hemingway, and in *A Moveable Feast* he mentions an evening when he went out for a drink, feeling virtuous at the end of a good day's work, and discovered that the Dôme was also full of people who had spent their time productively:

> *There were models who had worked and there were painters who had worked until the light was gone and there were writers who had finished a day's work for better or for worse, and there were drinkers and characters, some of whom I knew and some that were only decoration.*

Henry Miller's *Tropic of Cancer* also mentions Le Dôme: at one point, a character is unwilling to go there because he owes too much money – he'd prefer the Coupole, presumably until his debt in that establishment also reaches unacceptable levels.

These cafés are just a smattering of those available to the literary pilgrim: there's also Brasserie Lipp, close to Les Deux Magots, frequented by the French poets Paul Verlaine (1844–1896) and Guillaume Apollinaire (1880–1918) and later the scene of Baldwin's fracas with Wright; and Le Select, described in the 1920s by another expatriate American, journalist editor Harold Stearns (1891–1943) as 'a seething madhouse of drunks, semi-drunks, quarter-drunks and sober maniacs'. The list could go on ... and on. Unfortunately, many of these establishments are now upmarket restaurants that will expect you to pay for more than a lingering cup of coffee.

Some Parisian Cemeteries
Émile Zola, Guy de Maupassant and others

paris.fr/lieux/cimetiere-de-montmartre-5061
paris.fr/lieux/cimetiere-du-montparnasse-4082
paris.fr/dossiers/bienvenue-au-cimetiere-du-pere-lachaise-47

In 1800, Paris had the largest population of any city in continental Europe: at about 500,000, it lagged behind London, but was well ahead of Naples, Vienna, Amsterdam or anywhere else. Having recovered from the fall in numbers occasioned by the Revolution, it then continued to grow, with the result that it needed more room not only for the living but for the deceased. The vast Holy Innocents' Cemetery (the closure of which forms the backdrop to Andrew Miller's 2011 novel *Pure*) had been cleared in the 1780s; churchyards were full to overflowing; and Parisians were in urgent need of new spaces in which to bury their dead. The cemeteries that came into being around this time included Montparnasse to the south of the city centre, Montmartre to the north and, largest and eventually most famous, Père Lachaise to the east.

Montmartre Cemetery, as you might expect, is the last resting place of artists of all descriptions, including the Impressionist painter Edgar Degas and the great ballet dancer Vaslav Nijinsky, but literary pilgrims can find the novelist

Stendhal (see page 62), the poet and dramatist Alfred de Vigny (1797–1863) and the brothers Goncourt – Edmond (1826–1896) and Jules (1830–70), publishers and patrons of the literary prize that bears their name. The Zola family tomb is here too: it's one of the most handsome in Montmartre, an Art Deco affair of curlicues and carved foliage, with a bust of the author at its centre. Émile Zola (see page 34) was a national figure at the time of his death in 1902, his funeral attended by thousands, including a procession of miners following the coffin and chanting, 'Germinal, Germinal' – *Germinal* being the title of Zola's no-holds-barred 1885 novel about a miners' strike and the horrors of the miners' lives. More than a hundred years on, the Zola monument remains magnificent – and a popular destination for visitors, though its most famous occupant had the honour of being moved to the Panthéon in 1908, where he lies in the same crypt as Victor Hugo (see page 13) and Alexandre Dumas (see page 47).

Across the city and to the south of the Seine, Montparnasse houses the short-story writer Guy de Maupassant (1850–1893) and the twentieth-century philosophers and novelists Jean-Paul Sartre and Simone de Beauvoir (see page 23). Maupassant's life was cut short by syphilis, a disease that inspired some of his more macabre writing and led to paranoia, alienation and attempted suicide: although his tomb is eye-catching enough, his self-penned epitaph, 'I have coveted everything and taken pleasure in nothing', says it all. Long-term lovers Sartre and De Beauvoir are buried together in a less ostentatious grave, leaving us to speculate as to whether or not their turbulent relationship is being carried on into the afterlife.

For those who have time and inclination for only one cemetery, Père Lachaise is the must-visit. Named after Louis XIV's confessor, who had lived nearby in the seventeenth century, and covering 110 acres or 44 hectares, it was designed in the style of English landscape gardens of the period and, although you aren't allowed to picnic there, it is in many respects a tree-lined park that receives three million visitors a year and just happens to host almost 10,000 funerals.

Despite these impressive statistics, Père Lachaise had a shaky start. For one thing, it was a long way out of town (by the standards of the time: in modern terms it's about twenty minutes' drive from Notre-Dame and easily reached by métro); for another, Christians accustomed to having graves in consecrated ground were loath to be buried anywhere else. It took a marketing stunt in dubious taste to overcome these reservations: within months of Père Lachaise's opening, the authorities exhumed the poet and fable writer Jean de la Fontaine (1621–1695) and the playwright Jean-Baptiste Poquelin, known as Molière (1622–1673), both of whom had died over a century earlier, and moved them to the new cemetery. A few years later, they

Dying Beyond Your Means

l-hotel.com/rooms/oscar-wilde-suite/

Visitors attracted to Père Lachaise by Oscar Wilde should conclude their pilgrimage at L'Hôtel, previously L'Hôtel d'Alsace, in the Saint-Germain area, where the disgraced playwright spent his last days. L'Hôtel today describes itself as 'the world's first boutique hotel' and in the course of its post-Wildean life has boasted guests ranging from Elizabeth Taylor to Princess Grace of Monaco. The words 'opulent' and 'sumptuous' occur frequently on its website, and rightly so, given the luxurious drapery in the bedrooms and the spiral staircase carpeted in leopard print. The Oscar Wilde suite, no more understated than the rest of the hotel, covers close to 400 square feet (37 square metres) and has its own private terrace. If you want, as Oscar claimed he was doing, to 'die beyond your means', this may well be the place to do it.

did the same thing with the legendary twelfth-century lovers Abelard and Héloïse. This was an even more shameless piece of hype, as there had been some doubt about the couple's previous resting place, so it's impossible to be sure that their elaborate tomb in Père Lachaise actually contains their mortal remains. Subsequent visitors didn't seem to care, however: throughout the nineteenth century it was a popular spot for the lovelorn to leave letters in the hope of finding true love. (They were presumably also not turned off by the fact that Abelard was castrated by people who objected to his relationship with Héloïse.)

Today, visitors can still see the memorials to Molière, adorned with theatrical masks, and La Fontaine, as well as those to the novelists Honoré de Balzac (see next entry below), Marcel Proust (see page 45) and Colette (1873–1954), and the dramatist Alfred de Musset (1810–1857). Most famously, though, there's the exiled Irish writer and wit Oscar Wilde (see opposite and page 203). In a burial ground where conventional slabs and Christian crosses are the norm, Wilde's memorial stands out by virtue of being a 10-feet-high (3 metres) Jacob Epstein sculpture of the Sphinx. Installed in 1914 amid great controversy regarding the testicles on display (they were briefly covered by a bronze plaque in the shape of a butterfly and have since been removed altogether), it was soon bedecked with lipstick kisses and notes from admirers. Following his disgrace and imprisonment for 'gross indecency', Wilde had assumed that posteriority would revile him; he would surely have been gratified to know how wrong he was, and amused to learn that the impression of generations of lipstick caused so much damage to the stone that a glass barrier has been constructed to protect it. It seems a posthumous vindication of his maxim that one should always forgive one's enemies: 'Nothing annoys them so much.'

Maison de Balzac, Paris
Honoré de Balzac

maisondebalzac.paris.fr
Closed Mondays and some public holidays

For a man who spent his whole life struggling to keep out of debt – he was full of get-rich-quick schemes but a hopeless businessman – Honoré de Balzac (1799–1850) seems to have lived reasonably comfortably in the house in Passy which is now a museum devoted to him. Today Passy is very much part of Paris, but when Balzac moved there in 1840 it was a village known for its vineyards and quarries. He didn't rent the whole house, but had an apartment consisting of a living room, dining room and bedroom with access to the garden and the wine cellar. Not exactly starving in a garret, and very probably living beyond his means.

He was in Passy for seven years and during that period completed work on the seventeen volume collection of almost a hundred novels and stories that he came to call *La Comédie Humaine*. This massive output has established him as one of the great novelists of all time; an influence on Dickens, Flaubert,

Zola, Proust and others whose works are mentioned elsewhere in this book. Creating over 2,000 characters from every walk of life – wealthy but joyless misers, poor relations consumed with envy for their richer cousins, people who make loveless marriages for the sake of worldly gain – he painted a picture that has never been equalled of a French society in which money was more important than religion or politics, and if you had enough of it you could do what you liked.

Bestsellers such as *Eugénie Grandet* and *Le Père Goriot*, included in *La Comédie Humaine* but first published separately in the 1830s, had already made Balzac famous and should have made him rich, but he frequently spent more money on the changes he made to his proofs once he sent a book to the printer that he earned from sales. Working as many as fourteen hours a day, sleeping in the evening then getting up at midnight to work through till morning and keeping himself going on a diet of strong black coffee, he is said, on one occasion, to have completed the first draft of a book in seventy-two hours, then spent sixty nights re-writing it. You can see some of his scribbled-over texts in the museum; one commentator described them as 'a labyrinth of erasures, emendations and insertions' and you have to shudder at the thought of what the typesetters must have made of them – and how much they would have charged to do the work.

On a more domestic level, you can also see Balzac's cafetière, produced to his own specification from a porcelain factory in Limoges – *the* go-to city for porcelain manufacture; no cheap high-street purchases for our Honoré! It includes not only his monogram but also a tiny heater to keep the coffee warm during those long, sleepless nights.

Keeping his coffee warm in a luxurious container was far from being his only extravagance. Convinced that prosperity was just around the corner, he indulged in many of the accoutrements of success: another of the museum's treasures is the gold-topped and turquoise-studded cane for which he paid (in long-drawn-out instalments) 700 francs, more than a year's rent on his apartment. There's also a sketched design for a fan (probably never made) by Jean-Jacques Grandville, one of the foremost caricaturists of the day. It features Balzac as the centrepiece of a parade of admirers reading his works and of characters from his books. He brandishes a cane (he had quite a collection of them) as if he were Jupiter about to cast a thunderbolt, and there's a trumpet above his head as if to symbolise his power or perhaps his ascent into Heaven. It's the ultimate glorification of an author who didn't suffer from false modesty and once wrote of the impact he might have on posterity:

> *A man who disposes of thought is a sovereign. Kings command nations for a given time, the artist commands whole centuries, he changes the face of things.*

Balzac married a wealthy woman only months before his death, too late to sort out his financial difficulties. But his status was beyond dispute: he was buried at Père Lachaise cemetery (see page 29), where a bust on an imposing pedestal stands above a model of a copy of *La Comédie Humaine*, complete with quill pen.

There's no shortage of likenesses of Balzac in the museum itself, but for the most impressive image you need to cross the Seine to the Musée Rodin, where the larger-than-life-size bronze *Monument to Balzac* stands in the garden. The sculptor Auguste Rodin, who had been only nine when Balzac died, was commissioned to produce the statue almost forty years later. Used to working from life, he could only draw on the knowledge that Balzac had been short and fat and wore a dressing gown when writing through the night. The British

art historian Kenneth Clark, in the book associated with his seminal 1969 television series *Civilisation*, explained that Rodin 'also had to make Balzac look immense – the dominating imagination of his age, and yet transcending his age'. To achieve this from the limited information available, Rodin made five or six figures of a fat naked man, contemplated them for several months, then draped the one he liked best in a robe akin to the famous dressing gown. Thus, Clark continued, 'he contrived to give the figure both monumentality and movement'. Clark regarded the *Monument* as the greatest sculpture of the nineteenth century. Go to the Musée Rodin and judge for yourself. If you're lucky, one of the nude studies will be on display indoors and you can see what Balzac meant when he said:

I am not deep but I am very wide, and it takes time to walk around me.

Perhaps he had flashes of modesty – or at least of self-awareness – after all.

Zola's House/Dreyfus Museum, Médan
Emile Zola, Alfred Dreyfus

maisonzola-museedreyfus.com *Closed Mondays and Tuesdays*

In 1898 the novelist Émile Zola (1840–1902), one of the most famous writers in France, took up the cause of a Jewish army officer named Alfred Dreyfus who had been found guilty of spying for the Germans and sentenced to lifelong penal servitude on the notoriously harsh Devil's Island, off the northern coast of South America. Zola wrote an open letter to the President of France which was published on the front page of the newspaper *L'Aurore* and repeatedly used the now-famous words *J'accuse* – 'I accuse'. In it, he warned the President that the image of France would be sullied by the filth produced by the Dreyfus Affair, which he called a ghastly miscarriage of justice; he accused Dreyfus's accusers of 'demented fabrications' of evidence, of 'a cover-up of the most preposterous fantasies imaginable' and of blatant anti-Semitism. Some sort of treason had been discovered, Zola wrote, the powers that be had chosen a victim and thereafter moved heaven and earth to ensure he was found guilty. He admitted, at the end of his letter, in which he had named and shamed no fewer than seven senior army officers, that he was laying himself open to accusations of libel, and was perfectly prepared to take the consequences, if only justice could be seen to be done.

It was powerful stuff and it had two immediate effects. First, Zola was indeed accused of libel, found guilty and sentenced to imprisonment, which he avoided by escaping to England. Second, it provoked a campaign for a re-trial. Dreyfus was recalled from Devil's Island, tried again and once more found guilty, but – because of the huge public outcry there had been over the whole affair – pardoned. It took another seven years of campaigning for Dreyfus finally to be exonerated and the true identity of the spy acknowledged, and Zola didn't live to see it.

You can delve deeper into all this at the museum at Médan, in what was once Zola's country home. He bought the house in 1878, having acquired both fame and money thanks to the success of his novel *L'Assommoir;* Médan is now a dormitory suburb of Paris, about twenty miles or thirty-two kilometres from the city centre, but at the time it was a small and isolated village. Zola wrote to his friend and mentor Gustave Flaubert (see page 41):

> *I've bought a house, a rabbit hutch ... in a charming spot by the Seine, 9,000 francs, I tell you the price so that you aren't too impressed. Literature has paid for this modest country retreat.*

At the time, you would have been doing reasonably well for yourself if you earned a hundred francs a month, so, however unpresumptuous Zola was trying to sound, nine thousand would have bought quite a decent rabbit hutch. Nor was it to remain modest for long: he and his wife Alexandrine renovated and expanded it enormously, acquiring an extra 10 acres/4 hectares of land and laying out a park; they added towers to the house, naming new additions

after Zola's novels, so that there was a Nana Tower and a Germinal Tower. Out of doors, they created a pavilion, a greenhouse and a small farm. The Zolas subsequently entertained on a grand scale, inviting artists and writers including Paul Cézanne, Edouard Manet and Guy de Maupassant (see page 28) to what Maupassant described as 'les Soirées de Médan'. Following Zola's death, Alexandrine donated the house to the newly created Zola Foundation; after various incarnations, much restoration and the addition of a wing dedicated to the Dreyfus Affair, the current museum opened in 2021.

The furniture and décor are as nearly as possible as Zola would have known them and you can see that he lived a comfortable life, particularly in the spacious salon with its lavish stained-glass windows (designed, like everything else in the house, to Zola's specification). You can climb the narrow staircase to the study, which has a huge bay window overlooking the Seine and Zola's motto, 'Not a day without a line', painted above the fireplace. According to his great-granddaughter, he went up that staircase and wrote from 9 a.m. to 1 p.m., with the aim of producing four pages of manuscript, each and every day for twenty-four years.

But Zola's generous hospitality and admirable work ethic aren't what make him memorable. It's more his passionate commitment to justice – obvious in the novels that deplored the working conditions of miners or the poverty that drove so many to alcoholism and crime, but never more apparent than in his defence of Alfred Dreyfus. At Médan, in the Musée Dreyfus, you can read the entire text of 'J'accuse', but perhaps more importantly you can recoil at the reaction to it: at the caricature showing Zola as 'the King of Pigs', spreading muck – to put it no more coarsely – over the map of France. Or at the newspaper article describing him as a pornographer and 'the shame of our literature' whose support had been bought by the Dreyfus 'syndicate'. It's an article full of vitriol which sets more store by the fact that the supposed traitor was a Jew than by any solid evidence.

The contrast between comfortable salon and abuse in the gutter press has to set you thinking about Zola. This idyllic country retreat was designed to be everything he could possibly have wanted, and – at the height of his fame and approaching old age – he gave it up for what turned out to be a year of exile, because he was incapable of seeing a miscarriage of justice without trying to put it right.

Maison Forestière, Ors
Wilfred Owen

tourisme-cambresis.fr/maison-owen.html

Open 9.30–12.30, 14.00–17.30 from mid April to mid November, Wednesdays, Saturdays and Sundays during school terms; every day during school holidays

Of all the writers and artists who lost their lives in the First World War, perhaps the most tragic is Wilfred Owen (1893–1918): not only because he was a mere twenty-five years old and a poet of genius, but because he died on 4 November 1918, just a week before the Armistice that marked the end of hostilities. How *angry* he would have been. Because he was angry already, at the needless loss of life – the 'doomed youth' who, as he put it, 'die as cattle' – and at the propaganda that surrounded the war. In one of his most famous poems, he described the ancient Roman idea that it was 'sweet and honourable to die for one's country' as 'the old lie'.

His death becomes all the more tragic if you consider that he had spent very little time on active service: injured after only a few months in northern Europe, he was sent back to the UK for treatment for what we now know as PTSD and returned to France only in August 1918, determined to record the horrors of war for posterity.

Much of this was presumably in the mind of the Wilfred Owen Association when it commissioned visual artist Simon Patterson to create a Wilfred Owen Memorial in the Maison Forestière in Ors. It was here that the poet was staying the night before the assault on the nearby Sambre-Oise Canal – the battle in which he lost his life. Opened in 2011, the museum is a simple white building approached by a sweeping white walkway, its modern style intended to reflect the timeless nature of Owen's poetry. Be that as it may, the real point of the visit is to see the cellar.

It was from this unpretentious brick-lined and, on the night in question, smoke-filled space that Owen wrote his last letter home to his mother; extracts from that letter are engraved on the walls and read to you over the loudspeakers as you stand there. Owen thanks his mother for a parcel just received:

My servant & I ate the chocolate in the cold middle of last night, crouched under a draughty Tamboo [temporary shelter] roofed with planks. I husband the Malted Milk for tonight, & tomorrow night. The handkerchief & socks are most opportune, as the ground is marshy, & I have a slight cold!

Having assured her that the men who surround him are delightful, he continues:

It is a great life. I am more oblivious than alas! yourself, dear Mother, of the ghastly glimmering of the guns outside, & the hollow crashing of the shells.

There is no danger down here, or if any, it will be well over before you read these lines.

Within twenty-four hours he and about forty of his companions were dead. Did anyone else get to enjoy the remains of the Malted Milk? Probably not.

Signposted paths from the house take you on a pleasant ramble through the woods to the site of the battle and to the local cemetery where Lieutenant W. E. S. Owen MC of the Manchester Regiment is buried alongside his comrades. The headstone doesn't mention that he was a poet, but does include the first line and a half of this verse:

Shall Life renew these bodies? Of a truth
All death will he annul, all tears assuage?
Or fill these void veins full again with youth
And wash with an immortal water age?

They're from a poem called 'The End'.

The Maison Forestière is off the beaten track, a couple of hours' drive inland from Calais, and the visit won't take you long. But it's worth it. Take Kleenex.

Jules Verne Museum, Nantes
Jules Verne

en-julesverne.nantesmetropole.fr/home.html

Open every day during July and August; the rest of the year open Saturday mornings and every afternoon except Tuesdays

Mary Shelley's *Frankenstein*, published in 1818 (see page 97), is often called the first science-fiction novel, but the genre really took off half a century later when Jules Verne (1828–1905) published the first of more than fifty novels in a series his publisher called *Extraordinary Voyages*. Its goal, according to the

publisher, was 'to outline all the geographical, geological, physical, historical and astronomical knowledge amassed by modern science and to recount, in an entertaining and picturesque format ... the history of the universe'.

No pressure, then.

But fulfilling that vast brief is more or less what Verne did. What gave him such an edge was that he was interested in *everything*. He studied law, worked for a while in a theatre, dabbled in stockbroking, travelled widely and in between times spent as much time as he could in the National Library of Paris, researching recent scientific developments. In an age when barely a day passed without some breakthrough or other hitting the headlines, his brain must have been in a permanent whirl of excitement and speculation.

In fact, it always had been. Looking back on his childhood when he was in his sixties, he recalled:

I lived in the maritime bustle of a big commercial city which is the starting-point and goal of many long voyages. I still see the river Loire, whose numerous arms are connected by a league of bridges, its quays encumbered by freight in the shadow of huge elms ....

Ships two or three rows deep line the wharves. Others sail up or down the stream ... In those days the only kind of sailing-vessels we had were the lubberly merchantmen. ... How I longed to cross the swaying plank that connected them with the quay, and set foot on their deck!

In the same article he wrote that he had always had a taste for stories 'wherein the imagination gives itself free scope' and that his family had respected the arts and literature, 'whence I conclude that heritage accounts in a large measure for my instincts'. Put all that together and you begin to see how Verne's vast and varied *oeuvre* came into being.

The 'big commercial city' of his childhood was the thriving port of Nantes, and the impressive nineteenth-century building that today houses the Jules Verne Museum sits on a spot overlooking the Loire where – according to the later novelist Julien Gracq (1910–2007), much influenced by Verne – the young Jules 'must have come often to contemplate the river, at the point where it becomes the gateway to the open sea and the path to adventure'. The museum offers a 'journey through the writings of Jules Verne', with original books, manuscripts and documents (many of them in Verne's own handwriting), films, posters, games and more. They build a fascinating picture of the life and work of the man who wrote *Around the World in Eighty Days* at a time when going around the world at all was a barely imaginable feat; *Twenty Thousand Leagues Under the Sea* when the idea of an electrically powered submarine would have seemed like pure fantasy; and *From the Earth to the Moon* when space travel was nearly a century away. His attention to scientific detail and his accurate predictions of advances to come were, just as his publisher had boasted, extraordinary.

There's plenty more Verne-related exploring to be done in Nantes. Once you've visited the museum, you can head away from the river and take in the ornate Gothic church of Sainte-Croix where he was christened, then stroll the streets and view (from the outside) several houses where he lived as a child. But the real source of inspiration is a bench a few minutes' walk from the museum, also overlooking the Loire. Here you can sit beside a bronze version of the young Jules as he appears – from the pensive look on his face – to be imagining adventurous yarns about the sea-going vessels he is watching. He forms part of a double statue commissioned to mark the centenary of his death. The other half, based on an illustration from the first edition of

Twenty Thousand Leagues Under the Sea, shows Captain Nemo, mysterious and melancholic commander of that book's *Nautilus* submarine. Mirroring the young Jules's imaginings, Nemo has a sextant to his eye as he calculates the route he must take on his own great journey.

More than 150 years on, Verne's *Extraordinary Voyages* continue to enthral readers, film directors and television producers alike. The first motion-picture adaptation of one of his works – *Twenty Thousand Leagues Under the Sea* – was made as early as 1916; a television version of *Around the World in Eighty Days* appeared in 2021. It's a shame that little boy staring out over the Loire didn't live to see the development of these new media: his brain would have whirled more than ever.

Madame Bovary's Rouen
Gustave Flaubert

cathedrale-rouen.net *Closed Monday mornings*

It's strange to think that one of the most notorious sex scenes in all of literature – the carriage ride in *Madame Bovary* – should consist of little more than a list of streets. It's set in Rouen in Normandy, where the book's author, Gustave Flaubert (1821–1880) was born. Having studied briefly in Paris and travelled in the Middle East and North Africa, he returned to the hamlet of Croisset, across the River Seine from Rouen, and lived there for the last thirty-five years of his life, writing all his major works there.

The day before the scene in question takes place, Emma – the bored and frustrated Madame Bovary of the title – has accidentally met her former admirer, the clerk Léon, again and agreed to a rendezvous the following morning at the cathedral. Having decided she cannot after all have an affair with him, she writes to him to explain why, realises she doesn't have his address and feels obliged to turn up at the appointed time and hand her letter to him. Without reading what she has written, Léon asks her to come for a drive with him; when she suggests that this is improper, he overcomes her resistance by appealing to her snobbery and assuring her that it is done in Paris.

'Where to, sir?' asked the coachman.

'Where you like,' said Léon, forcing Emma into the cab.

And the lumbering machine set out. It went down the Rue Grand-Pont, crossed the Place des Arts, the Quai Napoleon, the Pont Neuf, and stopped short before the statue of Pierre Corneille.

'Go on,' cried a voice that came from within.

The cab went on again, and as soon as it reached the Carrefour Lafayette, set off down-hill, and entered the station at a gallop.

'No, straight on!' cried the same voice.

The cab reaches the Cours, goes along the towpath by the Seine, then crosses Quatremares, Sotteville, La Grande-Chaussee, the Rue d'Elbeuf and reaches the Jardin des Plantes. It passes by Saint-Sever, by various *quais*, out of town, back into town. The hot day wears on, the coachman wishes his passengers would stop somewhere – anywhere – so that he could get a drink. Passers-by wonder why anyone would choose to drive with the blinds down on a day like this.

The cab was seen at Saint-Pol, at Lescure, at Mont Gargan, at La Rougue-Marc and Place du Gaillardbois; in the Rue Maladrerie, Rue Dinanderie, before Saint-Romain, Saint-Vivien, Saint-Maclou, Saint-Nicaise – in front of the Customs, at the 'Vieille Tour', the 'Trois Pipes' and the Monumental Cemetery.

The only allusion we are given to what is going on (as if we didn't know) is this:

Once in the middle of the day, in the open country, just as the sun beat most fiercely against the old plated lanterns, a bared hand passed beneath the small blinds of yellow canvas, and threw out some scraps of paper that scattered in the wind, and farther off lighted like white butterflies on a field of red clover all in bloom.

So much for Emma's letter.

It's not until six o'clock that a veiled figure leaves the carriage. By that time, the thirsty cab driver has covered a route that takes in almost every landmark in Rouen, many of which you can visit today. The various churches are still there; if your taste runs to the Flamboyant style of architecture, Saint-Maclou, with its four chapels radiating out from an octagonal choir, is the one you shouldn't miss. Saint-Romain is the name given to one of the towers of the

cathedral; it was also once a magnificent specimen of the Flamboyant style but was badly bombed during the Second World War and what you see today is a loving reconstruction, decorated with golden suns that sparkle irresistibly on a bright day. Saint-Sever is now a shopping mall, while the Monumental Cemetery contains the grave of Flaubert himself, with an unostentatious headstone next to those of his parents.

Emma and Léon, of course, having other things on their minds, notice none of these sights. But the most remarkable building in Rouen is the cathedral of Notre-Dame itself, and here you can genuinely claim to be seeing what they saw: before Emma arrives at the rendezvous, Léon offends the beadle who offers to be his guide by 'taking the liberty of admiring the cathedral by himself':

> *The nave was reflected in the full fonts with the beginning of the arches and some portions of the glass windows. But the reflections of the paintings, broken by the marble rim, were continued farther on upon the flag-stones, like a many-coloured carpet. The broad daylight from without streamed into the church in three enormous rays from the three opened portals.*

Pick a sunny day (not the easiest thing to do in Rouen, unfortunately) and this is still what you will see.

When Emma arrives and, having handed her letter to Léon, takes refuge in the chapel of the Virgin, the beadle pounces:

> *'Madame, no doubt, does not belong to these parts? Madame would like to see the curiosities of the church?'*
>
> *'Oh, no!' cried the clerk.*
>
> *'Why not?' said she. For she clung with her expiring virtue to the Virgin, the sculptures, the tombs – anything.*

In other parts of Rouen, you can visit Flaubert's birthplace, now a museum dedicated more to the author's father, a surgeon, than to Gustave himself; it includes an exhibit of anatomical curiosities and a garden of medicinal plants. Across the river, the Pavilion Flaubert is all that remains of the house in Croisset; it too is now a small museum. But for a real taste of *Madame Bovary* and that famous carriage ride, the cathedral is the place. Flaubert was famous for his tireless pursuit of *le mot juste,* rewriting again and again until he was satisfied that what he had produced was just right. As you stand today in the chapel of the Virgin, you can't help wondering how long it took him to come up with something as perfect and as tragic as 'she clung with her expiring virtue'.

Illiers-Combray
Marcel Proust

proust-ink.com/illiers

There can't be many authors whose influence on the place where they spent childhood holidays is so great that the town has been renamed in their honour, but so it is with Marcel Proust (1871–1922). He based the fictional Combray, where the narrator of his seven-volume masterwork *In Search of Lost Time* grew up, on Illiers in Eure-et-Loir, southwest of Paris; to mark the centenary of his birth, the town's residents rechristened their home Illiers-Combray. Young Proust spent those formative summers in the house of his uncle and aunt, and this is now a museum, named La Maison de Tante Léonie, after the fictionalised version of that aunt. While Tante Léonie's house was closed for renovation in 2022, its collection of Proustian ephemera was transferred to a new museum, a few steps down the road, where two bedrooms – the aunt's and the child's –

have been recreated in loving detail. You can also find a magic lantern, the early form of slide projector that would have been in use in Proust's day and that features in *In Search of Lost Time* as a symbol of a new way of looking at the world.

Most of the events of the first volume, *Swann's Way*, take place during the narrator's childhood (he's never actually named, but we are told we can call him Marcel; Swann is a wealthy family friend) and their settings can be rediscovered all over Illiers. The highlight of the year for the Society of the Friends of Marcel Proust is Hawthorn Day, held on a Saturday in May, which includes a visit to the hawthorn hedge whose sight and scent intoxicated the young Marcel. Having first been overwhelmed by the way the plants have been used to decorate the church, he then encounters them outside:

> *The hedge resembled a series of chapels, whose walls were no longer visible under the mountains of flowers that were heaped upon their altars; while underneath, the sun cast a square of light upon the ground, as though it had shone in upon them through a window; the scent that swept out over me from them was as rich, and as circumscribed in its range, as though I had been standing before the Lady-altar, and the flowers, themselves adorned also, held out each its little bunch of glittering stamens with an air of inattention, fine, radiating 'nerves' in the flamboyant style of architecture ...*

If you can't make it at hawthorn time, you can still visit this garden, just across the River Loir (a tributary of a tributary of the larger and more famous Loire) from the museum. It was created by Proust's uncle, Jules Amiot, who took his inspiration from the Pré Catelan, a botanical garden in the Bois du Boulogne in Paris; although Uncle Jules's property was nowhere near the size of the Paris original, it was and is fairly substantial for little Illiers. Proust turned it into Swann's estate, Tansonville, with its ornamental water features, leafy glades, follies of various descriptions and lush plantings of stocks, jasmine, pansies, verbena and, of course, hawthorns.

Although the church is called Saint-Hilaire in the novel, it's Saint-Jacques (Saint James) in real life and was in medieval times a stopping-off point for pilgrims on their way to Santiago (also Saint James) de Compostela in northern Spain. As a result, one of its decorative motifs is Saint James's symbol, the scallop shell. Admiring these, you may feel inclined to indulge in a Proustian moment, recalling the famous occasion, when, as an adult, the narrator is having tea with his mother and, without thinking, crumbles his cake into his tea:

> *She sent out for one of those short, plump little cakes called 'petites madeleines', which look as though they had been moulded in the fluted*

scallop of a pilgrim's shell. ... No sooner had the warm liquid, and the crumbs with it, touched my palate than a shudder ran through my whole body, and I stopped, intent upon the extraordinary changes that were taking place. An exquisite pleasure had invaded my senses, but individual, detached, with no suggestion of its origin ... Whence could it have come to me, this all-powerful joy? I was conscious that it was connected with the taste of tea and cake, but that it infinitely transcended those savours, could not, indeed, be of the same nature as theirs. Whence did it come? What did it signify? How could I seize upon and define it?

There is much more to this effect, but no one admires Proust for his brevity, and you get the gist. What he's doing is remembering the many times during his childhood when his Aunt Léonie served him madeleines crumbled and soaked this way. And as this is a town utterly dedicated to its most famous son, you can buy madeleines for yourself (or order them for dessert in a local restaurant) and enjoy a similarly Proustian but probably less metaphysical moment as you dunk them delicately in your own tea.

Château de Monte-Cristo, Port-Marly
Alexandre Dumas

chateau-monte-cristo.com

Open from March to November; times vary with the seasons. Closed Mondays.

You've got to love Alexandre Dumas (1802–1870). An acquaintance once described him as large-hearted, amusing and egotistical and remarked that 'his tongue was like a windmill – once set in motion, you never knew when he would stop, especially if the theme was himself'. Later critics have remarked on the prodigious amount of money he earned and his 'fantastic ease at spending it'. Even the great Victor Hugo (see page 15), a contemporary and another colossus of nineteenth-century French literature, said, 'His successes were not merely successes, he made them triumphs; they had the brilliance of the brass band about them.' This was a man with an incomparable zest for life.

So it's no surprise that, with two hugely successful novels in quick succession under his belt – *The Three Musketeers* (1844) and *The Count of Monte Cristo* (1844–5, see page 53) – Dumas should have decided spend some of that money creating his dream home. And when you have his imagination, his extravagance and his ego, your dream house is likely to be something pretty special. He chose a site on the banks of the Seine, near Port-Marly, about twenty miles (thirty-two kilometres) west of Paris, and commissioned one of the leading architects of the day, Hippolyte Durand, to turn his ideas into reality. The result, named – with typical Dumas lack of diffidence – the Château de Monte-Cristo, is part Renaissance château, part Gothic castle, surrounded by a small moat and set in gardens in the so-called *style anglais*, complete with fountains, waterfalls, rockeries and grottoes. Understated it is not.

The Gothic part is a separate building in the park, designed to be Dumas's writing retreat and decorated with plaques bearing the titles of his works and sculptures of his most famous characters. He called this mini-castle the Château d'If, after the foreboding place of imprisonment in *The Count of Monte-Cristo*, but must have done so with reference to its isolation rather than its appearance – the real Château d'If is an unassuming structure by comparison.

Carvings on the facade of the main house – the Renaissance bit – pay tribute to Homer, Virgil, Dante, Shakespeare and other literary greats, though whether Dumas was acknowledging a debt to them or including himself in their number is unclear. The fact that his own image takes pride of place, over the principal entrance, may provide a clue. Inside, the highlight is the Moorish salon, originally decorated for Dumas by artisans in the service of the royal house of Tunis. Delicate Islamic tracery and gold motifs leave no surface untouched, while padded ottomans invite you to recline and enjoy a relaxing cup of mint tea or, more likely with Dumas as your host, a glass or three of champagne.

The Monte-Cristo housewarming party set the tone for Dumas's life there: the moment everything was ready in this rural idyll, he invited fifty friends to celebrate with him, only to have six hundred turn up. Two years of sumptuous living, plenty more extravagant parties and multiple love affairs followed, with hangers-on moving in and benefiting from the author's boundless generosity. But those two years were all it took for him to spend his way through a fortune; by 1848 the whole celebrity lifestyle bit had come crashing down around his head and he was forced to sell the estate and everything in it for a fraction of what he had paid for them.

Apparently undaunted, Dumas moved on and moved on again, keeping his creditors at bay as best he could. Already an indefatigable traveller, he subsequently spent time in Belgium, Russia and Italy, becoming involved in the campaign for Italian unification. He wrote *Impressions de Voyage ...* about various places he had visited; he compiled a *Grand Dictionnaire de Cuisine,* inspired by his own enthusiasm for cooking; and he produced a lively reminiscence of the many animals, from dogs to monkeys, that he had kept as pets. This is in addition to many novels, children's books, a seven-volume history of the Bourbon dynasty in Italy, and twenty-two volumes of memoirs. It's been estimated that his output totalled over 100,000 pages (to put that in context, the *Complete Works of Shakespeare* can fit into 1,300). Most of these works are forgotten now, but *The Three Musketeers* continues to be adapted, filmed and televised and to inspire would-be swashbucklers the world over.

As for the château, it fell into ruin and was about to be demolished in 1969 when supporters of Dumas's legacy banded together and determined to restore it to its former glory. And glorious it is, with Dumas himself still to be seen over the doorway, welcoming visitors to his parties and with his inexhaustible *joie de vivre* embodied in the motto carved on the facade: *J'aime qui m'aime* – 'I love anyone who loves me.'

Parc Astérix, Plailly
René Goscinny and Albert Uderzo

parcasterix.fr

Open every day July and August; check website for other times of year and for special events

Par Toutatis!, the park's website exclaims, referring to the Celtic god so often invoked by Goscinny and Uderzo's cartoon heroes and encouraging visitors to throw themselves into the spirit of the place. Julius Caesar famously wrote that all Gaul (the Roman province that encompassed modern France and various adjacent territories) was divided into three parts, but the Astérix books

of René Goscinny (1926–1977) and Albert Uderzo (1927–2020) are based on the premise that Caesar wasn't telling the whole truth. There is, they say, a fourth part: a single small village in Brittany where one indomitable group of Gauls continues to hold out against the invaders.

Parc Astérix is rather less remote – it's not much more than twenty miles (thirty-two kilometres) north of Paris – but the spirit of those Gauls from two millennia ago pervades all 400 acres/160 hectares of France's third-most-popular amusement park. Its visitor figures pale into insignificance behind those of the two vast Disney theme parks, but Parc Astérix can claim to be the first and the most homegrown. It opened in 1989, the brainchild of Uderzo, who was inspired to create a park based on his famous creations after visiting Disneyland in California a few years earlier.

Writer Goscinny and illustrator Uderzo met in Paris in 1951 and produced the first Astérix comic strips together for *Pilote* magazine in 1959. The first book, *Astérix the Gaul*, appeared in 1961, followed by a further twenty-three before Goscinny's untimely death. Two other collaborations were published posthumously, then Uderzo took over the writing for seven more. A new team has carried on the work since Uderzo's retirement and subsequent death, with a total of thirty-nine books published by the end of 2021. The adventures of Astérix and his friend, the menhir delivery man Obélix, have taken them all over the Roman world: to Britain, Belgium, Helvetica (Switzerland), Spain and, of course, Rome. They have met not only Caesar but Cleopatra, Brutus and other historical figures, always ending up in scrapes from which Astérix's cunning and Obélix's strength rescue them. They rescue galley slaves, expose Roman spies and compete (successfully, of course) in the Olympic Games. For those not in the know, the Gauls' druid Getafix (Panoramix in the original French) holds the secret of a magic potion which gives anyone who drinks it superhuman strength for a short time; Obélix fell into a cauldron of the stuff when he was a baby, so its effects are permanent and beating up Romans comes second only to eating vast quantities of wild boar on his list of pleasurable things to do.

Parc Astérix recreates many of the thrills and spills of theme parks the world over, all suitably adapted to the Astérix theme. One whirligig ride encourages you to imagine travelling on a discus that Obelix has thrown, while the water-based Menhir Express allows you to help him with his deliveries when he's running late. You can pretend to be a Roman spy and steal the recipe for the magic potion, or take up Caesar's challenge to see if you have what it takes to become one of his legionaries. Kids can drive dodgem cars designed to repel the Romans, or ride on a merry-go-round whose seats make them look as if they are tucked into Obélix's vast blue-and-white-striped trousers. Restaurants serve burgers made from wild boar and, as with Mickey Mouse in those other theme parks, you never know when you are going to bump into Astérix or one of the others just strolling through the Parc.

So yes, it's all very Disneyland and it's mostly designed for those who enjoy being hurtled around at high speeds, often upside down. But who cares? It has the genius of Goscinny and Uderzo as its starting-off point, and you can't go far wrong with that.

Tour de Montaigne, Saint-Michel-de-Montaigne, Dordogne
Michel de Montaigne

chateau-montaigne.com

Michel Eyquem de Montaigne (1533–1592) was born into a distinguished family of Bordeaux wine merchants and taught from early childhood by a tutor who spoke no French. This was part of his father's plan for the young Michel's education: the boy was obliged to converse with his tutor and the rest of his household in Latin. He studied law and served as a councillor to the court of Périgueux and later to the Parliament of Bordeaux. Then at the age of thirty-eight he gave up a promising career in public service, retired to the chateau where he had been born (and which he had recently inherited) and spent much of the rest of his life in its tower, writing in a form that hadn't existed before: the *essai* or essay. The word simply meant 'attempt' until Montaigne reinvented it; in his hands it became a sort of introspective memoir that dealt not with what he was doing but what he was thinking and feeling, as a way of considering what it meant to be human. By examining himself, he could improve his understanding of others, for, as he put it, 'each man bears the full form of the human condition'. The subjects of his *Essais* range from sorrow to the power of the imagination, from the custom of wearing clothes to the Roman statesman Cato the Younger, and include such musings as:

> *When I play with my cat, who knows whether she is passing the time with me more than I am with her?*

and:

> *However much we may mount on stilts, we still must walk on our own legs. And on the highest throne in the world, we still sit only on our own backside.*

Little though many of today's bloggers, vloggers and influencers may know it, anyone who writes about themselves and their feelings owes a debt of gratitude to Montaigne.

Anyway, there he sat in his tower, for most of the last twenty years of his life, churning out a huge number of words about anything and everything; you can visit the place where he did it and sample the estate's Appellation Bergerac Controlée wine. The castle itself is only nineteenth-century – the original burned down in 1885 – and it has one of those fairy-tale roofs that wouldn't be out of place in the Loire or Euro Disney. It was built by the politician Pierre Magne and is still owned by his descendants; it boasts a magnificent entrance hall, splendid fireplace and staircase and all sorts of other grand things, but they aren't why you're here. You're heading for the round tower at the far end of the courtyard and it is the real deal: fourteenth-century, with some extremely well-worn steps to be negotiated as you head for the upper rooms. Here, you can see Montaigne's library, his bedroom, his private chapel with its domed ceiling studded with stars, but most importantly his garret study. There's a bust of the writer, examples of his manuscripts, the desk at which he wrote; you can gaze out the window, as he must have done, musing on this and that, at his vineyards and the imposing park he himself had designed. But the truly fascinating aspect of this spartan room is that someone – Montaigne himself? His estate carpenter? – has gone to the considerable trouble of engraving some fifty-seven quotations from classical writers and the Bible into the beams of the roof. This one is from the Old Testament Book of Proverbs:

> *Do you see a person who is wise in their own eyes? There is more hope for a fool than for them.*

And this, from *On the Nature of Things*, written by the Roman poet Lucretius in the first century AD:

> *O miserable minds of men, o blind souls! In what shadows of life, in what perils is this age of yours have you passed!*

These are modern translations, of course; Montaigne's versions are in Latin and Greek, and they're all the sort of sentiment that inspired his own writing. You'd get a stiff neck if you tried to decipher them all, but you'd end up with a greater understanding of what Montaigne was about.

It's a modest place, when you consider that he had a whole castle at his disposal, but it obviously afforded him the peace and quiet in which he thrived. When he wasn't writing, he spent most of his time thinking. Nothing was too insignificant to be of interest to him – there's an essay on thumbs, for heaven's sake – and that very thought is also engraved above your head, in a quotation from the Roman dramatist Terence:

I am human: I consider nothing human alien to me.

It's not a bad maxim. Montaigne got three volumes of essays out of it, and left us with a literary form that has stood innumerable writers and philosophers in good stead ever since.

Château d'If, Marseille
Alexandre Dumas

chateau-if.fr

Open all year round; closed Mondays from October to March

infoelba.com

Near the beginning of *The Count of Monte Cristo*, the great thriller by Alexandre Dumas (see page 47), the sea captain Edmond Dantès finds himself being rowed across Marseille harbour by four gendarmes in 1815. Mystified, he asks his captors where they are taking him.

'You are a native of Marseille, and a sailor, and yet you do not know where you are going? ... That is impossible ... Look round you then.' Dantès rose and looked forward, when he saw rise within a hundred yards of him the black and frowning rock on which stands the Château d'If. This gloomy fortress, which has for more than three hundred years furnished food for so many wild legends, seemed to Dantès like a scaffold to a malefactor.

'The Château d'If?' cried he. 'What are we going there for?'

The gendarme smiled.

'I am not going there to be imprisoned,' said Dantès; 'it is only used for political prisoners. I have committed no crime. Are there any magistrates or judges at the Château d'If?'

'There are only,' said the gendarme, 'a governor, a garrison, turnkeys, and good thick walls.'

One of the things the Château lacks is a cemetery – 'they simply throw the dead into the sea, after fastening a thirty-six-pound [sixteen-kilogram] cannon-ball to their feet' – which gives you an idea of the tone of the place. Although he has indeed committed no crime (he's merely suspected of supporting Napoleon, which is excuse enough for the treatment he receives), this gloomy fortress is to be Dantès's home for the next fourteen years. After that time he escapes miraculously (by pretending to be the corpse of someone who has actually died) and sets out to revenge himself on all who have done him wrong. The escape happens only about a quarter of the way through this lengthy tome, but the memory of the Château hovers menacingly over the remainder of the narrative.

It hovers over Marseille harbour, too, though to be fair, if you catch it on a sunny day it doesn't look as threatening as all that. Now a twenty-minute ferry ride from the Old Port, it was built in the early sixteenth century, on the orders of King Francis I (reigned 1515–47), who realised that the tiny island of If could be of strategic importance in protecting the city against invasion. He

might well have wanted to keep an eye on its inhabitants, too, as Marseille had become part of France as recently as the 1480s and, after centuries of autonomy, still had mixed feelings about submitting to the French throne.

The Château is a good, chunky fortress, built in a traditional medieval style: three towers, a keep, a moat and a drawbridge. It was designed to accommodate soldiers and heavy artillery, but its impregnability and apparent inescapability (until Edmond Dantès came along, obviously) soon led to its being used as a prison. Real-life prisoners over the centuries included murderers, bandits, anyone who had been exiled from Marseille, Protestants caught practising their illegal religion, revolutionaries and, of course, supporters of Napoleon. A persistent rumour that the notorious author the Marquis de Sade (1740–1814) was also imprisoned here seems not to be true, although he did spend a fair part of his life in various other jails.

At Château d'If you can visit two tiers of cells: the windowless ones on the ground floor, where conditions were so bad that a prisoner's life expectancy was nine months; and the more spacious ones above where you had a bit of comfort if you could afford to pay for it. Traces of graffiti remain to remind you that this was indeed a prison, not just the product of a swashbuckling novelist's imagination. But if you've chosen the right day, you can lighten your mood by strolling around the walkway and enjoying stunning views over Marseille and out across the harbour to the Mediterranean.

As for Monte Cristo, it's another tiny island, this time in the Tyrrhenian Sea, off the northwest coast of Italy, and now usually spelt Montecristo. Dantès is told by a friend from prison (the one whose corpse he pretends to be) that a fabulous treasure is said to be hidden there, in one of the island's many caves. Montecristo is now a protected nature reserve and you can't visit it without a permit, but its landscape is extraordinary: it's a natural fortress of white granite that, as you approach, can seem to be floating above the clouds. Tradition has it that there was once a real treasure here, guarded by monks from the Monastery of San Mamiliano, whose ruins can still be seen. In the novel, Dantès finds the treasure after his escape and takes it away; more excitingly, perhaps, local legend maintains that it has never been discovered. It might be worth applying for that permit ...

Villa Arnaga, Cambo-les-Bains
Edmond Rostand

eu.arnaga.com

Open from April to November, with occasional 'exceptional closures' – check the website

If you've seen *Cyrano de Bergerac* – the tale of the self-sacrificing soldier with the big nose who helps his handsome but inarticulate comrade to woo the lady they both love – on the stage or in any of its numerous film adaptations, you'll probably associate its hero with words like *dashing* and *swashbuckling*. Or, if you have a smattering of French, *élan* and *panache*. *Panache* would be particularly appropriate, as it is thanks to *Cyrano* that the word entered the English language. We already knew it as a plume of feathers used to adorn a hat (Gérard Depardieu as Cyrano wore one in the 1990 film version); now it came to mean a flamboyantly dashing and confident manner.

Cyrano de Bergerac (1619–1655) was a real person: a soldier, duellist and poet whose best-known works include the satires *A Comical History of the States and Empire of the Moon* and *A Comical History of the States and Empire of the Sun*. In these the author visits both the moon and the sun, which means that, unfortunately, travelling in his footsteps is beyond the scope of this book.

However, the play that has immortalised his name was written by Edmond Rostand (1868–1918) and if you visit his home in the Basque country, you'll see that he employed a certain amount of *panache* there. He'd built a career of sorts in Paris, writing – without huge success – for the great tragic actress Sarah Bernhardt, but in 1897 *Cyrano* became an overnight sensation and he followed it with another huge success, *L'Aiglon*, in 1900. Three years later, beset by pleurisy, Rostand moved for the sake of his health to the southern spa town of Cambo-les-Bains. By this time he was rich enough to build himself a villa there and it's safe to say that he did not hold back. The exterior of Villa Arnaga – now the Edmond Rostand Museum – is neo-Basque, a style of architecture based on the local farmhouses, with symmetrical double-sloped roofs and half-timbering painted in ox-blood red. That's eye-catching enough, but wait till you see the gardens.

There are 37 acres of them (15 hectares), so they are not much smaller than the gardens of Buckingham Palace in London; quite sizeable for the grounds of a private house. And, fine though the Buckingham Palace gardens undoubtedly are, they can't offer you the Pyrenees as a backdrop. Despite his illness, Rostand had enough energy to design the gardens himself and created one in the French style and one in the English, so you have your choice of formal parterres, lavish plantings of azaleas and rhododendrons, fountains, pergolas

and – perhaps the highlight – a mirror-smooth lake whose water provides a perfect reflection of the house. It's no great hyperbole for the place to be known as the Versailles of the Basque Country.

Rostand also designed the interior of the house himself (what is it with these French Romantics? – see Victor Hugo, page 15) and one look at it makes you wonder how he found the time to write plays. The whole thing is deliberately theatrical: the Great Hall on the ground floor, where Rostand received guests, has appropriately grand portraits of the playwright and his family; from it, doors lead off in all directions. They bring you to the Chinese room with its dazzling gilded ceiling, the dining room featuring *trompe l'oeil* panelling and, beyond, the so-called Empire Office. This was originally designed for Rostand's home in Paris but taken apart and adjusted to fit the dimensions of the room at Arnaga: its walls and furniture are in lemon wood, decorated in bronze and featuring the classical themes and strict symmetry of the early-nineteenth-century Empire style, which gave the room its name. Wherever you go in the house there are elegant knick-knacks and painted panels, but almost every room is bathed in such glorious light that the effect, while hardly minimalist, never becomes oppressive.

When you've had enough of black lacquered panels and mirrored shutters, a magnificent, swirling staircase takes you upstairs to the bedrooms and private spaces notable mainly for their gorgeous views. But there's also

something you don't expect in a villa built in 1903: a hydrotherapy room. Equipped with two enamel bathtubs, something that today might be called a power shower, and sophisticated arrangements for the heating and disposing of water, it enabled Rostand to undergo the sort of masochistic treatment you'd pay good money for at a modern health spa, in an attempt to relieve his pleurisy. In this room, presumably to protect his modesty, the windows are frosted, so the poor man wouldn't even had been able to admire the view while he submitted himself to alternating jets of hot and freezing water.

In the end it wasn't pleurisy that caused Rostand's premature death, but the flu epidemic of 1918. Having returned to Paris to celebrate the Armistice, he died there less than a month later. A hundred years on, it's hard to conceive just how famous he had become. Responding to his death, a friend wrote: 'The whole world and the ages will celebrate your dazzling glory; your genius will enter into legend.' That was perhaps an overstatement: *Cyrano* is the only one of Rostand's works that is still widely known. But he has left another, more enduring legacy. No one who visits Villa Arnaga can fail to be captivated by its dazzling glory, its flamboyance, its *panache*.

BELGIUM
& THE
NETHERLANDS

Musée Hergé, Louvain-la-Neuve
Hergé

museeherge.be

Tintin, teenage reporter for *Le Petit Vingtième*, a conscientious journalist with a boy-scout, do-gooding spirit, first appeared in a comic strip in 1929; the following year, the first of twenty-four adventures in book form took him and his faithful companion, the pure-white fox terrier Snowy, to the newly formed Soviet Union, to report to his readers on what life was like there. Whatever he may have discovered about Soviet life, he returned permanently changed in one respect. Starting out on a journey in an open-topped car, he is neatly groomed; within a few pages the wind has blown his hair into its trademark quiff, and it never sits flat against his head again.

Le Petit Vingtième ('The Little Twentieth') was a real-life publication, a weekly supplement, launched in 1929 and aimed at younger readers, to the magazine *Le Vingtième Siècle* ('The Twentieth Century'). A budding cartoonist named Georges Remi (1907–1983), employed in *Le Vingtième Siècle*'s subscription department, had been given the job of designing, supervising and illustrating the new supplement, and the rest, in Tintin terms, is history. Remi created his pen name of Hergé by reversing his initials (it's what you get if you pronounce 'R G' in the French way).

Tintin's exploits, which have sold over 270 million copies in more than 110 languages, subsequently took him to the Congo, Egypt, Australia and Peru; with a growing group of companions, including the whisky-loving Captain Haddock and the not-quite-identical Thom(p)son Twins, he investigated drug smuggling (*Cigars of the Pharaoh,* 1934) and the international oil trade (*Land of Black Gold,* 1950). Most notably, perhaps, he went to the moon in 1953, sixteen years before Neil Armstrong took his giant leap for mankind.

So it's good to find the museum dedicated to his creator in a suitably futuristic building. Purpose-built under the auspices of Hergé's widow, it's situated in Louvain-la-Neuve, about twenty-five miles (forty kilometres) southeast of Brussels, at an address that is also purpose-built: rue Labrador 26, the location of Tintin's apartment in the early books.

Inside, there are multiple examples of finished albums, sketches, work in progress and a superb resin replica of the Shark Submarine invented by Professor Calculus in *Red Rackham's Treasure* (1944), on the absent-minded but conveniently wealthy professor's first appearance in the series. (For the uninitiated, Red Rackham was a pirate, and how better to search for the

treasure he is said to have left at the bottom of the sea than in a shark-proof submarine?) There's also copious evidence of Hergé's serious attitude to research: his red and white cigar-shaped moon rocket, cutting-edge at the time, owes a debt to both NASA and the German-turned-American aerospace engineer Wernher von Braun. He was meticulous about other forms of transport, too: it's easy to feel seasick just looking at the images from *The Shooting Star* (1942), with a steamship pitching and tossing in the Arctic Ocean as it bears Tintin and his friends towards the site where a mysterious meteorite has crashed.

Another impression you'll take from the museum is how modern Hergé remains. He seems to have had his finger on the pulse of many issues that matter to this day. In *The Red Sea Sharks* (1958), Captain Haddock is appalled that human trafficking is still going on in the twentieth century. Two years later, *Tintin in Tibet* features an Adorable – as opposed to Abominable – Snowman, which must make *Tintin* one of the first comic strips to address the question of animal versus human rights.

Away from the drawing board, Hergé seems to have been, at best, a mass of contradictions. Apparently mild-mannered and humorous, he fell out with colleagues throughout his life; after the Second World War he was accused (though acquitted) of collaborating with the Nazis; his work is undeniably guilty of the racial stereotyping that was common at the time. Yet he insisted on replying to all his fan mail personally, because not to do so would be to betray the children who wrote to him. He also obviously took great pleasure in his work. In the grounds of the museum you will find one of the most endearing statues to feature in this book: a bronze Hergé perches on a pile of books, a cigarette between his lips, his drawing board on his lap, sketching whatever he sees in his mind's eye. Tintin, no more than a quarter of his creator's height and with Snowy in his arms, stands on the same plinth, observing the work in progress, while Hergé's pet Siamese cat Thaïke crawls around its owner's neck and peers over his shoulder. The look on the artist's face is one of pure contentment. Dislikable in many ways, he had his redeeming features.

The Battlefield of Waterloo
Victor Hugo, William Makepeace Thackeray and Stendhal

waterloo1815.be

The Battle of Waterloo has gone down in history as being absolutely decisive: the last battle of the long-running Napoleonic Wars, it put an end to Napoleon's career, and the expression 'meeting your Waterloo' is used to this day to mean suffering a crushing defeat. It was a brutal encounter that resulted in some 65,000 human casualties (killed, wounded or missing) and the death of 7,000 horses.

Another horrific aspect, as featured in several literary accounts, was the noise. With cannons and other artillery forming a major part of the weaponry, the firing was audible in Brussels, some fifteen miles (twenty-four kilometres) away, and must have been deafening on the battlefield. In *The Charterhouse of Parma*, Stendhal (Marie-Henri Beyle, 1783–1842), portraying a scene of chaos, has his hero Fabrizio attempting to converse with a general:

> *But the din at that moment became so terrific that Fabrizio could not answer him. We must admit that our hero was very little of a hero at that moment. However, fear came to him only as a secondary consideration; he was principally shocked by the noise, which hurt his ears. The escort broke into a gallop; they crossed a large patch of tilled land which lay beyond the canal. And this field was strewn with dead.*

In *Vanity Fair*, William Makepeace Thackeray (1811–1863) tells us that on the morning of the battle, Sunday 18 June 1815, 'Much louder than that which had interrupted them two days previously ... the cannon of Waterloo began to roar' and, later, that 'All that day from morning until past sunset, the cannon never ceased to roar. It was dark when the cannonading stopped all of a sudden.'

Thackeray, as a Brit, is concerned largely with the fate of his British protagonists; in *Les Misérables,* Victor Hugo (1802–1885) understandably sees the battle more from the French point of view:

> *If it had not rained in the night between the 17th and the 18th of June, 1815, the fate of Europe would have been different. A few drops of water, more or less, decided the downfall of Napoleon. All that Providence required in order to make Waterloo the ending of Austerlitz was a little more rain, and a cloud traversing the sky out of season sufficed to make a world crumble.*[1]

Hugo goes on to describe the battlefield itself:

> *... let the reader picture to himself a vast undulating sweep of ground; each rise commands the next rise, and all the undulations mount towards Mont-Saint-Jean, and there end in the forest.*
>
> *Two hostile troops on a field of battle are two wrestlers. It is a question of seizing the opponent round the waist. The one seeks to trip up the other. They clutch at everything: a bush is a point of support; an angle of the wall offers*

them a rest to the shoulder; for the lack of a hovel under whose cover they can draw up, a regiment yields its ground; an unevenness in the ground, a chance turn in the landscape, a cross-path encountered at the right moment, a grove, a ravine, can stay the heel of that colossus which is called an army, and prevent its retreat. He who quits the field is beaten; hence the necessity devolving on the responsible leader, of examining the most insignificant clump of trees, and of studying deeply the slightest relief in the ground.

If you've never quite got to grips with the Napoleonic Wars, the Waterloo Memorial Museum, on the site of the battle, will help put them in context. Alongside numerous examples of the uniforms and the weapons, the exhibition details the battles leading up to this one and presents some of the European rulers as pieces on a giant chess board. There's also a vast panorama – 360 feet (110 metres) in circumference and 40 feet (12 metres) high – dating from 1912 and still very impressive, depicting a key moment at Waterloo when the French cavalry were forced into retreat. But most memorable of all is the short 4D film (for which special glasses are supplied) showing close-ups of the charges and the hand-to-hand fighting, and of the battlefield strewn with corpses. If you've never given much thought to the human cost of battle – or even if you have – this film will stay with you.

When you've seen this, take the stiff climb (200+ steps) up to Lion's Mound, admire the massive lion monument, symbolic of the victory of the anti-Napoleon coalition, and look down on the battlefield. Pick your day and exhibitions of cannon fire will add to the effect, but it's perhaps more moving to find a few moments of silence. Read the sign boards and see how the various troops were deployed and how the lie of the land dictated how the battle developed. Hugo's image of 'two wrestlers seizing each other round the waist' will never have seemed more real; but thinking of the loss of life may also bring back Thackeray's two bald sentences, summarising the end of that fateful day:

No more firing was heard at Brussels – the pursuit rolled miles away. Darkness came down on the field and city: and Amelia was praying for George, who was lying on his face, dead, with a bullet through his heart.

1 The Battle of Austerlitz had been a decisive victory for Napoleon ten years earlier – as with Waterloo for the British, it was triumphant enough for a railway station in the capital to be named after it.

Anne Frank House, Amsterdam

Anne Frank

annefrank.org

The Diary of a Young Girl by Anne Frank (1929–1945) must be one of the most poignant works of literature ever, and her house one of the most chilling of museums. It's only a house, but you feel as if something bad happened here.

The first thing that strikes you is how small it is. Not the building itself: the houses that line Amsterdam's main canals are typically tall and narrow, and this one is no different. It's in the part called the Secret Annex, where Anne and seven others were hidden from the Nazi authorities by well-wishers, that the walls seem to crowd in on you.

To begin at the beginning, Anne Frank was given a diary for her thirteenth birthday, 12 June 1942. Her first entry describes waking at six o'clock on the morning of that day – an hour before she is supposed to get up – and her excited anticipation of her presents, which she goes on to list: 'masses of things from Mummy and Daddy' plus a party game, sweets, a puzzle, a brooch. What could be more normal for a thirteen-year-old girl on her birthday? But normality was not to last much longer.

Anne was Jewish, and by 1942 Amsterdam had been occupied by the Nazis for the past two years. The Franks were, in fact, German; Anne had been born in Frankfurt and her father Otto – already aware that there was no future and no safety for Jews under the Nazi regime – had moved his family to Amsterdam when Anne was four years old. The lack of safety soon followed them: less than a month after that first girlish entry in the diary, the family was forced to go into hiding after Anne's elder sister Margot, aged just sixteen, received a 'call-up' notice from the SS, requiring her to report for relocation to a work camp. Over the previous few months the family had been stealthily and gradually moving their possessions into Otto's office on Prinsengracht, with a view to going into hiding there when they had to; Margot's call-up meant that the move had to happen immediately, earlier than planned and without much dignity:

> *We put on heaps of clothes as if we are going to the North Pole, the sole reason being to take clothes with us. No Jew in our situation would have dreamed of going out with a suitcase full of clothing. I had on two vests, three pairs of pants, a dress, on top of that a skirt, jacket, summer coat, two pairs of stockings, lace-up shoes, woolly cap, scarf and still more.*

The four Franks were to share their new accommodation with four others: Otto's business partner Hermann van Daan (van Pels in real life, but this is the name that Anne uses) with his wife and son; and, later, a family friend called Fritz Pfeffer.

Anne's diary describes her new home in matter-of-fact detail:

A wooden staircase leads from the downstairs passage to the next floor. There is a small landing at the top. There is a door at each end of the landing, the left one leading to a storeroom at the front of the house and to the attics. One of those really steep Dutch staircases runs from the side to the other door opening onto the street.

The right-hand door leads to our 'Secret Annexe'. No one would ever guess that there would be so many rooms behind that plain grey door. There's a little step in front of the door, and then you are inside.

There is a steep staircase immediately opposite the entrance. On the left a tiny passage brings you into a room which was to become the Frank family's bed-sitting-room, next door a smaller room, study and bedroom for the two young ladies of the family. On the right a little room without windows containing the washbasin and a small W.C. compartment. ... If you go up the next flight of stairs and open the door, you are simply amazed that there could be such a big, light room in such an old house by the canal.

More chilling is the fear that they will be overheard and discovered. The business premises next door are deserted after hours:

...but even so, sounds could travel through the walls. We have forbidden Margot to cough at night, although she has a bad cold, and make her swallow large doses of codeine. ... I can't tell you how oppressive it is never to be able to go outdoors, also I'm very afraid that we shall be discovered and be shot. That is not exactly a pleasant prospect.

For added security, the Secret Annexe was hidden behind a bookcase that swung out on its hinges and opened like a door. Its shelves were filled with box files to make it look like an ordinary piece of office furniture: just what visitors see today. The hinged bookcase; the steep staircase behind it leading up to the living area; the overcrowded living room that during the day accommodated eight people, with Mr and Mrs van Daan's bed in the corner; the unsatisfactory and not exactly private washing and bathing arrangements.

You stop to consider how uncomfortable it would be to spend a week here. Then you remember that the Franks and their companions were here for two

solid years. Supplies were brought by loyal friends, but as Anne had remarked early on, the fugitives never went out; they never even looked out the window. It doesn't bear thinking about.

It's the day-to-day preoccupations of a girl entering adolescence that make the diary so poignant: Anne's lack of self-confidence, her perpetual complaints that her mother doesn't understand her, her crush on Peter van Daan. Couple this familiar teenage angst with the constant fear of discovery, the anxiety and gloom that are cast over the whole group if, as happens on one occasion during dinner, someone knocks on the wall next door.

Then couple that with the knowledge of what happened in the end. In August 1944 someone betrayed the hiding place to the authorities. The eight occupants were carried off to various camps, from which only Otto Frank returned; Anne and Margot ended up in Bergen-Belsen, where they died of typhus (brought on by the squalid conditions) in early 1945, a few weeks before the camp was liberated.

Stand on that staircase, just beyond the hinged bookcase, a moment longer. That initial impression wasn't wrong. Something bad did indeed happen here.

Tulipa purpurea calice
pallescente.
IV.
Tulipa ex pallido tota vi,,
rescens.
III.
Tulipa flo sulphureo,,
lore pallescentibus, lituris pro,,
pe apices roseis flammiformib.
Tulipa niuei coloris
ris rubeo purpurasce
II.
Tulipa florib. reflexis, inferi,
miniatis, exterius herbaceis
margine ex cinnabari ru

Tulip Museum, Amsterdam
Deborah Moggach

amsterdamtulipmuseum.com

The history of global economics is littered with disasters. From stock market crashes to bursting South Sea Bubbles, wild speculators and more cautious investors alike could lose a fortune overnight; what had been a valuable commodity yesterday couldn't be given away today. But there can be few stranger examples of boom and bust than what happened with the tulip in Amsterdam in the 1630s – the story at the heart of Deborah Moggach's *Tulip Fever*.

Amsterdam was at the time one of the richest cities in Europe. People with money to spend fell in love with the rare and exotic tulip, especially the so-called 'broken' form, whose variegated petals produced broken patterns resembling flames and feathers. We now know that this colouring is caused by a viral infection altering the pigments in the cells; in the seventeenth century it simply added to the flower's desirability. Tulipmania, according to the merchant Cornelis in *Tulip Fever*, 'enslaved people from all ranks':

> *'Great fortunes have been made and lost. These new hybrids they have been growing – they fetch the most astonishing prices ... Why, one Semper Augustus bulb – they are the most beautiful and the most valuable – one bulb was sold last week for six fine horses, three oxheads of wine, a dozen sheep, two dozen silver goblets and a seascape by Esaias van de Velde!'*

As he goes on to explain, the tulip is a native of Turkey, but the Dutch are a 'green-fingered, resourceful people' who have developed ever more spectacular varieties:

> *'No wonder people have been losing grip of their senses, for even in death a tulip is beautiful.'*

But it's not the beauty of the tulip that matters in *Tulip Fever*; it's the value of the bulbs. The novel is basically a doomed love story: a wealthy merchant commissions a portrait of himself and his young wife; she and the artist fall in love; they need money to run away together, but in Amsterdam in the 1630s you don't rob a bank, you speculate in the tulip market:

> *Jan has joined the big league now. He is trading in the white, in tulip futures. He and I speak like experts. We have lost sight of the bulbs; they have become an abstraction. We are buying bulbs we have never seen and for which we have not yet paid, gambling on new varieties, that their price will rocket,*

The Doll's House of Petronella Oortman, Rijksmuseum, Amsterdam

rijksmuseum.nl

If you're visiting the Rijksmuseum because of *Tulip Fever* (see page 69), you might also take the opportunity to check out the doll's house of Petronella Oortman, inspiration for *The Miniaturist* by Jessie Burton (born 1982). Like *Tulip Fever*, *The Miniaturist* is set in seventeenth-century Amsterdam and concerns a young woman married to an older and wealthy man. In Burton's work, Nella's husband Johannes gives her an extraordinary wedding gift – a miniaturised version of their home, whose accuracy she finds decidedly eerie. From the loft where firewood is stored to the two kitchens and the hidden cellar below, every detail is perfect and 'even the touch of the velvet curtains suggests a certain power'.

The gift causes unease in the household: Nella's frugal sister-in-law dislikes it on principle; Nella herself is faintly uncomfortable, not sure what her aloof husband means by it. But whatever your emotional reaction, you have to admit that the original in the Rijksmuseum is extraordinary. The difference between it and Burton's version is that the real Petronella – married to a wealthy merchant – commissioned the doll's house herself, from a Frenchman working in Amsterdam. But as with Burton's description, what is most striking is the attention to detail, and luxurious detail at that. There are marble floors and rich fabric wall coverings; the first-floor sitting room is wainscoted with oak and walnut, its soft furnishings a lush scarlet; the curtains round the bed in the master bedroom are a delicate green velvet. Porcelain displayed in the dresser in the kitchen was specially commissioned from the Dutch East India Company in China; the linen in the laundry room is embroidered with Petronella's initials. Everything is precisely to scale.

The one detail that seems not to have concerned Petronella is expense. By the time it was fully furnished, the house cost 30,000 florins – millions of pounds or dollars or euros in today's money. She could have bought the (full-sized) house she lived in on the Herrengracht for that.

trading onwards and upwards. Bulbs have been bought and sold ten times in one day without anyone laying eyes on them.

The artist, whom Moggach (born 1948) calls Jan de Loos, is a real-life figure also known as Jacob van Loo; you can see some of his works in Amsterdam's Rijksmuseum (and in the Danish National Gallery in Copenhagen and the Musée des Beaux Arts in Lyon, if your travels take you there). But for more about tulips, you need to head north along Prinsengracht to the Amsterdam Tulip Museum.

Here, you won't learn just about Tulipmania: you'll be carried eastward to the realm of the sixteenth-century Turkish Sultan Suleiman the Magnificent, an early devotee of the tulip, and back to Holland for the story of Carolus Clusius, the pioneering botanist who first recognised the potential of the broken form. You'll see how striking the flowers are in the rugged mountain landscapes that are their natural home, and learn about the present-day commercial bulb trade, one that expects you to pay sensible prices and actually grow the flowers. The museum is both a riot of colour and an engrossing piece of history – and you can visit all year round, whereas the (undeniably beautiful) outdoor tulip fields are available for only a few weeks in the spring.

That thought brings us back to the feeling of passing beauty, the *memento mori* that underlies *Tulip Fever*. When Cornelis is asking for a vase of tulips to be included in the painting, he muses:

'Do they not remind us of the transitory nature of beauty, how that which is lovely must one day die?'

It's an echo of the remarkably unscientific words of the scientist Carolus Clusius, describing the broken forms:

... any tulip thus changing its original colour is usually ruined afterwards and so wanted only to delight its master's eyes with this variety of colours before dying, as if to bid him a last farewell.

So as not to give too much away, let's just say that not everything in *Tulip Fever* ends as happily as it does in Moggach's *Best Exotic Marigold Hotel*. Also that, to the uninitiated, a tulip bulb looks rather like an onion; a valuable specimen shouldn't be entrusted to anyone who can't tell the difference.

Delft
Tracy Chevalier

vermeerdelft.nl
oudeennieuwekerkdelft.nl
Closed Sundays

If you want to see the original of Johannes Vermeer's painting *Girl With a Pearl Earring*, you have to go to the Mauritshuis museum in The Hague (and it is very much worth the trip). But if your interest has been sparked by the novel of that name by Tracy Chevalier (born 1962), you need to head a few miles south, to the smaller Dutch city of Delft. It's here that Vermeer was born in 1632 and where he spent the majority of his short life. One of the few outdoor scenes he painted, *View of Delft*, is also in the Mauritshuis, but the joy of Delft itself is that has changed so little since Vermeer's time that you can imagine yourself in the pages of the novel – and in the painter's life – just by walking around and taking in its most famous sights.

In the book's opening section, the narrator Griet walks across town from her home to Vermeer's house, where she is to be employed as a maid. The year is 1664 and she is crossing the Market Square:

To my right was the Town Hall, with its gilded front and white marble faces gazing down from the keystones above the windows. To my left was the New Church, where I had been baptised sixteen years before. Its tall, narrow tower made me think of a stone birdcage. Father had taken us up it once. I would never forget the sight of Delft spread below us, each narrow brick

house and steep red roof and green waterway and city gate marked for ever in my mind, tiny yet distinct.

In the centre of the square, now as then, is an eight-pointed star set inside a circle. Each point indicates a different part of Delft, and towards the end of the novel Griet stands in the middle and turns round and round, willing the star to help her choose what to do with the rest of her life, to decide which of the eight paths she should follow. If you aren't facing that sort of quandary, you may opt simply to buy a piece of the famous blue and white Delftware pottery; the eight-pointed star is a popular design.

Crossing the Market Square today still takes you between the Town Hall (early seventeenth century) and the New Church (built in stages from 1381 to 1655). On a clear day – and if you can cope with the 376 steps – you can climb the church tower and see Delft spread out beneath you, much as Griet did; you can also pick out Rotterdam and The Hague in the distance. The church is the last resting place of William the Silent, founding father of the independent Netherlands, remembered by a white marble monument that Griet mentions when she goes to worship there. Creeping into this magnificent building because plague prevents her going to her usual church, she feels 'like a mouse hiding in a rich man's house … the ceiling so high above me it could almost be the sky'.

In an odd quirk of fate, the original Town Hall burned down in 1618 while a final phase of work on the New Church was in progress, so the same architect – Hendrick de Keyser – was commissioned to replace it. Although it was much altered over the years and restored to its Renaissance grandeur only in the twentieth century, the Town Hall still stands at the west end of the square, facing up to the New Church on the east side as if the two buildings were chess pieces on opposite sides of a huge stone board.

The Old Church, dating from 1246, stands just across one of Delft's many canals from the Market Square and it's here that Vermeer and various members of his family are buried. The church is best known for its skewed tower, known as 'Old John' or 'Skewed John' (or, fancifully, 'Holland's Tower of Pisa', although the resemblance is minimal); but the insides, notably the stained glass, the soaring ceiling and the lavishly carved memorial to the Dutch naval hero Maarten Tromp, shouldn't be overlooked. No one knows exactly whereabouts in the church Vermeer lies: he died in debt and was largely forgotten for two hundred years, so he didn't merit anything as spectacular as Tromp's monument. A plaque in the floor gives only his name and dates, with more information supplied by an 'exhibition table' nearby.

Back outside, many of Delft's streets are as Griet would have known them. As she approaches Vermeer's house for the first time, she observes:

> *It was an end house … a little wider than the other houses in the street. It felt less pressed in than many of the houses in Delft, which were packed together in narrow rows of brick along the canals, their chimneys and stepped roofs reflected in the green canal water.*

There may be a few more bicycles today, but that same feeling of being packed into a limited space prevails.

Sadly, Vermeer's own house was destroyed long since; it would be nice if the Vermeer Centre were based there, but you can't have everything. Instead, it can be found in a reconstruction of the headquarters of the Guild of St Luke, the artists' trade union of which he was a prominent member. The Centre does a great job of recreating the feel of Vermeer's life and times, but just walking the streets with Chevalier's novel to hand is the truly enriching experience.

GERMANY & POLAND

Literary Berlin
Christopher Isherwood, Emanuel Geibel and Robert Walser

visitberlin.de

When the American writer Mark Twain (1835–1910) was living in Berlin in the early 1890s, he stayed in a hotel so upmarket that it refused to serve beer to its patrons on the grounds that it was 'too vulgar'. He dubbed the city 'the Chicago of Europe', obviously intending a great compliment:

> *There is no other city, in any other country, whose streets are so generally wide. Berlin is not merely a city of wide streets, it is the city of wide streets. As a wide-street city it has never had its equal, in any age of the world. Unter den Linden is three streets in one; the Potsdamer Strasse is bordered on both sides by sidewalks which are themselves wider than some of the historic thoroughfares of the old European capitals.*

Unter den Linden, running from the Brandenburg Gate to the Lustgarten Park on what is now Museum Island, is Berlin's most famous street, and it's undeniably wide. But Christopher Isherwood (1904–1986), an English-born American living in Berlin in the early 1930s, took a less rosy view than Twain's. In *Goodbye to Berlin*, published in 1939, he described the buildings along Unter den Linden as 'the self-conscious civic centre ... carefully arranged'; here, he said, the buildings – parliament, museums, the opera house, various embassies – were all very dignified and correct:

> *... all except the cathedral, which betrays in its architecture a flash of that hysteria which flickers always behind every grave, grey Prussian façade. Extinguished by its absurd dome it is, at first sight, so startlingly funny that one searches for a name suitably preposterous – the Church of the Immaculate Consumption.*

That isn't the kindest of descriptions – he's also unnecessarily dismissive of the mighty Brandenburg Gate – but it's not entirely inaccurate. The copper dome of the Catholic St Hedwig's Cathedral frankly looks as if it belongs to another building, as if at the last minute someone thought that this conventional neoclassical structure needed a bit of cheering up and plonked something eye-catching but entirely inappropriate on top of it.

Isherwood famously wrote at the start of *Goodbye to Berlin*:

I am a camera with its shutter open, quite passive, recording, not thinking.[1]

So you don't expect him to be very enthusiastic about anything, and that includes Berlin's 'green lung', the Tiergarten, which he dismisses as 'a small damp black wood'. This really is unjust, but fortunately there are other, more lyrical descriptions to be had. Stretching westward from the Brandenburg Gate, the Tiergarten, with its tree-lined walks and substantial lawns, was originally a royal hunting ground. The park had only recently been opened to the public when, in 1837, the Romantic poet and playwright Emanuel Geibel (1815–1884) waxed eloquent about its 'countless treetops, which autumn had clad in the most colourful of garbs'. By 1911, 'the harmless Sunday pleasure-seeking' public were flocking to it, as Robert Walser (1878–1956) reflected in his short story 'Tiergarten', delighting in the 'enchanting pleasure' of sitting on one of its benches:

The image of the Tiergarten as a whole is like a painted picture, then like a dream, then like a circuitous, agreeable kiss.

Today, a carillon equipped with sixty-eight bells serenades passers-by on a Sunday, and an open-air museum celebrating the gas lighting that once illuminated Berlin's streets (and in some places still does) is open twenty-four hours a day, every day.

One reason for Isherwood's moroseness, of course, is that he was writing just as the Nazis were coming to power. He watched with horror as Jews were beaten up in the street, aware that, as a gay man, he might equally easily be the victim of unprovoked attacks. At the time one of the most popular gay bars in Berlin was the Dorian Gray; without openly acknowledging the Oscar Wilde connection, Isherwood visits the (fictional) Lady Windermere bar, whose walls 'were covered with sketches on menu-cards, caricatures and signed theatrical photographs'; it's here that his most famous creation, the

1 When the dramatist John Van Druten (1901–1957), another English-born American, adapted the book into a play in the 1950s he called it *I Am a Camera*; it went on to inspire the musical *Cabaret*.

wannabe actress Sally Bowles, sings, badly but surprisingly effectively, 'her arms hanging carelessly limp, and a take-it-or-leave-it grin on her face'. Later Isherwood drops in to another bar, the Salomé, where 'the whole premises are painted gold and inferno-red – crimson plush inches thick, and vast gilded mirrors' and 'young men with plucked eyebrows' stand at the bar and guffaw – 'supposed, apparently, to represent the laughter of the damned'.

Perhaps what this shows is simply that Berlin, like all large, multi-cultural cities, is a place of contrasts. Isherwood's cool detachment, Geibel's enthusiasm or Walser's unashamed romance – *Willkommen, bienvenue, welcome*. There's room for it all.

Alexanderplatz, Berlin
Alfred Döblin

> *To list them all and describe their destinies would be daunting, only a few instances would be possible. The wind sprinkles all of them with bits of straw. The faces of the eastbound are in no way distinguishable from those of west-, south- or northbound persons, they exchange roles, and the ones now crossing the square towards Aschinger's can be found later in front of the vacated premises of Hahn's ... They are as indistinguishable as those others sitting in trams and buses. They all sit in different postures, adding to the declared weight of the carriage.*

It could be a description of any faceless horde of commuters in almost any big city in the world. In fact, it's Berlin in the 1920s, as described in the free-wheeling masterpiece *Berlin Alexanderplatz* by Alfred Döblin (1878–1957). A huge bestseller in its day, it has been hailed as doing for Berlin what James Joyce's *Ulysses* did for Dublin (see page 204).

On the surface, Alexanderplatz – Alex, as it is popularly known – was in its heyday at the time Döblin was writing. Its department stores were new and glamorous, its advertising billboards a sophisticated novelty. Its position as a transport hub gave it status rather than mere usefulness, and it was the centre of a buzzing, cosmopolitan city:

> *Bars and restaurants, greengrocers and grocers, delicatessens and haulage businesses, painters and decorators, ladies' outfitters, flour and grain products, garages, insurance: the advantages of the fuel injection engine are simple design, ease of use, light weight, no clutter ... Plumbing goods, window cleaners, sleep is medicine, Steiner's paradisal bed.*

But you can't help noticing the irony. Like so many who have written about Berlin, whether German-born or expat, Döblin is well aware of the city's dark side: in listing the attractions on offer on Alex, he recalls the promises of 'peace, freedom and bread' made to the German people at the end of the First World War, only ten years earlier, and concludes that 'never has a people been more shamefully deceived'. It's always windy on Alex (hence the straw being blown into people's faces); everywhere you turn, someone is selling something – tobacco, newspapers, sex, bananas – and the general impression is decidedly tacky:

> *Give your kids bananas. The banana is the most sanitary of fruits, its peel protects it from insects, worms and germs. (Except such insects, worms and germs as penetrate the peel.)*

Then there's:

> *... fine sausage, home deliveries possible, cheap liver sausage, blood sausage.*
>
> *The highly interesting Magazine retails for 20 pfennigs instead of 1 mark. Marriage, highly interesting and saucy, 20 pfennigs ... Here's an old man with a set of doctor's scales: check your weight, 5 pfennigs.*

All human life is here, in other words. But it isn't a happy life, not least for Döblin's protagonist, Franz Biberkopf. He's just out of prison; we're told in the

novel's opening paragraph that he did time for 'some stupid stuff', and he's now determined to 'go straight'. However, as the very next paragraph tells us:

> *To begin with, he succeeds. But then, though doing all right for himself financially, he gets involved in a set-to with an unpredictable external agency that looks an awful lot like fate.*

No matter how hard he tries to escape, Biberkopf finds himself drifting back to that centre of petty and not-so-petty crime, Alexanderplatz and its surrounds.

Today, as in the 1920s, you're unlikely to spend much time in Berlin without visiting Alexanderplatz. Three of the U-Bahn (underground) and three S-Bahn (rapid-transit rail) lines converge here, and trams and buses galore pass through. Badly damaged during the Second World War and substantially rebuilt in the Soviet era, it is now dominated by the Fernsehturm television tower, erected in the 1960s as a symbol of communist power, and by a number of high-rise buildings dating from the same era. Various subsequent plans to redesign it have, for one reason or another, never come to fruition. It's a major shopping centre, though not the most glamorous one: if you want Gucci and Prada, you need to head west to Kurfürstendamm. Said to be the most visited area in the city, Alex is busy, important and just a bit soulless. But there are echoes still of Döblin's poignant, tongue-in-cheek epilogue, apparently written by someone travelling through on a bus:

> *Look out, and you're amazed to see the human tide crossing the road. Where can they all be coming from? Well, the ones on the left, they've had business in the court or with the police, and on the right they're coming from the market, and then there are some that are heading for the train station, oh, do stay, it's quite nice in Berlin.*

The Berlin Wall
John le Carré

mauermuseum.de

If you didn't live through it, it must be hard to imagine that for nearly thirty years – from 1961 to 1989 – there was a wall, patrolled by sentries, armed with searchlights and covered in barbed wire, running through the centre of Berlin. It surrounded the area known as West Berlin, an enclave of the Federal Republic of Germany – commonly known as West Germany – and divided it from the Russian-occupied, communist East. Between the end of the Second World War

(1945) and the time the Wall was built, perhaps 2.5 million Germans, including substantial numbers of skilled workers, professionals and intellectuals, had fled from East Germany to the 'free' West; if such a brain drain were allowed to continue, the communist leadership reasoned, the East German state would cease to be economically viable. The way out had to be, if not entirely cut off, at least strictly controlled; building a wall seemed the way to do it. Its existence didn't stop people trying to leave, however. It's estimated that over the years more than 200 people lost their lives in failed escape attempts.

The Wall became a powerful emblem of the 'Cold War' of the period, and no part of it was more potent than its checkpoints, the points where authorised persons could legally cross. There were three of these, named by the West according to the letters of the NATO alphabet: Checkpoint Alpha, Checkpoint Bravo and, most important because it was the most central, Checkpoint Charlie, at the junction of Friedrichstrasse with Zimmerstrasse and Mauerstrasse.

It sounds like the stuff of which spy literature is made and indeed 'Cold War thrillers' were a major genre, in which the smuggling of people, arms and secrets across the Wall were a significant feature. The greatest exponent of such works was John le Carré (1931–2020) and the greatest example was probably his breakthrough novel, published in 1963, when the Wall was newly built. Everything about *The Spy Who Came in from the Cold* is chilling, but for pure menace le Carré's description of the checkpoint – not yet nicknamed Charlie – stands out:

> *There was only one light in the checkpoint, a reading lamp with a green shade, but the glow of the arclights, like artificial moonlight, filled the cabin. Darkness had fallen, and with it silence. They spoke as if they were afraid of being overheard. Leamas [the spy of the title] went to the window and waited, in front of him the road and to either side the Wall, a dirty, ugly thing of breeze blocks and strands of barbed wire, lit with cheap yellow light, like the backdrop for a concentration camp. East and west of the Wall lay the unrestored part of Berlin, a half-world of ruin, drawn in two dimensions, crags of war.*

The Wall was famously torn down in 1989, but you can visit the Mauermuseum – the Wall Museum or Museum House – to brush up on its history. Intriguingly, the museum's origins can be traced to as early as 1962, when an anti-communist resistance fighter named Rainer Hildebrandt began to record the stories of the first refugees. Within a year, his fledgling museum had relocated to its present site adjacent to Checkpoint Charlie. Here you can see some original pieces of the Wall, a selection of fake and genuine documents that helped people to persuade the authorities to let them pass, and an escape car with a compartment in the boot for hiding contraband; you can also read about the escape made in 1979 in a home-made hot-air balloon.

Almost as iconic as Checkpoint Charlie, a few miles to the north are the remains of a stretch of Wall on Bernauerstrasse – the spot where the first section was built and the first segments broken off when it was torn down. Now a largely open-air installation known as the Berlin Wall Memorial, it includes 200 feet (60 metres) of Wall, a five-storey observation tower, a Chapel of Reconciliation and a replica of the bronze Statue of Reconciliation, created by the English sculptor Josefina de Vasconcellos for the University of Bradford but now also to be found in Coventry, Belfast and Hiroshima. The statue depicts a man and woman embracing, presumably after lengthy and frightening separation: a ray of hope that would have been totally alien to John le Carré's characters. The final scene of *The Spy Who Came in from the Cold* (unforgettably recreated in the film starring Richard Burton) takes place at another key point in the Wall, a bit further north:

> *Before them was a strip of thirty yards. It followed the wall in both directions. Perhaps seventy yards to their right was a watch tower; the beam of its searchlight played along the strip. The thin rain hung in the air, so that the light from the arclamps was sallow and chalky, screening the world beyond. There was no one to be seen; not a sound. An empty stage.*

The watch tower's searchlight began feeling its way along the wall towards them, hesitant; each time it rested they could see the separate bricks and the careless lines of mortar hastily put on. As they watched the beam stopped immediately in front of them. Leamas looked at his watch.

'Ready?' he asked.

She nodded.

There's nothing like le Carré's terse, no-nonsense prose for alerting you to the fact that something is about to go horribly, tragically wrong.

Theater am Schiffbauerdamm, Berlin
Bertolt Brecht

berliner-ensemble.de *Guided tours Sundays only*

If you want to go to the theatre in Berlin, what better place than the one that was for many years under the direction of Germany's greatest twentieth-century playwright? Jewish and left-wing, Bertolt Brecht (1898–1956) fled his native land after the rise of the Nazis, spending the war years in the United States. He returned in 1948 and settled in East Berlin, intending (perhaps naively) to offer his support to the fledgling socialist state against a supposed fascist threat. Whatever the rights and wrongs of his politics, he remained there for the rest of his life and founded – in collaboration with his wife and long-term business partner, the actor and artistic director Helene Weigel – the Berliner Ensemble theatre company. In 1954 they moved the company into the Theater am Schiffbauerdamm, which is its home to this day.

The theatre had opened its doors in 1892 and, under various managements, staged everything from modern drama to operetta, eventually establishing a reputation for plays dealing with contemporary social issues. Brecht and Kurt Weill's *Threepenny Opera* premièred there in 1928; Brecht and Weigel's management saw revivals of his *Mother Courage and Her Children* and *The Caucasian Chalk Circle* and, after his death, there were premières of several plays for which he had failed to find backers during his lifetime, including *The Resistible Rise of Arturo Ui*.

The building itself is imposing neo-Baroque, not as over the top as others in the style, perhaps (see Paris Opera House, page 17), but an impressive symbol of Germany as an emergent imperial power. The main auditorium is all gilt and red plush, with each pillar topped by a carving of a scantily clad

Muse. Guided tours take you behind the scenes to make-up, costume and props departments, and downstairs, where one of the points of interest is the revolving stage. The Theater am Schiffbauerdamm was the first to use this feature as a dramatic device (in Max Reinhardt's 1905 production of *A Midsummer Night's Dream*); during the Soviet era Weigel's contacts within the occupying forces enabled them to expand it, running it on thirty-two wheels salvaged from a disarmed Russian tank. In a more modern touch, the curtain bears a representation of Picasso's *Dove of Peace*, originally hung by Brecht as a warning against war in general and recently restored specifically as a symbol of solidarity with Ukraine.

The *platz* on which the theatre stands is now named after Bertolt Brecht, and a statue of him seated on a bench was installed there in 1988 to mark the ninetieth birthday he didn't live to celebrate. He sits at the edge of an attractive green space, but doesn't look happy. But then he wouldn't. Being happy is not what Brecht is about. This is the man who pioneered the concept of plays that were intended not to entertain but to make the audience think, who wanted us to be appalled by monsters such as Arturo Ui and Mack the Knife. 'I don't write for slobs who want me to warm the cockles of their hearts', he once said. He also wrote, in his poem 'To Posterity':

He who laughs
Has not yet heard
The terrible news.

If you can cope with that, his theatre is worth the trip.

Lübeck (1)
Thomas Mann

buddenbrookhaus.de/museum/museum
Closed for refurbishment; scheduled to reopen in 2028
museum-behnhaus-draegerhaus.de/home
Closed Mondays

'Without a birthplace there can be no cosmopolitanism,' wrote the novelist Heinrich Mann (1871–1950) in 1945. Born in Lübeck but *persona non grata* there under the Nazi regime, he was living in exile in the United States, having had his books burned in his homeland for being 'contrary to the German spirit'. Mann was part of a wealthy Lübeck family of merchants which had, from the nineteenth century onwards, also spawned a number of writers, actors and film-makers. From solid conservatism, the Manns' political views moved steadily towards the left and they gradually drifted away from the home town where they had once been extremely powerful.

It's Heinrich's younger brother Thomas Mann (1875–1955) who is best remembered today. His most famous novel, *Buddenbrooks*, published in 1901 when he was only twenty-six and always described as semi-autobiographical, concerns various generations of a family which, at the start of the book in 1835, is at the height of its powers as a dynasty of successful grain merchants. Over the following decades, misplaced ambition, ill health, various unhappy marriages and the activities of a wastrel son bring the Buddenbrooks and their business interests to their knees. The book's subtitle, *The Decline of a Family*, has warned us: over its seven-hundred-plus pages we watch helplessly as the various strands of their fortune unravel.

When the current refurbishment is completed you'll be able to investigate all this and more at the Buddenbrook House/ Heinrich and Thomas Mann Centre at 4 Mengstrasse, Lübeck. (At the moment you have to content yourself with visiting various Mann-related exhibitions at the Museum Behnhaus Drägerhaus, but this is an excellent art gallery housed in two eighteenth-century mansions, so there's plenty to help you pass the time.) Number 4 Mengstrasse is the house that Thomas's grandparents bought in 1841 and which he knew as a child (it was sold to the city after his grandmother's death in 1890). One of its must-sees is the glorious 'landscape room' on the first floor, the so-called *bel étage*, which Mann evokes so vividly:

> *The room was hung with heavy, resilient tapestries put up in such a way that they stood well out from the walls. They were woven in soft tones to harmonize with the carpet, and they depicted idyllic landscapes in the style of the eighteenth century, with merry winemakers, busy field-workers and gaily beribboned shepherdesses who sat beside crystal streams with spotless lambs in their laps or exchanged kisses with amorous shepherds. These scenes were usually lighted by a pale yellow sunset to match the yellow coverings on the white enamelled furniture and the yellow silk curtains at the two windows.*

The mission of the revamped Buddenbrook House will be to act as a centre for scholarship on the Mann family, while encouraging visitors to explore and discover on their own. Following in Mann's spirit, the Centre is for both 'the few [...] and the many': for the few experts and the many interested individuals. As such, it offers everything from conferences to literary walks, concerts and 'Christmas with the Buddenbrooks', a ritual that the older generation of Buddenbrooks (or was it the Mann grandparents?) observed faithfully:

> *They gathered in the landscape-room with due solemnity ... The smell of the Christmas tree was already coming through the crack in the great white folding doors; and the Frau Consul took the old family Bible with the funny big letters, and slowly read aloud the Christmas chapter; and after the choir-boys had sung another carol, everybody joined in 'O Tannenbaum' and went in solemn procession through the hall into the great salon, hung with tapestries that had statuary woven into them. There the tree rose to the ceiling, decorated with white lilies, twinkling and sparkling and pouring out light and fragrance; and the table with the presents on it stretched from the windows to the door.*

If you find yourself wondering where *Buddenbrooks* ends and the history of the Mann family begins, don't worry. It has been said that in this museum, as in the novel, the line between fact and fiction is 'spectacularly blurred'.

Thomas Mann was awarded the Nobel Prize in Literature in 1929, making him the first of three Nobel laureates to have emerged from this modestly sized city. West German Chancellor Willy Brandt (1913–1992) won the Peace Prize in 1971, and then in 1999 the Literature Prize came to Lübeck again ...

Lübeck (2)
Günter Grass

grass-haus.de
Open all year; closed Mondays from January to March
st-marien-luebeck.de

Like many writers from his part of the world, Günter Grass (1927–2015) went through a number of sea changes in the course of his life. He was born in what was then the Free City of Danzig; by the time he was twenty it had become the Polish port of Gdansk. Having served in the Waffen-SS (a fact which understandably upset his left-wing admirers when he revealed it late in life), he came to regard the Nazi regime as having been so full of 'mistakes and madness' that, when he turned to writing, he found that his subject matter had been more or less chosen for him. His first and most famous novel, *The Tin Drum* (1959), is a magic realist fantasy that starkly portrays the madness of the Nazi era, and his writing remained political and controversial throughout his career.

So it comes as a bit of a surprise to find that his former home in Lübeck, now the Günter Grass House museum, should be – on the outside, at least – a quaint historical building in a narrow street in the old town, complete with charming garden and courtyard. Inside, it's more modern. The entrance hall is impressive, with many editions of Grass's books in different languages hanging from the ceiling; the walls are decorated with a timeline of his life and

work and with quotations about him by fellow authors and friends. There's an endearing quirkiness about some of these. You expect the ones along the lines of 'the best German writer since Thomas Mann' and others that praise his political engagement; perhaps not the one that talks about him swimming like a shark in the swimming pool on the capitalist block, or the suggestion that he should wear a collar and tie, as it would make him look younger.

He may have been careless of his appearance, but Grass was a multi-talented man, a lifelong sculptor and graphic artist as well as a writer. He drew the cover illustrations for his own novels, and the museum's collection includes many of these, with various sculptures on display in the garden and courtyard. As you approach the front door (redolent with the scent of roses and lavender if you've chosen the right time of year), you're greeted by a bronze forearm standing upright and grasping a solid and surprised-looking fish. (Fish were a recurring feature of Grass's work, notably the flounder that was the title of a 1977 novel – another source of controversy, as it was seen by many as being anti-feminist.) Two bronze heads, one appreciably squatter than the other, also emerge from the gravel, while a collection of seven bronze birds, tall, slender and vaguely goose-like, stand on a plinth nearby.

Not ten minutes' walk from the house is the third-largest church in Germany, Marienkirche (St Mary's Church). It has all the glories you'd expect in a thirteenth/fourteenth-century basilica built when Lübeck was the centre of the rich and powerful trading confederation known as the Hanseatic League. It boasts a seven-hundred-year-old font; medieval frescoes that were the subject of a forgery scandal when they needed to be restored after the Second World War; and an astronomical clock that would have had Goethe's tongue hanging out in envy (see page 99). It's a wonderful place. Then, tucked away in the northwestern corner, are paintings by – yes – Günter Grass, including the 'Tree of Life', depicting a crucifix by which you are invited to light a candle or say a prayer.

If you want to go a bit further afield, an app called 'Tour de Grass' will guide you along the Elbe–Lübeck canal. A two-hour cycle ride takes you to Mölln, a small town surrounded by lakes and associated with Till Eulenspiegel ('Owl Mirror'), the practical joker of medieval folklore who had a reputation for exposing vices. Mölln and the surrounding countryside are worth the trip in themselves, but the point of the app is to take you through Grass country, listening to stories and poems inspired by the landscape and stopping to admire the places that he chose to paint. If all you knew about Grass before you came to this part of Schleswig-Holstein was that he wrote about a disturbed young man who beat a drum in protest against the world around him, you are in for a treat.

Karl Marx House, Trier

Karl Marx

trier-info.de/en/museums/karl-marx-house

Germany's oldest city, founded by the Roman Emperor Augustus in 16 BC, draws visitors for all sorts of reasons. Situated on the banks of the Moselle River and surrounded by some of the most beautiful countryside in Germany, it has the best preserved Roman city gate north of the Alps; the grandiose Romanesque cathedral (the oldest church in the country, founded by the Emperor Constantine in the early fourth century) is a must-see for anyone interested in art or architecture; the Market Square offers an abundance of flowers, fruit and vegetables six days a week, not to mention a wine stall showcasing the best of the local vineyards. Looking for a single word to sum up Trier, you'd probably waver between picturesque, romantic and charming. You wouldn't necessarily have guessed it was the birthplace of the world's most famous revolutionary socialist.

But so it is. Karl Marx (1818–1883) was born into a comfortable middle-class family in the building that is now the Karl Marx House museum, part of a handsome Baroque terrace on Brückenstrasse (Bridge Street). In fact, he lived in this house for only fifteen months (when his family moved to a more luxurious house near the Roman gate) and after he went to university in Bonn at the age of sixteen he spent little time in Trier. By the time he was twenty-five his radical left-wing views had made it prudent for him to move first to Paris – where he met Friedrich Engels (1820–1895), with whom he was to collaborate on *The Communist Manifesto* – then to Brussels and, in 1849, to London, where he spent most of the rest of his life and famously researched his most significant work, the four-volume *Das Kapital*, in the Reading Room of the British Museum.

Despite all this, Trier retains its claim to him. The museum is more about Marxism than it is about Marx. It's disappointingly short on personal stuff: there's not much more than Marx's pocket watch and the well-worn and uncomfortable-looking reading chair in which he is said to have died, but there's a lot about the philosophical works that made his name and the impact that his thinking continues to have on the world today. If it feels just a little didactic, you can relax afterwards in the walled garden and contemplate the bust that shows him with a flowing beard and hair receding from a noticeably high forehead. It's hard not to be impressed: even in bronze he has quite a presence.

Oddly enough, although there's an imposing sculpture of him and Friedrich Engels in the park in Berlin named after them, Trier didn't see fit to display a memorial to Marx until 2018, the bicentenary of his birth. Even then the statue was a gift from the Chinese. Some 15 feet (4.5 metres) high, it shows him gazing confidently into the future. If you're inclined to worship at the man's feet, this is the place to do it.

Walking from the museum to the statue, you'll have passed Kasino Kornmarkt, now a modern entertainment venue that you can hire for parties, but formerly a dance hall where the young Marx and his wife Jenny were regulars. Sadly, most of the building was destroyed during the Second World War, but they'd have recognised the gleaming white facade, the only part to survive unscathed.

Trier isn't a large city and wandering around it is a pleasure. There is one oddity, though, that often confuses visitors. Another of the many attractions is the second-century Roman bridge and, as it was at one time the only bridge across this stretch of the Moselle, the street approaching was called Bridge Street. Fair enough. But when, in 1947, the authorities decided to honour Marx by naming a street after him, they renamed the part of Bridge Street nearest the river. What remains of Bridge Street is now only a short stretch about half a mile (eight hundred metres) from the bridge itself. So Bridge Street doesn't go to the bridge, and Karl Marx's House isn't on Karl Marx Street. Logic played an important part in Marx's philosophy and it's worth spending a frivolous moment imagining what he might have made of this.

Gutenberg Museum, Mainz
Johannes Gutenberg

mainz.de/microsite/gutenberg-museum
Closed Mondays

It's been said that Johannes Gutenberg's innovations in the field of printing – the printing press and the mass production of metal type – are the most important breakthroughs of the second millennium. Before Gutenberg (*c*.1400–1468), the number of books in the world numbered a few hundred

Incipit prologus sancti iheronimi
presbiteri ī parabolas salomonis

Iungat epistola quos iūgit sacerdoti-
um: immo carta non dividat: quos
xp̄i nectit amor. Cōmētarios in osee.
amos. ⁊ zachariā malachiā. quoq;
poscitis. Scripsissē: si licuisset pre vali-
tudine. Mittitis solacia sumptuum.
notarios nr̄os et librarios sustenta-
tis: ut vobis potissimū nr̄m desudet
ingeniū. Et ecce ex latere frequēs turba
diversa poscētiū: quasi aut equū sit me
vobis esurientibꝫ aliis laborare: aut
in racione dati et accepti. cuiq̄ꝫ preter
vos obnoxiꝰ sim. Itaq; lōga egrota-
tione fractus. ne penitus hoc anno re-
ticerē. ⁊ apud vos mutus essem. triduū
opus nomini vr̄o consecravi. interp̄-
tationē videlicet triū salomonis vo-
luminū: masloth qđ hebrei parabolas.
vulgata editio proūbia vocat: coeleth.
quē greci ecclesiasten. latine cōcionatorē
possumꝰ dicere: sirasirim. qđ ī linguā
nr̄am vertit̄ canticū cāticoꝝ. Fertur et
panaretos. ihū filii sirach liber: ⁊ aliꝰ
pseudographus. qui sapientia salomonis inscribit̄. Quoꝝ priorē hebra-
icum reperi. nō ecclesiasticū ut apud la-
tinos: sed parabolas p̄notatū. Cui iūcti
erāt ecclesiastes. et canticū canticoꝝ: ut
similitudinē salomonis. nō solū nu-
mero librorū: sed etiā materiaꝝ gene-
re coequaret. Secūdus apud hebreos
nusq̄ꝫ est: quia et ipse stilus grecam
eloquētiā redolet: et nōnulli scriptoꝝ
veteꝝ hūc esse iudei filonis affirmāt.
Sicud ergo iudith ⁊ thobie ⁊ macha-
beoꝝ libros. legit quidē eos ecclesia. sed
inter canonicas scripturas nō recipit:
sic ⁊ hec duo volumina legat ad edi-
ficationē plebis: nō ad auctoritatem
ecclesiasticoꝝ dogmatū cōfirmandam.

Si cui sane septuaginta interpretum
magis editio placet: habet eā a nobis
olim emēdatā. Neq; enī nova sic cu-
dimꝰ: ut vetera destruamꝰ. Et tamē cū
diligētissime legerit. sciat magis nr̄a
scripta intelligi: que nō in tercium vas
trāsfusa coacuerit: sed statim de prelo
purissime cōmēdata teste: suū saporē ser-
vaverit. Incipiūt parabole salomōis

Arabole salomonis
filii david regis isrl̄:
ad sciendā sapienti-
am ⁊ disciplinā: ad
intelligenda verba
prudentie et suscipi-
endā eruditationē doctrine: iusticiā
et iudiciū ⁊ equitatē: ut detur parvulis
astutia: et adolescenti sciencia et intel-
lectus. Audiēs sapiēs sapientior erit: ⁊
intelligēs gubernacula possidebit. Ani-
madvertet parabolam et interpretatio-
nem: verba sapientiū ⁊ enigmata eoꝝ.
Timor dn̄i principiū sapiētie. Sapien-
tiam atq; doctrinam stulti despiciūt.
Audi fili mi disciplinā pr̄is tui et ne
dimittas legem m̄ris tue: ut addatur
gracia capiti tuo: ⁊ torques collo tuo.
Fili mi si te lactaverint peccōres: ne ac-
quiescas eis. Si dixerit veni nobiscū.
insidiemur sāguini. abscōdamꝰ tedi-
culas cōtra insontem frustra. degluti-
amus eū sicud infernus viventē ⁊ inte-
grum. quasi descēdentē in lacū: omnē
preciosā substanciā reperiemꝰ. implebimꝰ
domus nr̄as spoliis. sortem mitte no-
biscum. marsupiū sit unum omniū
nr̄m: fili mi ne ambules cū eis. Pro-
hibe pedem tuū a semitis eoꝝ. Pedes
enī illoꝝ ad malū currūt: ⁊ festināt ut
effundant sāguinem. Frustra autem
iacit̄ rete ante oculos pēnatoꝝ. Ipsi q̄ꝫ
contra sanguinē suū insidiantur: et

thousand; by 1500, only fifty years after his printing press was set in motion, there were nine million; today there are billions. His first books, the so-called Gutenberg Bibles, were in Latin, the language of the educated, wealthy and powerful, and he probably printed no more than 180 copies of them. This is all a long way from mass production, mass literacy or taking a few seconds to download an e-book on to your Kindle, but 180 copies still represented an enormous leap forward from the tiny numbers of labour-intensive, hand-written texts that preceded them. They paved the way for, basically, everything in the world of books and news media that came afterwards.

So it's perhaps surprising that the museum celebrating Gutenberg's accomplishments should be situated in Germany's thirty-eighth-largest city, Mainz. But that happens to be where he was born and where he did his most important work.

Another possible surprise: if you thought that printing began with Gutenberg, think again. The Gutenberg Museum takes you back four thousand years to cuneiform inscriptions in the Middle East; it includes the woodblock printing known to the Chinese in the third century and the early uses of paper that had emerged in various parts of Asia by the ninth. Carrying on through to the technology of modern typesetting and including a history not only of the printing press but of the techniques of bookbinding and papermaking, it's quite a journey.

That said, the majority of the museum does focus on Mainz's most famous son. We know tantalisingly little about him: he was born into a wealthy family, which left Mainz for political reasons when Johannes was about eleven; he probably worked as a goldsmith; he did much of his pioneering work on printing in Strasbourg. But he was back in Mainz by 1448, and in 1450 the printing press which made his name was up and running. The museum has reconstructed his workshop, including a printing press based on contemporary woodcuts, and gives frequent demonstrations of type-casting, typesetting and printing Gutenberg style.

The jewels of the museum's collection are its two copies of the Gutenberg Bible, and you have to look quite closely at them to realise that they aren't medieval manuscripts. Each page is set in two columns, with important sentences in red, ornate initial capitals at the start of each chapter and plenty of the sort of decoration in which clerical monks of the period delighted. Considering it was a first attempt at this style of printing, it is surprisingly professional and surprisingly gorgeous.

Apart from Gutenberg, there's what the museum describes as the most beautiful book of the Renaissance era: the snappily titled *Hypnerotomachia Poliphili* ('Poliphilo's Strife of Love in a Dream'), probably written by a fifteenth-century Italian priest called Francesco Colonna. Published in Venice in 1499, its elegant woodcut illustrations rank among the finest of the period. There's a copy of the eighth-century *Dharani Sutra*, a Buddhist text scroll that is one of the oldest surviving examples of woodblock printing. There's an example of the Columbian Printing Press, manufactured in Germany in the nineteenth century following a design by the American George Clymer. Made of cast iron and highly decorated, it was operated by a lever that meant – the advertisers claimed – that even a child could work it; it also increased output from three hundred to four hundred sheets per hour.

This isn't a large museum: its floor area of around 40,000 square feet (3,700 square metres) would fit twice into the Turbine Hall of London's Tate Modern and about twenty times into the Louvre. But it's a gem. Take yourself to Germany's thirty-eighth-largest city and marvel at the legacy of the man who made all the other works mentioned in this book available to you.

The German Fairy Tale Route
The Brothers Grimm

deutsche-maerchenstrasse.com
hann.muenden-erlebnisregion.de/en/poi/sleeping-beauty-castle-sababurg

Warning: you're going to have to suspend a bit of disbelief here. The so-called German Fairy Tale Route – 'where fairy tales come alive' – takes you on a journey through some delightful countryside and picturesque towns to the places where 'fairy tales can be personally experienced'.

OK, some of it may be a bit twee. But channel your inner child and go with it.

The Brothers Grimm – Jakob (1785–1863) and Wilhelm (1786–1859) – were inveterate collectors of folk tales from an early age; it's thanks to them that our childhood reading included Hansel and Gretel, Snow White, Little Red

Arthur Rackham.

Riding Hood and many others. They were born about fifteen miles (twenty-four kilometres) from Frankfurt, in what was then the booming goldsmiths' centre of Hanau. There's a fine bronze sculpture of them in the main square there, with Wilhelm seated poring over an open book, Jakob standing and apparently reading over his shoulder. There's also a small exhibition dedicated to them within the Castle Philippsruhe, with fairy-tale-themed activities for children, and every summer a Brothers Grimm Festival in the castle's glorious parkland.

You'll find other Grimm Museums – and other towns calling themselves 'Brothers Grimm City' – along the Fairy Tale Route. There's Steinau, about thirty miles (fifty kilometres) to the northeast of Hanau, where the brothers lived as small children. There's Marburg, where they were students, dominated by the hilltop Castle of the Landgrave and festooned with half-timbered houses, narrow alleys and steep steps. Fairy-tale sculptures peer out at you at every turn. In Kassel, where they stayed for thirty years, working as librarians and doing much of the work on the tales that made their names, you can do a guided tour 'in the footsteps of the Brothers Grimm' or, if you pick your time right, attend another annual Brothers Grimm Festival (July/August) or the Christmas market which is dedicated each year to a different fairy tale. Jakob and Wilhelm later worked in Göttingen, where a statue of their Little Goose Girl in the market square is described as 'the most kissed in the world'.

But the brothers' life is far from being the only thing highlighted along the Fairy Tale Route. Between Steinau and Kassel, along the Schwalm River valley, is Rotkappchenland, or Little Red Riding Hood Country. The Museum der Schwalm includes an exhibition of the region's traditional textiles and explains the significance of their colours. An unmarried girl wore her hair tucked modestly into – you guessed it – a little red hood.

Then there's Bad Wildungen, a spa town said to have been the inspiration for Snow White and the Seven Dwarfs. In the sixteenth century a local maiden called Margaretha apparently caught the eye of the future King Philip II of Spain. This would have been such an unsuitable match that the girl clearly had to be disposed of. By poison, admittedly, rather than by instructing a servant to take her into the forest and abandon her, but the bare bones of the story are there. A nice touch in the process of history-turning-into-folk-tale is that Margaretha's family owned the local copper mine, whose working conditions stunted the miners' growth.

Continuing northward along the route brings you to Sababurg, and specifically to Dornröschenschloss or Briar Rose Castle. Briar Rose is the original name of the tale we now usually call Sleeping Beauty; the castle, dating from the fourteenth century, was, in the Grimms' time, a ruin overgrown with thorns: a perfect setting for the story of a princess who fell asleep for a hundred years and could not be rescued by the many princes who tried to reach her, 'for the thorns and bushes laid hold of them, as it were with hands; and there they stuck fast, and died wretchedly'. That, by the way, is one of the milder examples of how gruesome the tales can be. Never mind the upbeat tone of the film adaptations, you may want to consider editing the originals before you read them to children.

Today, Briar Rose's thicket has been replaced by a sumptuous rose garden; the local council is developing the restored castle (which operated for a while as a hotel) into an attraction that will further exploit its fairy-tale connections. While waiting for this to open, you can visit on Fridays, Saturdays and Sundays in the summer, be greeted by Sleeping Beauty and her prince, and see an open-air performance of the tale amid some of Germany's most romantic ruins.

So it goes on. In Hamelin – another picture-postcard town of half-timbered houses and medieval churches – a plaque on the wall of the Rattenfängerhaus or Rat Catcher's House (now a restaurant) claims to give an eyewitness account of the legend of the Pied Piper:

> *A.D. 1284 – on the 26th of June – the day of St. John and St. Paul – 130 children – born in Hamelin – were led out of the town by a piper wearing multicoloured clothes. After passing the Calvary near the Koppenberg they disappeared forever.*

Tours of the town are conducted, inevitably, by a guide dressed as the Piper himself.

Equally picturesque are Nienburg (whose non-fairy-tale attractions include an asparagus museum) and Verden (where an amusement park offers a fairy-tale forest and a gingerbread house straight out of Hansel and Gretel); the route concludes, after about four hundred miles (six hundred and forty kilometres) of fantasy, in Bremen, where the Grimms' famous musicians – a donkey, a rooster, a dog and a cat – are commemorated in another statue.

You can do as much or as little of this trail as you like, and the timber-framed houses and cobbled streets of nearly every town on the route make it a delight even without the fairy-tale connections. But enter into the spirit of it and you can be guided wherever you go by beautiful princesses, handsome princes and brightly clad rat catchers. What's not to like?

Castle Frankenstein, Mühltal
Mary Shelley

eberstadt-frankenstein.de
great-castles.com/frankensteinghost.html

The ground-breaking Gothic novel *Frankenstein* was famously written when Mary Godwin (1797–1851), her future husband the poet Percy Bysshe Shelley and their friend Lord Byron were holidaying in Switzerland in the summer of 1816: the weather was unseasonably dreadful and they set themselves a creative-writing task to pass the time. But while the story was conceived and largely set in Switzerland, the title comes from some three hundred miles (four hundred and eighty kilometres) further north, where the ruins of Frankenstein Castle sit atop a 1,300-foot/400-metre hill and loom over the Rhine Valley just south of Frankfurt. The novel's protagonist Victor Frankenstein doesn't carry out his experiments here, but he does travel through the region and describes it precisely:

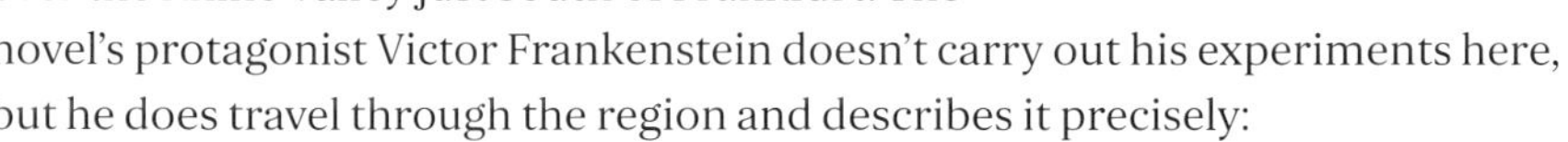

> *We saw many ruined castles standing on the edges of precipices, surrounded by black woods, high and inaccessible. This part of the Rhine, indeed, presents a singularly variegated landscape. In one spot you view rugged hills, ruined castles overlooking tremendous precipices, with the dark Rhine rushing beneath; and on the sudden turn of a promontory, flourishing vineyards with green sloping banks and a meandering river and populous towns occupy the scene.*

The castle is known to have existed in 1252 and to have been the residence of the (real-life) aristocratic Frankenstein family for four hundred years. They sold it in the 1660s and it was never properly cared for again. By the time Mary Shelley (as she is known to posterity) visited the region in 1814, it was more or less in ruins, as it is today. It was never large by castle standards and exploring the remains won't take you long. There's a towering curtain wall; a gate-tower that dates from around 1400 where you can see slits for the chains that

raised and lowered the drawbridge; and a well-preserved kitchen area. You can clamber about to your heart's content, and the views over the woodlands below and the plains beyond are spectacular.

But what probably left more of a mark on Shelley was the reputation of an earlier resident. The controversial theologian Johann Dippel was born in the castle in 1673 and, a century before Shelley's time, he was practising alchemy and producing an unpleasant-sounding substance called Dippel's oil. This, he claimed, was the alchemist's dream, the elixir that promised eternal life. (The fact that it was more effective as an insect repellent or at making water undrinkable seems not to have discouraged him.) Dippel is known to have dissected and experimented on a variety of animals, but there's no evidence that he worked on human cadavers, nor that he proved his theory that a soul could be transferred from one corpse to another using a funnel. Shelley would have heard the rumours, though, and the lack of scientific proof was no deterrent when she later came to dream up an imaginative Gothic novel.

As a brief digression, Dippel wasn't the only scientist to fire Shelley's imagination. The work of the Italian Luigi Galvani was much discussed at the time: he had discovered, probably by accident, that if you put an electric charge through the muscles of a dead frog, the muscles would contract and the animal would appear to come back to life. This concept of 'animal electricity' – an intrinsic force in living creatures – is the science, or pseudo-science, behind the re-animation of Shelley's 'Creature'.

To return to Shelley's trip to the Rhine, she would also have heard about a medieval knight called Lord Georg of Frankenstein who slew a dragon that was upsetting the local peasants; in the course of the fight the dragon stung him with the poisonous spine in its tail and he died three days later. An effigy of Georg with his foot atop the fallen dragon can be seen in the church at nearby Nieder Beerbach.

So, while Shelley did no more than pass through the area, and the only connection between the castle and her novel is the title, there is lots to spark the imagination. Go in bad weather and you can readily conjure young Victor Frankenstein conducting his doomed experiments. The idea of his laboratory being in a ruined castle with thunder crashing around it owes more to Hollywood and Hammer Films than it does to Mary Shelley, but don't let that worry you. Better yet, go at Halloween, when the local restaurant organises special events. Think back to Victor's description of 'the demoniacal corpse to which I had so miserably given life':

> *Oh! no mortal could support the horror of that countenance. A mummy again endued with animation could not be so hideous as that wretch. I had gazed on him unfinished; he was ugly then; but when those muscles and joints were rendered capable of motion, it became a thing such as even Dante could not have conceived.*

In other words, be prepared to be very afraid.

Goethe Museum, Weimar
Johann Wolfgang von Goethe

klassik-stiftung.de/en/goethe-national-museum
Closed Mondays
frankfurter-goethe-haus.de
auerbachs-keller-leipzig.de

You may know him as the author of *Faust*, as a major figure in the *Sturm und Drang* ('Storm and Stress') movement or as the man who first expressed the opinion that life is too short to drink bad wine. Or for any number of other reasons, because as well as being a poet, playwright and novelist – unarguably the most important figure in all German literature – Johann Wolfgang von Goethe (1749–1832) was also, at various times, a lawyer, scientist, geologist and statesman. He met Napoleon, was the first to identify the intermaxillary bone in the human jaw, and understood enough about Isaac Newton's work to attempt to refute his theory of light. Quite a man.

His birthplace in Frankfurt is now a museum, showing the comfortable setting in which he spent his childhood and wrote his first works, notably the play *Götz von Berlichingen*, about a brilliant young man in conflict with society, and the novel *The Sorrows of Young Werther*, about a brilliant young man brought to a tragic end by an unhappy love affair. (If you think you're spotting a pattern here, wait till you get to *Faust*, the play written some thirty years later and dealing with a brilliant older man who sells his soul to the devil.) A highlight of the house is an astronomical clock dating from 1746, an exquisite piece of furniture, elegantly carved and some eight feet (2.4 metres) tall. It shows not only the time and date but phases of the moon and the position of the sun in terms of signs of the zodiac, and you can imagine it fascinating the budding polymath mind of the young Goethe.

After university in Leipzig Goethe moved to Weimar, at the time a tiny independent dukedom, where he became a councillor to the young duke. He lived in Weimar for the rest of his life, and his house there is another museum. It's a handsome Baroque building which he altered to suit his own taste and his position in life. Most noticeably, there's a passageway across the courtyard at first-floor level, linking the formal rooms at the front of the house with the more private ones at the back. Inside the house is a shallow-stepped staircase with niches containing classical sculptures: inspired by the staircases he had seen on a visit to Italy, Goethe wanted to create a staircase 'one would never tire of climbing up and down'.

Members of the royal family Goethe served could mix informally with writers, artists and other guests in the salon he called the Yellow Room, painted in that colour because he had studied the theory of colour and considered that this would make the room 'cheerful, lively and mildly stimulating'. (He was writing about colour in 1810 and it's worth noting that, a good two hundred years later, contemporary colour theorists would agree with him.) The house is almost as he would have left it, so you can see where he slept, where he ate and where he wrote *Faust*, a work that occupied him on and off for half a century.

You can also admire some of the vast numbers of classical sculptures and paintings of all kinds that he collected during his long life.

He may have lived in the same house in the same small place for over half a century, but Goethe was an inveterate traveller. A map on the wall of the Weimar museum shows the places he visited, and it's been calculated that he covered enough distance to have gone all the way around the globe at the equator. 'For natures like mine,' he wrote, 'which like to establish themselves firmly and hold fast to things, a journey is invaluable; it animates, instructs and cultivates.' Clearly, like Montaigne (see page 51), he took the view that nothing human was alien to him, and there seems to have been no limit to what his brain could encompass.

Goethe doesn't only dominate German literature; his memory dominates much of the southeastern part of Germany where he lived. If you find yourself in Leipzig rather than Frankfurt or Weimar, you can still indulge yourself in his legacy. The town's Auerbach's Keller restaurant dates from the sixteenth century, although it has been much modernised since; Goethe drank there as a student and used it in a scene from *Faust*. Two *Faust*-related statues stand outside: one of the hero with Mephistopheles (the devil), the other recalling a scene from the play in which Mephistopheles bewitches a group of drunken students. You can't expect your wine to catch fire in Auerbach's as it did when Mephistopheles was showing off his powers, but that may be just as well. If it did, Goethe's spirit would doubtless emerge from the ether, taking notes and working out how it was done.

Literary Dresden
Friedrich Schiller and others

museen-dresden.de

Open April to October, weekends and public holidays only; special tours on request

dresden-magazin.com/en/culture/literary-walk

> *Dresden. The entire city was an artwork. The sum of thoughts too big to be conceived by one person alone, greater than anything an entire generation could conceive.*

Funnily enough, that lyrical description – which goes on to say that Dresden became 'more exquisite' with every new thing that was built and with each century that passed, and that the only European city to rival it was Florence – was written not by a German, nor by a Pole or a Czech, both of whose countries lie within easy reach of Dresden. It's from *The Bell in the Lake* by

the Norwegian Lars Mytting (born 1968), published in 2018 but set in the last years of the nineteenth century. Nor is Mytting the only one to have likened Dresden to Florence. The Russian novelist Ivan Turgenev (1818–1883) spent time in the city and mentions it in *Fathers and Sons*. His character Pavel Petrovitch, the bourgeois who aspires to become an aristocrat, contemplates leaving Russia and can think of only two places he would like to live: Dresden or Florence. The Germans themselves called it 'Florence on the Elbe' and Mytting's description would have remained largely accurate until February 1945, when British and American bombing devastated more than two and a half square miles (six and a half square kilometres) of the city centre.

Dresden had been a hub of literary society in the eighteenth century, and one of the many houses demolished by the 1945 bombing had belonged to Christian Gottfried Körner (1756–1831), a lawyer and patron of the arts who opened his home to writers and musicians and held a salon where new works could be read or played. Goethe (see page 99) and Mozart were among his guests, as was Körner's close friend and one of Germany's greatest poets and playwrights, Friedrich Schiller (1759–1805). A number of Schiller's plays had their first performances in the small theatre Körner had had built on to his house.

That house may have gone, but Körner was wealthy enough to own another, smaller property with accompanying vineyard to the east of the city centre, and it lives on. Schiller stayed here for several months in 1785, writing the play *Don Carlos* (later adapted into an opera by Verdi). The Schillerhäuschen or Schiller Pavilion, as it is now called, is one of Dresden's smallest museums, containing pictures and manuscripts from the playwright's time there, as well as mementos of that period when Dresden was a mecca for so many artists.

Borders in that part of Europe have always been, let's say, fluid ... so there's nothing odd about finding a museum in Dresden devoted to a Polish writer. Józef Ignacy Kraszewski (1812–1887), credited with more than two hundred novels and nearly as many novellas and short stories, is the most prolific of all Polish authors and, because of his political activism, one of the most significant Polish figures of the nineteenth century. Forced to flee his home country after the 1861 January uprising against Russia, he lived in Dresden for several years, in the house on Nordstrasse which is now dedicated to his memory and to the memory of other Polish émigré writers of the period. A neoclassical building with a high-pitched roof reminiscent of a Swiss chalet, it looks like a comfortable suburban home with a charming garden: pretty, certainly, but nothing out of the ordinary. Yet, as a bi-national museum with an emphasis on all things Polish, it is a first in Germany, and you can see manuscripts and early editions of many of the works Kraszewski produced during his years here – works in which his adopted city and its culture played an important role.

Those fluid borders attracted Russian authors, too. Turgenev's great rival Fyodor Dostoevsky (1821–1881) lived here for a couple of years around 1860, in between health-related trips to various spa towns. He never learned German and is said to have had an ambivalent relationship with Germany itself, admiring its culture but never warming to its people. He must have left his mark, though: there's a statue of him on the Elbe Embankment in Dresden, looking like a man who doesn't want strangers to wander up and chat; on the other side of the river, you'll find a restaurant named Raskolnikoff, after the central character in *Crime and Punishment*.

Among all these visitors and immigrants, you can find one Dresden native: Erich Kästner (1899–1974), satirist and author of the children's novels *Emil and the Detectives* and *Lottie and Lisa* (later twice filmed in English as *The Parent Trap*). Kastner was born here, but the house preserved as his museum belonged to the uncle he often visited as a child. Fitting into one modest-sized room, the museum focuses on the author's early years and

encourages visitors, young and old, to interact with and read anything that takes their fancy. Outside, a statue of the young Erich reflects a scene from his autobiographical *When I Was a Little Boy*, showing him perched on a wall and looking out onto the wider world.

Dresden has been rebuilt twice since the bombing: once in the 1950s and again following the collapse of the Soviet Union and the reunification of Germany. Much of the Soviet-era architecture has gone and a fortune was spent on rebuilding the Baroque Frauenkirche or Church of Our Lady, topped with a golden orb and cross. Delightful or a bit fake? You decide. But these surviving buildings and their literary collections are enough to give a flavour of Florence on the Elbe in its artistic heyday.

Literary Kraków

Joseph Conrad, Stanisław Wyspiański, Czesław Miłosz and others

katedra-wawelska.pl
skalka.paulini.pl
muzeumkrakowa.pl/oddzialy/rydlowka
Closed Sundays and Mondays

With all due deference to the residents of Warsaw, most people would agree that if you had time to visit only one city in Poland, it should be Kraków. The country's capital for six centuries until 1609, it boasts some of the finest Italian Renaissance architecture outside Italy. The finest of all is to be seen in Wawel Cathedral, with its three splendid towers and the graves of almost all the Polish monarchs, a number of whom boasted endearing names such as Wladyslaw the Elbow-High and Zygmund the Old. There's also a collection of prehistoric bones, including the shin bone of a mammoth and the skull of a woolly rhinoceros, said to protect the cathedral just as ravens protect the Tower of London. In his play *Liberation* the dramatist Stanisław Wyspiański (1869–1907), a lifelong resident of Kraków, gives Wawel Cathedral a central role in Polish identity:

> *Here, everything is Poland, every stone and every little thing. Whoever enters it, becomes himself part of Poland ... You are surrounded with Poland, eternally immortal.*

Literary grave-hunters should make a point of seeking out the cathedral's Crypt of National Poets, where they'll find Adam Mickiewicz (1798–1855), widely regarded as Poland's finest, and the great Romantic Juliusz Słowacki (1809–1849). Both died abroad – Mickiewicz in Turkey and Słowacki in France – and their remains were moved to Wawel decades later in symbolic gestures: as with the Panthéon in Paris, being laid to rest in Kraków's cathedral was an honour accorded only to those of national importance, and the poets lie in close proximity to noblemen, generals and other luminaries.

In addition to all this, Kraków was the first continental European city to be designated a UNESCO City of Literature (Edinburgh, Dublin and – yes, really – Norwich were ahead of it). This is an accolade acknowledging the recipient's cultural heritage, in which literature, poetry and drama play an important role. The Cities of Literature website describes Kraków as 'the cradle of the Polish language and literature'; it is certainly the centre of Polish publishing, has more than its share of bookshops, and hosts two major literary festivals each year.

The Conrad Festival, held in October, honours Joseph Conrad (1857–1924), who was born Józef Teodor Konrad Korzeniowski in what is now Ukraine but spent chunks of his life in Kraków. Conrad is acclaimed for, among many other things, writing in a language (English) that he didn't learn until he was in his twenties, and his festival is a chance for writers from all over the world to celebrate literature in many aspects and languages. Conrad's childhood home has disappeared under the city's civic centre, but a plaque on one of the buildings claims that he 'introduced the Polish spirit into English literature, whose treasure he became'. It goes on to quote a passage from the writer's *Notes on Life and Letters* in which, writing towards the end of his life, he looks back on his youth in Kraków:

> *It was in that old royal and academical city that I ceased to be a child, became a boy, had known the friendships, the admirations, the thoughts and the indignations of that age.*

The other festival, held in July, is named after one of Kraków's Nobel Prize-winning poets, Czesław Miłosz (1911–2004). Miłosz was renowned as much for his outspoken criticism of Stalinism (notably in his 1951 work *The Captive Mind*) as for his poetry, and spent much of his adult life as a political exile. He became an American citizen and was able to return to Poland only after he won the Nobel Prize in 1980. He settled in Kraków in 2000, where, after his death, he was honoured with a state funeral. He's buried in the crypt of the Catholic church of Skałka (also known as the Church on the Rock), part of a monastery founded by the legendary medieval chronicler Jan Dlugosz (1415–1480), also buried here. Miłosz's sarcophagus is inscribed with the words 'The cultivation of learning, too, is love', though he might have preferred the tribute to his spiritual home that he wrote while he was still in exile:

> *And the city stood in its brightness when years later I returned.*

Stanisław Wyspiański – also buried in Skałka – was a designer as well as a writer, and the twenty-first-century pavilion named after him, one of the few modern buildings in the Old Town, displays three stained-glass windows conceived by him. He had originally intended the works, which depict early Polish rulers, to be displayed in the cathedral, but the cathedral's loss is the pavilion's gain.

There are traces of Wyspiański all over the city, including in the National Museum and the smaller Szołayski Museum, but if you're interested in the literary aspects of his work it's worth heading a little way out of town to the Bronowice district. Here, what is now the Young Poland Rydlówka Museum was in 1900 a private house where Wyspiański attended a friend's wedding. His best known play, *The Wedding*, opens with this description of the scene:

> *A November night; the sitting room of a well-to-do Polish peasant hut. The hut is white-washed in light blue, almost sky-blue, so that the furniture and all the people who pass through are enveloped in a greyish tone of pale blue. Through an open door on the side toward the vestibule, a boisterous wedding band can be heard ...*

There may not be a boisterous wedding band playing when you visit, but otherwise the setting is just as it used to be.

Poland's borders have always been a moveable feast – many of its authors were born in what are now Ukraine, Belarus and Lithuania. Its government and censorship laws have also often been repressive, so that its writers and intellectuals have been forced, or have chosen, to live elsewhere. Yet through it all Kraków seems to have drawn people in and inspired them to write.

SCANDINAVIA

1870
2000
1900
L. Frölich

Copenhagen and Odense
Hans Christian Andersen

hcandersenshus.dk

Open all year; closed Mondays from November to March

The statue of the Little Mermaid is a must-see for any visitor to Copenhagen: a beautiful young woman cast in bronze, sitting on a rock in the harbour and gazing mournfully out to sea. She's surprisingly small – just four feet (1.25 metres) high, excluding the rock – and you can't get very close, so it takes a second look to notice that below the knees her legs fuse into the fin-like appendage that marks her not as human but as a mermaid. She has every reason to be mournful. Forget the sanitised animated film version; in the original story by Hans Christian Andersen (1805–1875), the unnamed mermaid dies when the prince she loves marries someone else – though, in the improving tone common to nineteenth-century tales for children, she does turn into a spirit with the chance of attaining eternal life.

Endings like this – sorrow in this world with the promise of better things in the next – are typical of Andersen's tales. Yes, the Little Match Girl freezes to death, but then she and her grandmother are carried off to a place where there was 'neither cold, nor hunger, nor anxiety'. Karen in 'The Red Shoes' has to have her feet cut off because the shoes – which she wore in defiance of all that was right and proper – wouldn't stop dancing. Even so, she ends up with her heart 'so full of sunshine, peace, and joy, that it broke' and her soul flies on the sunshine to God. The Ugly Duckling, who has been prepared to die rather than face a lifetime of rejection, turns out to have been a swan all along and cries joyfully and from the bottom of his heart, 'I never dreamed of such happiness as this.'

Two larger-than-life statues of Andersen can be found in Copenhagen: one in Rådhuspladsen (City Hall Square), the other in the rose garden of the city's oldest park, the Rosenberg Castle Gardens or King's Garden. Both show him seated with a book in his hand, as if he were reading us a story. There's a Hans Andersen Experience in the Ripley's Believe It Or Not museum and a Hans Andersen Fairy Tale House in the Tivoli Gardens. This is Denmark's most famous literary son – they make the most of him.

Andersen's story is a rags-to-riches one. He was born in poverty in Denmark's third-largest city, Odense, now a couple of hours' drive to the west of the capital but at that time much more remote; his father (also called Hans) was a shoemaker, his mother a washerwoman. At fourteen, following his father's death and his mother's remarriage, young Hans moved to Copenhagen to seek his fortune, publishing his first story when he was seventeen. He travelled widely, became known as much for his travelogues as for his stories, and achieved the patronage of royalty and the status of a national treasure. He never lived in Odense again but, like Copenhagen, it is keen to celebrate him.

Andersen's childhood home is a little yellow half-timbered house, not far from Odense's cathedral. You can still see the shoes on Hans Senior's workbench and shiver at the thought of the budding author lying on the floor trying to sleep while his father was dead in his bed in the same room. On a more cheerful note, there's a peaceful courtyard garden where the young Hans discovered the wonders of nature that feature so strongly in his stories. One of the lesser-known tales, 'The Happy Family', begins:

> *Really, the largest green leaf in this country is a dock-leaf; if one holds it before one, it is like a whole apron, and if one holds it over one's head in rainy weather, it is almost as good as an umbrella, for it is so immensely large. The burdock never grows alone, but where there grows one there always grow several: it is a great delight, and all this delightfulness is snails' food.*

It must have taken a while just sitting and observing in an unpretentious garden to come up with those words.

There's much here that is charming, but perhaps nothing desperately surprising. The truly original tribute to Andersen – also in Odense – is to be found in the H. C. Andersen House, opened in 2021, which claims to be the first museum of its kind in the world. It's not about the life and times of Hans Christian Andersen, but about the way his work speaks to us now, his way of looking at the world. It emphasises the recurring motif of the stories – that the moment of deepest despair is also the moment of redemption or transformation – and encourages us, as Andersen did, to take a new perspective on the world. In this it is helped both by the architecture of the building and by the natural world, so that, for example, the way light plays through the water means you see the Little Mermaid in different ways depending on the seasons, the weather, even the time of day. You walk along paths lined by high hedges where contrasts between light and dark, and ever-changing scents and colours, inspire the imagination. Encouraging visitors to look at familiar stories from a new angle shows – the museum's curator tells us – that they are deeper and more magical than we might have realised.

If that sounds a bit airy-fairy, try re-reading that piece from 'The Happy Family'. The museum's ethos reflects Andersen's view of the natural world and the magic to be found even in dock leaves and burdock.

Kronborg Castle, Helsingør
William Shakespeare

kongeligeslotte.dk/en/palaces-and-gardens/kronborg-castle.html

The twelfth-century scholar Saxo Grammaticus may not be a household name around the world, but he unknowingly made a massive contribution to world literature when he wrote the first major history of Denmark, the *Gesta Danorum* or 'Deeds of the Danes' and included the story of Amleth, a Danish prince whose father was murdered by his own brother. The brother subsequently married Amleth's mother, leading the son to feign madness in order to avoid the same fate.

Sounds familiar? Yes, it's the basis for the most performed play in the world: William Shakespeare's great tragedy, *Hamlet*. You may remember that Shakespeare's version opens at night on 'a platform before the castle' in Elsinore, where nervous sentries are discussing having seen a ghost who resembles the late king. A few scenes later, on a more remote part of the same

platform, Hamlet and the ghost get together, Hamlet learns that his father was murdered and the whole thing kicks off from there.

Translated into Danish, Elsinore becomes Helsingør, a port city to the north of Copenhagen. It's best known for its castle, Kronborg, which is, by general consent, the inspiration for the setting of *Hamlet*.

It's a fine place, Kronborg, a UNESCO World Heritage site whose turrets, adorned with gilded globes, offer views across the narrow strait that separates this part of Denmark from Sweden. There's been a fortress on the site since the 1420s, but Kronborg owes its magnificence to King Frederick II (reigned 1559–88), who converted it into the splendid example of Renaissance architecture you see today. He built what was then the largest ballroom in Northern Europe – two hundred feet (sixty metres) long, with a marble floor and walls hung with specially commissioned tapestries depicting a thousand years of Danish heroes and monarchs. Frederick, seated under a magnificent canopy of purple silk, presided over lavish entertainments, during which cannons fired to accompany the many toasts he proposed. To help fund this extravagance he had his cannons pointed out into what he dubbed 'the King's Sound' to encourage any ship that wanted to sail past to pay its dues.

Despite his taste for luxury, Frederick hadn't forgotten that the early part of his reign had been marked by conflict between Denmark and various other Northern European countries. As a precaution against any recurrence of hostilities, he had a maze of passages known as casements built under his castle, with room for soldiers and horses to barricade themselves in. According to legend, the Danish national hero Holger Danske – Ogier the Dane – sleeps here, as he has done for many centuries, ready to awaken and raise his sword on the day his country is threatened by enemies. A statue of him – a copy of a bronze original now in the western Danish town of Skjern – sits in the casements, apparently wide awake and not to be messed with.

Holger's duties are confined to fending off enemies, however: he's no proof against natural disasters. So in 1629 he couldn't prevent a fire destroying much of the castle and its furnishings. Although the then king, Frederick's son Christian IV (reigned 1588–1648) immediately set about a massive rebuilding project that repaired the exterior, the interiors were never quite the same. Restoration over the centuries has ensured that the royal apartments and the ballroom are again magnificent, and the casements authentically gloomy and dark. But only the chapel, which escaped the flames, shows Frederick's taste at its flamboyant best.

So where does Shakespeare (1564–1616) fit into this? He probably never visited Denmark, but the heyday of Kronborg spans his lifetime and Frederick is known to have entertained travelling players, some of whom might have come from England. Word of the luxury of the Danish court would certainly have reached London, and it's possible that Shakespeare met two Danish nobles with names remarkably like those of Hamlet's treacherous friends Rosencrantz and Guildenstern when they visited in the 1590s. He would have known the Amleth legend, and it may well be that he simply decided to set his Danish story in the most famous place in Denmark.

Whatever the reason, *Hamlet* has been part of the fabric of Kronborg for a long time. Amateur players performed it here in 1816, to mark the bicentenary of Shakespeare's death; a professional performance by the Danish Royal Theatre took place a hundred years later; and since 1937 it has been a regular event, attracting actors of the calibre of Laurence Olivier and Simon Russell Beale. Shakespeare's scene-setting directions aren't very explicit – he never specifies anything grander than 'a hall in the castle' – but it's not hard to imagine the ghost drifting around one of the turrets, plotting his revenge, or Hamlet and Laertes fighting to the death on that beautifully restored marble floor.

Ibsen Museum, Oslo
Henrik Ibsen

ibsenmt.no

There is precious little in the work of Henrik Ibsen (1828–1906) to raise a smile. He may be the second most performed playwright in the world today (after Shakespeare), but he didn't go in for weird and wonderful. So the weird, wonderful and smile-inducing Peer Gynt Sculpture Park, to the northeast of Oslo city centre, is a surprise. *Peer Gynt* (1867) was one of Ibsen's early successes: it's based on an old fairy tale, and its first production had incidental music by Ibsen's compatriot Edvard Grieg that is today probably more famous than the play itself. The story concerns a young peasant who sets out confidently on a series of adventures (including abducting a bride from her wedding) only to fall into one disaster after another and eventually be redeemed by the love of a devoted woman. The park and surrounding area contain more than twenty sculptures by different artists, each depicting a scene from this narrative. Their titles, including *The Devil in the Nut*, *Trolls with Pig Heads* and *Peer Meets Begriffenfeldt at the Mental Asylum*, give you an idea of just how rich and varied Peer's adventures were.

Peer Gynt has that rarity in Ibsen plays, a happy ending. Most of his greatest works end, if not with death, at least with disaster and misery. They are also scathing indictments of the small-mindedness of Norwegian society, in

ARackham

particular of the restrictions placed on women. In *Ghosts* (1881), the widowed Mrs Alving had stayed with her unfaithful husband for fear of turning herself and her son into social outcasts. In *Hedda Gabler* (1890), the aristocratic Hedda's stifling marriage to someone of lower social status is one of the driving forces behind her destructive – and ultimately self-destructive – behaviour. Worst of all, Nora in *A Doll's House* (1879), in what has been described as the most famous door-slam in theatre, leaves her husband and children simply because she is unhappy. 'I must try and educate myself,' she tells her disbelieving husband. 'I must stand quite alone, if I am to understand myself and everything about me. It is for that reason that I cannot remain with you any longer.'

A bit dated now, perhaps: in the twenty-first century these women could leave their husbands halfway through Act One and the audience could go home. But it was shocking stuff in nineteenth-century Europe.

Ibsen wrote most of these plays while in voluntary exile. Disgruntled with life and lack of success in Norway, he moved first to Italy and then to Germany. With only a few brief return visits, he stayed away for twenty-seven years. But gradually he built up a reputation and by the time he moved back to Kristiania (now Oslo) in 1892 he was internationally famous and something of a national treasure. It doesn't seem to have lightened his mood, though – *The Master Builder* (1892) and *John Gabriel Borkman* (1896), his great plays from this period, are as humourless as ever.

But he could at least afford a luxurious apartment, the first in the city to have indoor plumbing. Today this is part of the Ibsen Museum on, appropriately enough, Henrik Ibsens Gate, near the Royal Palace. In the last few decades the apartment, reached via a dark and narrow staircase that must have suited Ibsen's general state of mind, has been restored to how it was during his last years; great efforts have been made to track down and re-acquire original furnishings that had been dispersed after his wife's death in 1914. The highlight is perhaps the Blue Parlour, where the playwright received his guests: it's a splendid affair of chandeliers, gilded chairs and mirrors. But the Salon boasts an impressive number of portraits, including one of Ibsen, swathed in a black academic gown and louring down at visitors. These formal rooms are generally over-furnished, hung with dark velvets and brocades, and claustrophobic – not unlike the set of many an Ibsen play. There are artefacts, letters and books galore for those interested in his life and work; if you prefer to delve into more intimate matters, the original bathtub is there too, taps, pipes and all.

The facade of the museum is unimposing and would be easy to miss if it weren't for a rather forbidding life-sized statue of Ibsen on the pavement outside. He sits – or rather perches; his feet don't touch the ground – clutching his cane, hat on head, imposing beard bristling and looking very much like a man who doesn't want you to venture into his home and disturb his work.

That is probably an accurate assessment, for he was a man of rigid habits. After working all morning, at 1 p.m. every day he walked the same route past the palace and the National Theatre to the Grand Café, where the same table was always waiting for him. There's no record confirming that he ate the same thing every day, but it's impossible to believe he didn't. The painter Edvard Munch was also a customer, and his portrait of Ibsen in the café is on display in the Munch Museum, half an hour's walk away, down towards the harbour. The café is still there (part of the Grand Hotel which each year hosts the celebratory dinner for the Nobel Peace Prize), but much modernised: it's hard to picture Ibsen reading the paper in these immaculate surroundings. But you may still enjoy recalling a tale that Munch told about the great man, and captured in a pen-and-ink sketch that is also in the Munch Museum. The artist was in the café with his friend, the art critic Jappe Nilssen. Spotting Ibsen at a nearby table, they thought it would be fun to invite him to join them. Clearly not realising that Ibsen didn't do fun, Nilssen approached, only to be told curtly: 'I'm not used to being disturbed by strangers in cafés.' When Nilssen returned to his own table, he and Munch agreed to carry on drinking and not mention the incident again. Which is almost certainly how Ibsen would have wanted it.

Harry Hole's Oslo
Jo Nesbø

vigeland.museum.no
Closed Mondays
restaurant-schrøder.no
royalcourt.no
Open in the summer only, for guided tours

You know you're onto a good thing when you open a novel to find a map of its setting. That's what happens when you enter the world of Jo Nesbø (born 1960). Oslo and surrounds – with everything from the Royal Palace to the bars where fiction's most self-destructive detective, Inspector Harry Hole (pronounced *Hoo*-leh), too often drinks himself into oblivion – are laid out in black and white in front of you. As with Donna Leon's Venice (see page 143), the city is an essential part of the novels, almost a character in itself. If you haven't come across Harry Hole, you might visit the Vigeland Sculpture Park – part of the much larger Frogner Park – to admire the wonderfully life-like bronze 'Angry Baby', stamping his foot and clearly throwing a tantrum. You might well

be aware of the swimming-bath complex in the same park. But once you've read *The Leopard* (2009), the place takes on a whole new meaning: you'll find yourself shivering at the memory of the woman who is forced to jump from the diving board with a rope around her neck and is found decapitated on the bluish-white porcelain of the floor of the pool.

Similarly, normal tourists go to Egertorget Square to shop and to enjoy its outdoor cafés. In Harry Hole land, you listen out for shots and expect to see a young Salvation Army officer, interrupted in the middle of a carol concert, drop dead in front of you, as he does in *The Redeemer* (2005). The city is so intrinsic to the novels, you struggle to separate the two.

With Harry Hole's Oslo, the weather is key, too. In summer, we are told in *Knife* (2019), there is an abundance of growth and life, while the autumn is the finest in the world. It's only spring that lets you down: in the Vår Freslers Cemetery, just north of the city centre and the scene of some of the horrors of the novel, the smells after the snow has melted are of scorched metal from nearby roadworks, 'decaying flowers and wet earth. And dog shit'.

The cemetery is as good a place as any to start a Harry Hole tour. It's the last resting place of many distinguished Norwegians, including playwright Henrik Ibsen (see previous entry) and artist Edvard Munch; the views over the city are magnificent and the site itself green and beautiful. But it's also slightly eerie: you can imagine that there have been many dark goings-on here in the course of its two-hundred-year history.

Vår Freslers is conveniently close to Harry's local, Restaurant Schrøder, which, if you've seen the 2017 film of *The Snowman*, starring Michael Fassbender, you may recognise as one of the locations. As we learn in *Knife*, from Harry's point of view 'restaurant' is something of a misnomer. Although the café does serve Norwegian specialities, such as pork chops and dripping, the emphasis is on drinking and the décor hasn't changed in twenty years:

> *The biggest change Harry could remember was when the smoking ban came into force in 2004 and they repainted the bar to get rid of the smell of smoke. The same colour as before. And the smell of smoke never went completely.*

This unappetising description hardly does justice to Schrøder's menu (go on a Tuesday for the 'Taste of Norway' special including reindeer steak), but the Fosnes paintings of local neighbourhoods which Harry mentions are still there and the restaurant is proud of being one of Oslo's last surviving 'brown cafés', so the walls are indeed still brown.

Harry's other local, The Underwater Pub, has sadly closed down, so the next stop is his apartment building on nearby Sofies Gate. He lives on the third floor of number 5.

Moving upmarket at bit, the Royal Palace, a short walk to the south, is worth a stop even for non-Nesbø fans. It's situated in what must be Oslo's most beautiful green space (even in spring), the Slottspark (Palace Park), on a rise appropriately known as the Belle Vue: the view down Oslo's main thoroughfare, Karl Johans Gate, towards Egertorget Square is another of the city's delights.

You can visit the palace during the summer, and marvel at the magnificence of the Great Hall or Ballroom, almost 4,000 square feet (380 square metres) in area and 35 feet (10.6 metres) high. Each of the four chandeliers (copies of the originals, which were sold off in 1903 when electric light was installed) weighs over 1,300 lb (590 kg). It's not the sort of place Harry Hole would expect to be invited, but in *The Redbreast* (2000) he finds himself foiling a plot to assassinate the Crown Prince, so he's moving in more exalted circles than usual.

Every now and again Harry leaves Norway: the first book in which he features, *The Bat* (1997), is set in Australia; at the start of *The Leopard* (2009) he is in Hong Kong; but for most of the series (thirteen novels at the time of writing) it is Oslo, Oslo, Oslo. Wherever you go in this beautiful city, you can find Harry Hole surrounded by violent death and feeling – yet again – that he shouldn't get involved.

Grimstad, Norway's 'Town of Poets'
Henrik Ibsen and Knut Hamsun

en.visitsorlandet.com/grimstad

Situated on the Skagerrak strait, which separates Norway from Denmark, about one hundred and seventy miles (two hundred and seventy kilometres) southwest of Oslo, Grimstad earns its nickname from having been the home for a few years in the 1840s of the playwright Henrik Ibsen (see page 115) and for three decades in the twentieth century of the Nobel Prize-winning novelist Knut Hamsun (1859–1952).

Ibsen moved here from his birthplace in Skien in 1843 or 1844: he was fifteen and had just left school. He worked as an apprentice pharmacist, but also began writing plays. Nothing he wrote was performed until he had moved to Oslo six years later, but Grimstad is proud of its claim that this is where 'Ibsen became Ibsen'. The Ibsen Museum there is housed in the building where he lived and worked: you can see not only the pharmacy, but also the room where he wrote his first play, *Catilina*. You can also read about the financial hardships that forced him to pursue a career so alien to his literary ambitions, and about the love affair that produced his only child, a son whom he supported for many years but never met. Lots of insight into an

unhappy period of his life, and perhaps into why he went on to write so many depressing plays.

Before hitting the big time as a playwright, Ibsen was more famous for a dramatic narrative poem called *Terje Vigen*, set during the Napoleonic Wars and concerning a young fisherman who tries to penetrate the British blockade of Norway and row all the way to Denmark to feed his starving family. (Don't try this for yourself: the Skagerrak is a busy shipping route with notoriously difficult sailing conditions; Terje was at sea for three days and didn't get anywhere near his destination.) The poem was written years after Ibsen had left Grimstad but was clearly inspired by local legends he picked up during his time there; it was hugely popular and for a long time was part of every Norwegian schoolchild's curriculum. Today, you can take a cruise around the various small islands near Grimstad, soak up the atmosphere and listen to a guide reciting the poem. Or visit Apotekergaarden, a highly regarded local hostelry, and take part in a *Terje Vigen*-themed pub quiz, accompanied by Pilot's Bacalao, a fish dish based on the local clipfish (a sort of cod) and said to be inspired by the poem.

So not all gloom, then. To finish on a high note, a short walk out of town brings you to 'Ibsen's herb garden', a collection of the medicinal plants that would have been in use in his pharmaceutical days. It's part of Dømmesmoen Arboretum, a gem of a park that includes a five-hundred-year-old hollow oak tree measuring 23 feet (7 metres) in circumference, with a gap in its bark large enough for children to crawl through and see the tree from the inside: very much worth a visit, however scant your interest in medicinal plants may be.

Who would have thought that the morose Ibsen would turn out to be the more endearing of Grimstad's attractions? The innovative and influential novelist Knut Hamsun moved here in 1918 and settled at Nørholm farm, on the outskirts of town, looking for peace and quiet in order to write. He may have become a Nobel laureate, but he was an unashamed racist and supporter of National Socialism who wrote a glowing obituary of Hitler. ('A preacher of the gospel of justice for all nations'? Not a view many Norwegians would have shared.)

There are a number of literary excursions available in Grimstad, one of which is a guided walk in the surrounding hills. The downside is that the theme of the walk is Hamsun's last book, the controversial *On Overgrown Paths*. Published in 1949, when he was ninety, it was controversial because it was, in part, an apologia for the pro-Nazi views that had led to his arrest for treason in 1945. Hmm. Enjoy the countryside: it is undeniably charming. If you're here on a Wednesday there's also a guided tour/lecture in Hamsun's farmhouse that dwells, among other things, on the massive library that he collected in the course of his long life.

Hamsun was awarded the Nobel Prize in 1920, well before all this unpleasantness hit the headlines, and another way of remembering him is to book yourself a Nobel banquet at Grimstad's elegant Smag & Behag restaurant. The seven-course meal recreates what was served in Stockholm after the award ceremony; it's accompanied by a lecture on *The Growth of the Soil*, the 1917 epic novel that was a weighty factor in his earning the prize.

Grimstad may be only a small place, but it's in an idyllic location and it certainly knows how to inveigle visitors into celebrating its literary past: throw food and drink at 'em. Can't go wrong.

Lisbeth Salander's Stockholm
Stieg Larsson

kvarnen.com

Stieg Larsson (1954–2004) spent most of his adult life in Stockholm, so it is no surprise that the city should come vividly to life as a setting for his novels. The three volumes of the Millennium series that he completed before his untimely death, though published only posthumously – *The Girl with the Dragon Tattoo* (2005), *The Girl Who Played With Fire* (2006) and *The Girl Who Kicked the Hornets' Nest* (2007) – had sold over eighty million copies worldwide by 2015 (and probably a few more since) and had been published in more than fifty countries. So it's also no surprise that tourists flock to see the places where antisocial computer hacker Lisbeth Salander – the 'girl' of the titles – and her on-off investigative partner, journalist and publisher Mikhail Blomkvist, live, work, eat and drink. You can take a guided tour, buy a Millennium map from the City Museum or just wander around under your own steam: none of these sites is far from the others and two of them involve opportunities to stop for refreshment.

Lisbeth Salander frequents a long-established beer hall and restaurant called Kvarnen (The Mill) in Tjärhovsgatan, in the Södermalm district. She goes there primarily to drink and to discuss men, music and politics; you can, if you prefer, dine on reindeer steaks or traditional Swedish meatballs in a room which at various times in its history has been modelled on a Bavarian bierkeller and an English pub (complete with dartboard), but which now reflects what a typical Stockholm restaurant might have looked like when it first opened in 1908. The high ceilings and arched windows are very much in the style of the mill that once stood on the site and that gave the restaurant its name.

A few minutes' walk away to the north, Lisbeth's home in the later books is a luxury penthouse at Fiskargatan 9, which she buys with money stolen from a corrupt businessman; it consists of twenty-one rooms of which, we are told, she uses only three. Rather than her own name on the door, she has V. Kulla: it's an abbreviation of Villa Villekulla, the address of another fictional Swedish heroine, Astrid Lindgren's Pippi Longstocking. (Larsson is reported as saying that part of Salander's character is based on his idea of what Pippi Longstocking would have been like when she grew up.)

Fiskargatan 9 is an Art Nouveau-inspired building, once known as 'the House of Scandal' because, shockingly, its height meant it overshadowed the nearby Katarina Church. Today, unless you can wangle an invitation to visit someone who lives there, you have to imagine the glorious views that Lisbeth would enjoy over the Old Town and the island of Djurgården. Except, of course, that Lisbeth Salander isn't the sort of person to enjoy views.

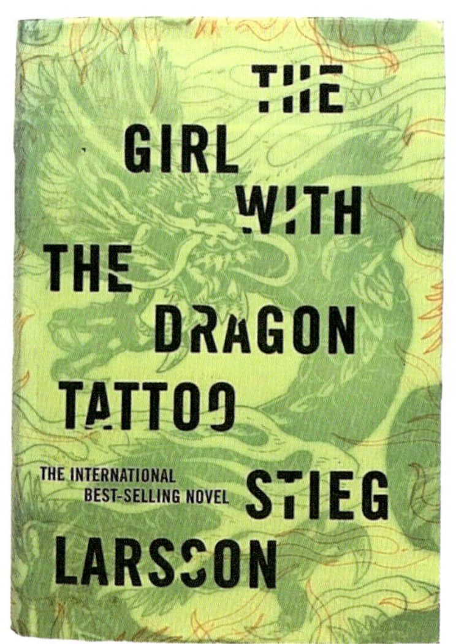

Mikhail Blomkvist also lives in an apartment you can't imagine he could afford. It's in a handsome seventeenth-century building on Bellmansgatan; he acquired it cheaply 'at the end of the go-go eighties, during a period when he had a steady job and a pretty good salary', when the previous owner suddenly moved abroad. It, too, is an attic with views:

> *... two dormer windows and a gable window with a view of the rooftops towards Gamla Stan, Stockholm's oldest section, and the water of Riddarfjarden. He had a glimpse of water by the Slussen locks and a view of City Hall.*

At one point when Blomkvist is in need of money and faces the prospect of having to sell the apartment, we're told that this would break his heart. It's good to know that at least one of Larsson's characters can take pleasure from looking out the window.

Blomkvist part-owns the magazine *Millennium*, which gives the series its name, and you can identify its headquarters, too: on the busy shopping street Götgatan, with the fashion store Monki on the ground floor. Although Greenpeace has moved on now, at the time Larsson was writing it did occupy part of the building, as is mentioned in *The Girl with the Dragon Tattoo*.

Finally, there's the café where Blomkvist hangs out, Kaffebar, on the corner of Hornsgatan and Bysistorget. It's here that, at a crucial point towards the end of *The Girl with the Dragon Tattoo*, Lisbeth tries to borrow 120,000 kronor from him – in the region of £9,000 or €10,000 at the time of writing – and casually lets slip the fact that she has hacked into his bank account to check that he can afford it. Downstairs from the offices of the real-life anti-racist magazine *Expo* that Larsson helped to found, Kaffebar has made a reputation as Larsson's local, the place where he sat and wrote the novels whose stupendous success he didn't live to enjoy.

Wallander's Ystad
Henning Mankell

The pretty little harbour town of Ystad in southern Sweden boasts two fine thirteenth-century buildings: a monastery, now an art gallery and museum, set in delightful rose and herb gardens; and the brick Gothic church of St Mary. It has some great beaches and colourful half-timbered houses. It is undeniably beautiful in summer, but, as with the Brontës' parsonage in Haworth (see page 193), to go there on a sunny day is rather to miss the point. For in 1991 – some years before Harry Hole began drinking his way round Oslo (see page 118) or Lisbeth Salander first hacked into a computer in Stockholm (see page 123) – Ystad gave birth to Scandi noir and neither the town nor the genre has ever looked back.

It is here in Ystad that Henning Mankell (1948–2015) set his series of novels featuring the gloomy Inspector Kurt Wallander. It's also here that both Swedish and British television adaptations – a total of forty-four episodes, plus a handful of feature-length films – were made; if you've seen any of these, many streets and buildings in the town will look familiar, particularly in the worst of weather. Whatever is going on in his life, Wallander seems to spend much of his

time leaving home while it's still dark, having the car door wrenched out of his hand by the wind and wishing he had worn a warmer jacket.

An obvious place to start your tour is at the Ystad Studios, where not only *Wallander* but parts of *The Bridge* and numerous other films and television series have been made. The interactive visitor centre allows you to sit in the armchair in Wallander's living room, explore his office and even try on his jacket; you can also record a scene in the greenscreen studio; and experiment with stop-motion techniques in the animation studio.

Back on the streets, Wallander's favourite café, Fridolfs Konditori, will be happy to sell you coffee and a pastry or some of the sandwiches that are an important feature of the inspector's notoriously unhealthy, eat-on-the-hoof diet. Just a few minutes' walk away, the red-brick former railway station served as the police headquarters in some of the films, but is now a B & B. You can sleep in Wallander's office, and you'll do it in more comfort than he did, on those desperate occasions when he retrieved a mattress from the basement in order to snatch a few hours' rest before refuelling on coffee and dashing off to pursue the next phase of his investigation. Close at hand is the Continental du Sud; founded in 1829, it is Sweden's oldest hotel and in the novels is a convenient place for Wallander's team to gather when they want to get away from the office. Wallander's house, described as being in Mariagatan, can be viewed only from the outside, but he lives in something akin to squalor, rarely making his bed or washing up his coffee cups, so that may be a good thing.

For a spectacular change of scene, a drive of about twenty minutes east along the coast will bring you to Ales Stenar (Ale's stones), near the village of Kaseberga. This is a magnificent and mystical early Iron Age monument consisting of fifty-nine vast boulders laid out in the form of a ship. Perhaps three thousand years old, they're a mystery. No one knows who put them there, or why. But they're an excellent excuse to head up into the hills and enjoy (on a clear, unWallander-like day) a stunning view over the Baltic. It's here that Wallander comes when he needs to do some serious thinking. In *Faceless Killers* (1991), puzzling over a case and putting off the always uncomfortable business of visiting his father, he turns off the main road to visit what he calls 'a stone circle of contemplation ... an invitation to solitude and peace of mind'. He has no inclination towards introspection, meditation or worrying about the meaning of life. Those aren't Wallander things at all. But a few minutes of solitude, just looking out to sea, are a different matter:

> *It was the vast peace that lay hidden in not having to think at all. Just listen, observe, sit motionless.*

It's a rare moment of calm in the life of a troubled man who sometimes feels (as he says in *The Man Who Smiled*, 1994) that we go through life 'with one foot in a rose garden and the other in quicksand'. When you sit among Ales Stenar, or perhaps when you're having a pastry in Fridolfs, you might catch a glimpse of the rose garden. Come November, when the wind gets up and the temperature plummets, you'll be back in the metaphorical quicksand that you may think is more in keeping with Scandi noir.

Moominland
Tove Jansson

moominworld.fi
Open summer only – check the website
icecave.fi/ice-cave
Open April to August

Outside her native Finland, Tove Jansson (1914–2001) is best known as the creator of the Moomins, a family of friendly and affectionate trolls (in their cartoon form they look rather like white hippopotamuses) in a series of children's books and a comic strip. The Moomins' adventures – like those of many Finns – are closely connected with their country's extreme climate; in *Moominsummer Madness* (1955), for example, they are flooded out of their home (following a volcanic explosion which spreads soot over everything just after Moominmamma has hung out the washing), but typically they land on their feet, moving into an abandoned theatre and learning how to put on a play.

The child of a sculptor and a graphic designer, Jansson was an artist as well as a writer, illustrating much of her own work. You can see many of her Moomin artworks at the Art Museum in Tampere, a couple of hours' drive inland from Helsinki. To the west, on an island just off the coast at Naantali, is Moominworld, a theme park centred around the five-storey bilberry-coloured Moominhouse, which is full of Magical Experiences; and if you venture further inland from Tampere you can find the Moomin Ice Caves at Leppävirta, where the scary character Groke – whom the kindly Moomins discover to be not wicked but lonely – has created eternal winter in its most enjoyable form: there are ice sculptures, an ice chute, a sleigh-go-round and husky rides.

If you want to get under the skin of Tove Jansson, though, you should investigate the books she wrote for adults – the semi-autobiographical *Sculptor's Daughter* (1968) and *The Summer Book* (1972), and the succinct,

evocative short stories collected in English as *A Winter Book* (2006). These were all inspired by Pellinge, a group of small islands in the Gulf of Finland where she spent summers first as a child and later with her partner, the artist Tuulikki Pietilä. Like the Moomins, the young Tove was at the mercy of the weather:

> *If the water rises, there'll be a storm. If it falls very quickly and sharply, there might be a storm too. A ring around the sun may be dangerous. And a smoky, dark-red sunset bodes no good either. There are many more things like this, but I can't be bothered with them just now. If it's not one thing, it's another.*

That's the beginning of the story 'Flotsam and Jetsam' and it expresses a feeling you can sympathise with if you visit today. The islands – accessible by frequent ferries in the summer – are rocky, exposed and either low-lying or protected from the sea by sheer, unscalable cliffs. You can see why people fall in love with them. They are great for hiking and for discovering the wildflowers that captivate Grandmother (a version of Jansson herself) in *The Summer Book*. There is always the chance you will find her magic forest, where the trees, exposed for hundreds of years to the teeth of every storm, have come to form 'a tangled mass of stubborn resignation'. Then there is the seashore itself, as explored by young Tove in *Sculptor's Daughter*:

> *The seaweed only shines in the evening. You walk and walk and walk and the morning wind begins to get up. The second bay is full of reeds and when the wind blows through them they rustle, and swish and sigh and whisper and whine softly and gently and you go right into the reeds and they brush you on all sides and you go on and on, thinking of nothing at all. The reeds are a jungle that goes on and on right to the end of the earth. The face of the earth is covered by nothing but whispering reeds and all human beings have died and I am the only one left and I just walk on and on through the reeds.*

The Finnish summer days are long, of course – apparently endless to a small child – but then inevitably there comes the moment when everything changes, when 'summer is no longer alive' but 'autumn is not yet ready to begin'. This is when the packing-up chores start. The tent and the water pump are brought indoors; the boat is pulled ashore on a cradle; soon the family will be heading back to Helsinki for the winter, as Jansson did throughout her life. In the city you can see samples of her art, with some important frescoes in the Art Museum; you can visit what is now Tove Jansson Park, where she used to play as a child, and in Esplanade Park she is – legend has it – the model for a mermaid in the fountain sculpted by her father Victor Jansson. In Hietaniemi cemetery, you can visit her grave, topped by another of Victor Jansson's sculptures. You can follow the 'Life Path of Tove' offered online by the Art Museum and taking you to, among other places, her elementary school (now the Design Museum) and her studio, not open to the public but identifiable by yet another of Victor's works, a plaque showing her face as a young girl.

In other words, you can do a fairly major *hommage* to Tove Jansson without leaving Helsinki. You can also have a lot of family fun in the various Moomin-themed locations. But it may be that that is a rather superficial approach to her, and that her heart is out there on those bleak little islands, waiting for spring to come around again.

AUSTRIA, SWITZERLAND & THE CZECH REPUBLIC

Prater Vienna
Graham Greene and Elfriede Jelinek

praterwien.com

The amusement park is open mid-March to end October, with some businesses open in the winter, depending on the weather. Check the website for details

There's been a public park in the heart of Vienna since 1766, occupying a space that was once the heavily wooded hunting ground of the sixteenth-century Emperor Maximilian II. After it was opened to the public, coffee houses, bars, bowling alleys and carousels sprang up. It hosted a World's Fair in 1873, and became a place for elegant carriage rides and secret assignations after the amusement area Venedig in Wien ('Venice in Vienna') – canals and all – was established in 1895. The iconic Riesenrad or Giant Ferris Wheel was introduced two years later. To be clear, the Wiener Prater or Prater Vienna is the formal name given to the whole park; the amusement area within it is the Wurstelprater, or simply the Prater.

The whole area was badly damaged during the Second World War, and it was immediately after that – in a grey and desolate Vienna – that Graham Greene (1904–1991) set his novella *The Third Man*. Although the Prater has

always been intended for 'public enjoyment', there's not much gaiety in the park of the story (nor in the famous 1949 film), where the American visitor Holly Martins is waiting for ... someone:

For an hour he waited, walking up and down to keep warm, inside the enclosure of the Great Wheel; the smashed Prater with its bones sticking crudely through the snow was nearly empty. One stall sold thin flat cakes like cartwheels, and the children queued with their coupons. A few courting couples would be packed together in a single car of the Wheel and revolve slowly above the city, surrounded by empty cars.

Austrian novelist Elfriede Jelinek (born 1946) sets part of *The Piano Teacher* in the Prater of the 1980s, and she sees an even seamier side to it, the ground strewn with empty cans, betting tickets and all sorts of other detritus 'that Nature cannot digest'. Then when evening comes, there are the sex workers, the 'people who have lost out on life' and who must make the most of their young bodies, because no one will want them when they are older: 'The whores hustle and the hustlers whore through the Prater.'

It's fair to say that the Prater can be more fun than either of these descriptions suggests. Today the attractions include a museum, a planetarium, Vienna's Madame Tussauds and the world's first rollercoaster restaurant, where food and drink are brought to your table via a series of rollercoaster loops and rails. There are plenty of woods to stroll in, or you can hire a horse and explore that way. The centre of attention is still the revitalised 212-foot-diameter (nearly 65 metres) Riesenrad, the ferris wheel that gives you splendid views over the whole park or enables you to gaze down, like Harry Lime in *The Third Man*, on all the little dots of people below:

Harry took a look at the toy landscape below and came away from the door. 'I never feel quite safe in these things,' he said. He felt the back of the door with his hand, as though he were afraid that it might fly open and launch him into that iron-ribbed space ...

The car swung to a standstill at the highest point of the curve and Harry turned his back and gazed out of the window. Martins thought: One good shove and I could break the glass, and he pictured the body falling, falling, through the iron struts, a piece of carrion dropping among the flies.

It doesn't happen, but it makes you feel you want to be careful who you travel with. Or stay on the ground and enjoy a beer or a pastry in safer surroundings.

SIDNEY PAGET
1893

Reichenbach Falls
Arthur Conan Doyle

myswitzerland.com/en-gb/experiences/reichenbach-falls-funicular

Open May to October

sherlockholmes.ch

Museum open afternoons only, all year round

It is indeed, a fearful place. The torrent, swollen by the melting snow, plunges into a tremendous abyss, from which the spray rolls up like the smoke from a burning house. The shaft into which the river hurls itself is an immense chasm, lined by glistening coal-black rock, and narrowing into a creaming, boiling pit of incalculable depth, which brims over and shoots the stream onward over its jagged lip. The long sweep of green water roaring forever down, and the thick flickering curtain of spray hissing forever upward, turn a man giddy with their constant whirl and clamour. We stood near the edge peering down at the gleam of the breaking water far below us against the black rocks, and listening to the half-human shout which came booming up with the spray out of the abyss.

This is Doctor Watson's description of the Reichenbach Falls in the 1893 Sherlock Holmes story 'The Final Problem'. We know, because Watson has told us, that this is the last story he will ever write about Holmes, so we're expecting something powerful, but this word-picture still provokes a shudder.

The falls, near the village of Meiringen, some fifty miles (eighty kilometres) east of Bern, are in superb hiking country, though it's possible that Holmes's creator, the athletic Sir Arthur Conan Doyle (1859–1930), arrived on skis. Visiting Switzerland for the sake of his wife's health, he was almost single-handedly responsible for introducing skiing there. Already a high-level cricketer, footballer and boxer, he knew that people skied in Norway, decided that the Swiss terrain would lend itself to the sport and sent to Norway for skis in order to try it out.

The less energetic can – from May to October – reach the falls by funicular railway; it's a tough hour-long slog on foot from the lower station to the upper one if the train isn't running. But the view is worth all the pain of getting there: viewing platforms offer a stunning vista over the Haslital valley below, with the falls at the centre of a narrow gorge.

In Meiringen itself there is, perhaps inevitably, a Sherlock Holmes museum. Based in the English church, it offers a reconstruction of the sitting room at 221B Baker Street. Outside, a life-sized statue of Holmes himself, thoughtfully puffing on his trademark meerschaum, presumably contemplates a three-pipe problem. If you want to test your own detecting skills you can buy a 'crime pass' and follow an interactive trail of clues around the village, attempting to solve a Holmes-style mystery.

Meiringen, as its name suggests, is also said to be the home of meringues. There's no suggestion in Conan Doyle's texts that Holmes was a foodie, but that doesn't stop the village offering 'Sherlock meringues' for sale.

But really, the point of a visit here – for Holmes fans at least – is the waterfall. It drops an impressive 820 feet (250 metres) over multiple tiers, and the water seems to have worn a hole in the cliff, creating a bizarre zigzag effect. Embedded into the cliff itself is a plaque, commemorating (in three languages) the fact that 'at this fearful place', Sherlock Holmes vanquished Professor Moriarty on 4 May 1891. But of course Dr Watson doesn't know this: he believes his friend has perished along with his arch-enemy. So a last word from him, as he returns to the spot:

> *The blackish soil is kept forever soft by the incessant drift of spray, and a bird would leave its tread upon it. Two lines of footmarks were clearly marked along the farther end of the path, both leading away from me. There were none returning ... I lay upon my face and peered over with the spray spouting up all around me. It had darkened since I left, and now I could only see here and there the glistening of moisture upon the black walls, and far away down at the end of the shaft the gleam of the broken water. I shouted; but only the same half-human cry of the fall was borne back to my ears.*

Heidi Country, Bündner Herrschaft

Johanna Spyri

myswitzerland.com/en-gb/destinations/buendner-herrschaft
heididorf.ch

> *The pretty little Swiss town of Mayenfeld lies at the foot of a mountain range, whose grim rugged peaks tower high above the valley below. Behind the town a footpath winds gently up to the heights. The grass on the lower slopes is poor, but the air is fragrant with the scent of mountain flowers from the rich pasture land higher up.*

So begin the adventures of Heidi, the little orphaned girl adopted by her grandfather and reared in the Swiss Alps, that have charmed millions of children since they were first published in 1881. Author Johanna Spyri (1827–1901) came from a different part of Switzerland but spent summer holidays

here as a child and clearly fell in love with the place: Heidi's delight in the sparklingly clean air, the wild flowers of the alpine pastures, and the rosy red of the mountains in the first sunset she has ever seen leaps from the page.

Heidi's story has sparked a huge tourist industry centred on the wine-growing region of the Bündner Herrschaft, in an area now known unofficially as Heidiland. So closely intertwined are the region's two industries that you can do a Heidi Wine Tour which promises 'family fun' – despite the fact that the little heroine is five when the book begins, no more than eleven when it finishes and spends much of her time in the mountains drinking fresh goat's milk.

Perhaps more appropriately, you can walk from Maienfeld (to use the modern spelling) to what is now called Heididorf (Heidi Village) and follow the Heidi Adventure Trail to take in her house, her friend Peter's house and the Heidi Museum. You can also visit small herds of mountain goats like those that Peter tended, and see cheese being made from their milk. The trail is a four-mile circuit (six and a half kilometres) whose highlight is a spiral staircase leading up into the treetops, giving spectacular views over the valley. (The website rather delightfully recommends this only for 'those who are free of dizziness'; those who are less keen on heights can content themselves with the views from the terrace of the Heidihof hotel and restaurant – still pretty impressive.) En route you'll also see the Heidi fountain, built in 1953 to commemorate the area's most famous daughter: it shows our heroine clambering rather clumsily over a rock, perhaps to rescue the goat that seems to have become stuck in this unfamiliar terrain.

Heidi, in fact, had two houses – one in the mountains where she and Grandfather spent the summers, and one down in the village where they lived in winter and she attended school. The winter house is the genuine article, insofar as it is three hundred years old. Up the hill a bit, the summer hut is a modern replica, but it prides itself on reproducing exact details from the book: a bearded man doing carpentry outside, as Grandfather did; indoors a single downstairs room, with Grandfather's bed in the corner; a big pot hanging over the fireplace; a ladder (well, more of a fixed staircase these days, as Health and Safety demand) leading up to the hayloft where Heidi slept. The fact that you can hire the place for parties perhaps detracts slightly from the feeling of authenticity, but it's a small price to pay.

All this happens against the stunning backdrop of the Eiger and the Jungfrau, which tower cliff-like above the vineyards. *Heidi* won't be to everyone's taste nowadays. A generation brought up on the more robust attitudes of Tom Gates may find her way of spreading sweetness and light wherever she goes a touch twee. But there's no denying the beauty of the country that inspired her story.

Kafka Museum, Prague

Franz Kafka

kafkamuseum.cz/en/

One morning, when Gregor Samsa woke from troubled dreams, he found himself transformed in his bed into a horrible vermin.

Someone must have been telling lies about Josef K.; he knew he had done nothing wrong but, one morning, he was arrested.

Two of the most haunting opening lines in the business, from *Metamorphosis* (1915) and *The Trial* (written 1914–15, published 1925), and they are typical of the author's writing. With Franz Kafka (1883–1924) the world is a mysterious, threatening place, throbbing with nightmarish questions that no one seems willing to answer. So ubiquitous are these themes in Kafka's work that his name has passed into the language: you don't have to have read a word he wrote to understand the meaning of *Kafkaesque*.

It's no wonder that Kafka had this overwhelming fear of authority. In a letter to his father written when he was thirty-six, he recalled an occasion from his childhood when he had called out in the night, asking for a glass of water. His furious father had lifted him out of bed and put him outside on the balcony to freeze until morning. 'I was quite obedient after that period,' Franz wrote, with chilling understatement, 'but it did me so much incalculable inner harm.'

This inner turmoil – the feeling that an innocent individual has somehow strayed into a world of pointless, tortuous bureaucracy and malign fantasies – is reflected in the Franz Kafka Museum. Housed in a former brickworks on the bank of the River Vltava in Prague's Old Town, it is predominantly dark, with some of the display cases brightly and harshly lit, as if they were under interrogation. A red-lit staircase leads you down to ... where? Black filing cabinets line the walls, some of their drawers standing open. Might they contain secret dossiers about you? Three-dimensional installations depict elements of Kafka's life and works, their musical soundtrack decidedly haunting. As you'd expect, there are first editions of the author's books, letters, diaries and the like, but they hardly matter: what matters is that you're in a Kafkaesque nightmare.

Kafka rarely named the places he was writing about, but it's widely believed that he was generally thinking about Prague. There's a cathedral in *The Trial* that is presumably Prague's landmark St Vitus's; in the 1912 short story 'The Judgment', he describes a view from a window that could easily be the view from his own family home. But it might not be. There's no way of knowing. In *The Castle* (1926), the mysterious and inaccessible castle was probably inspired by one in the modern ski resort of Spindleruv Mlyn. Gregor Samsa lives in Charlottenstrasse, opposite an 'endless, grey-black building' which is a hospital – but there isn't a Charlottenstrasse in Prague, and the hapless Gregor could be anywhere. That's the point, and the museum makes that point – to disturbing effect.

Outside the museum, a bronze statue graphically entitled *Piss* shows two men urinating into a lake shaped like the Czech Republic. Elsewhere in the city, two further statues more specifically commemorate the author. The *Statue of Franz Kafka* by Jaroslav Rona on Dusni Street (cross the Klarov Bridge from the museum and bear left-ish towards the Spanish Synagogue) depicts two human figures. The lower one, vast and headless, is effectively an empty suit, with a much smaller, recognisable likeness of Kafka perched on its shoulders. The inspiration is one of Kafka's earliest stories, 'Description of a Struggle', in which a young man, having met a stranger at a party, spends much of the rest of the story riding on his acquaintance's back as if he were a horse, the landscape changing around him at a whim. Fifteen minutes' walk further south, outside the Quadrio shopping centre, you'll find an extraordinary 35-foot-tall (11-metre) artwork by David Cerny, installed in 2014. Known as *The Head of Franz Kafka*, it consists of a mirrored base on which sit forty-two reflective panels which rotate independently and are said to reflect Kafka's tortured feelings of self-doubt.

If, when you look at any of these statues, you find yourself thinking 'Why?', just remember you are in Kafka country. The land of unanswered questions.

For a burst of normality, take yourself to the picturesque Café Louvre a few minutes' walk from the rotating head, on Narodni (National) Avenue. The student Kafka used to hang out here with his friend and fellow author Max Brod (Albert Einstein was a regular a few years later). Treat yourself to anything from a cup of hot chocolate to a three-course meal and give thanks to Brod, who ignored his friend's dying wish that all his works be destroyed. Brod saw to it that not only the novels and stories, but also the letters and soul-baring diaries were published. Without him, dictionaries wouldn't feature the word *Kafkaesque,* and posterity wouldn't have known about the sufferings, or the genius, of the man who never quite recovered from wanting a glass of water after lights out.

ITALY

Venice's Underbelly
Thomas Mann, Donna Leon and others

Can there be anyone who has not had to overcome a fleeting sense of dread, a secret shudder of uneasiness, on stepping for the first time or after a long interval of years into a Venetian gondola? How strange a vehicle it is, coming down unchanged from times of old romance, and so characteristically black, the way no other thing is black except a coffin – a vehicle evoking lawless adventures in the plashing stillness of night, and still more strongly evoking death itself, the bier, the dark obsequies, the last silent journey! And has it been observed that the seat of such a boat, that armchair with its coffin-black lacquer and dull black upholstery, is the softest, the most voluptuous, most enervating seat in the world?

This is from Thomas Mann's *Death in Venice* (1912), and his central character, Gustav Aschenbach, probably has a gloomier view of the city than most. Nonetheless, it's remarkable, given how extraordinarily beautiful Venice is, how many writers have emphasised its darker side. To be fair to Aschenbach, the Lido – the resort where most of his story takes place, a short *vaporetto* ride from the city centre – can look pretty gloomy in the off season these days. Hotels behind forbidding fences all seem to be under renovation, though the rows and rows of beach huts, in blocks of differing colour and design denoting the hotel they belong to, suggest that in summer the demand for sun and sand is as high as ever. At the time of Edith Wharton's *The Glimpses of the Moon* (1922), the Lido's now rather faded Art Nouveau hotels would have been at the peak of their glamour and the Bright Young Things of the novel could well have been right in thinking that Venice afforded 'exceptional opportunities for bathing and adultery'.

The German Mann (1875–1955) and the Europhile American Wharton (1862–1937) are far from being the only foreigners inspired to live and write in Venice. Another Europhile American, Henry James (1843–1916), wrote both *The Aspern Papers* (1888) and *The Wings of the Dove* (1902) here. You can admire the Palazzo Barbaro, which features in the latter and where he stayed with wealthy friends, from the Grand Canal: it's just to the east of the Ponte dell' Accademia and is one of the finest surviving examples of Venetian Gothic design. The palazzo in *The Aspern Papers,* though, is past its best: James describes it as overlooking a 'clean, melancholy, unfrequented canal' and as having 'an air not so much of decay as of quiet discouragement, as if it had rather missed its career'.

James refers to the streets of Venice as 'little winding ways' and as 'dusky labyrinthine alleys'; no newcomer to the city can fail to be baffled by them.

They are – almost literally – the death of John, the English hero of *Don't Look Now*, a 1971 novella by Daphne du Maurier (1907–1989):

> *Wait a minute, the church itself had a familiar appearance ... Surely it was only a stone's throw from the Riva degli Schiavoni and the open wide waters of the San Marco lagoon, with all the bright lights of civilisation and the strolling tourists? ... Wasn't that the alley-way ahead?*

He decides it must be, and that it would be quicker to follow it until he gets his bearings once more, rather than retrace his steps and risk getting lost again. Alas, it turns out not to be simple at all. If you've seen the 1973 film version, you probably won't be able to wander down these narrow lanes without looking out fearfully for a little figure in a red coat. Be warned, though: in the original text John's nemesis wears not a red coat but a pixie hood of unspecified colour – you can't assume that anyone wearing black or green or blue is not a homicidal maniac.

Today's most popular portrayer of Venice – another American – is perhaps not as paranoid as that, but she is still under no illusions about her adopted home. In her crime novels featuring Commissario Guido Brunetti, Donna Leon (born 1942) uses the labyrinthine streets as a metaphor for the web of vice, intrigue and corruption beneath the city's glamorous surface. Even Brunetti, a Venetian born and bred, frequently has to consult the *Calli, Campielli e Canali* directory in order to pin down an address. As for his Sicilian boss, Vice-Questore Patta, we are told in *Doctored Evidence* (2003) that, after years in Venice, he has never been able to find his way alone through the narrow *calli*:

> *... but he had at least learned to send Venetians ahead to lead him through the labyrinth of rancours and animosities that had been built up over the centuries, as well as around the obstacles and wrong turnings created in more recent times.*

It isn't all despondent, though. For all his general tendency to pessimism, Henry James – again in *The Aspern Papers* – isn't blind to the beauty and theatricality of Venice:

> *Without streets and vehicles, the uproar of wheels, the brutality of horses, and with its little winding ways where people crowd together, where voices sound as in the corridors of a house, where the human step circulates as if it skirted the angles of furniture and shoes never wear out, the place has the character of an immense collective apartment, in which Piazza San Marco*

is the most ornamented corner and palaces and churches, for the rest, play the part of great divans of repose, tables of entertainment, expanses of decoration ... As you sit in your gondola the footways that in certain parts edge the canals assume to the eye the importance of a stage, meeting it at the same angle, and the Venetian figures, moving to and fro against the battered scenery of their little houses of comedy, strike you as members of an endless dramatic troupe.

But it's perhaps a couple of minor characters in *The Glimpses of the Moon* who best catch the true nature of the Queen of the Adriatic. They are 'reverently if confusedly aware that they were in the presence of something unique and ineffable, and determined to make the utmost of their privilege'. In their place, most of us would feel the same.

Shakespeare in Verona
William Shakespeare

casadigiulietta.comune.verona.it
Closed Mondays

'T*wo households, both alike in dignity,*
In fair Verona, where we lay our scene ...'

So begins the Prologue to *Romeo and Juliet*, going on to explain about the tragedy of the 'pair of star-cross'd lovers' that we are about to witness. 'Fair Verona' has been a byword for a romantic city ever since, but that's because Shakespeare (1564–1616) put it on the map, rather than because it had any particular romantic associations beforehand. That said, it's a beautiful place, whose tiers of surrounding hills make you feel as if you're in an amphitheatre, and whose genuine Roman amphitheatre, used today for lavish presentations of opera, is one of the best preserved in the world.

Shakespeare set almost a third of his plays in Italy and scholars have argued for centuries about whether or not he visited the country: there's no evidence to prove that he did. He almost certainly read about Romeo and Juliet's doomed romance in a 1562 poem by a largely forgotten poet called Arthur Brooke, inspired by earlier Italian sources. Again, there's no evidence that the story was based on fact. We know that there were families named Montecchi and Capuleti (the origins of Shakespeare's Montague and Capulet) in Verona in the fourteenth century: Dante's *Divine Comedy* (published in 1472 but written 150 years earlier; see page 149) mentions them being in Purgatory, victims of the political upheavals of the period. But there's no reason to suppose that they had offspring who fell in love.

Whatever the truth of the story, what the tourist authorities today promote as 'Juliet's house' in Verona is a thirteenth-century building known to have belonged for many years to a family called Capello or Cappelletti. The name translates as 'little hat'; a stone bas-relief of a hat, above the entrance arch, is traditionally said to be the family's coat of arms. Outside the house, visitors routinely – and surely inappropriately – stroke the right breast of a statue of Juliet, in the belief that it will make them lucky in love. Be warned, though: this is an extremely popular tourist site, with huge crowds gathering for selfies beside the statue or to leave messages of love on the removable panels. (You used to be able to write directly onto the walls, but this got so out of hand that it was damaging the structure and is now forbidden.)

If you want a bit more peace, pay the very reasonable entrance fee and go inside. Here you'll find a museum that features a reconstruction of Juliet's bedroom, including the bed used in Franco Zeffirelli's 1968 film, some costumes from the same film, and a hall said to be the scene of the party where Romeo lays eyes on Juliet for that first, fateful time (*'Did my heart love till now? forswear it, sight/For I ne'er saw true beauty till this night'*).

Most importantly of all, the house has a balcony, from which it is more or less compulsory to declaim, 'Romeo, Romeo, wherefore art thou Romeo?' Cynics will point out that the balcony is a twentieth-century addition; romantics will ignore that and continue:

What's in a name? That which we call
a rose,
By any other name would smell as
sweet …

They can then move on, happily and with a tear in their eye.

The play's text refers to 'the great rich Capulet' – Juliet's father – but the historic Montagues must have been people of substance, too: 'Romeo's house', just round the corner from Juliet's but tucked away in an alley, is almost a castle, red brick and crenellated. It's privately owned, so you can view it only from the outside, but you can see how, when the tragic deaths are discovered, Romeo's father can – in Shakespeare's version – afford to offer to raise a statue to Juliet in pure gold. (Cynics will point out that the existing statue is in bronze, which is probably just as well – gold wouldn't have lasted long with all that breast-rubbing.)

Finally, take a walk of about fifteen minutes south to the thirteenth-century church and monastery of San Francesco al Corso, which purports to house Juliet's tomb. It's a magnificent place, boasting imposing cloisters, a reconstruction of a hall from a sixteenth-century palace with accompanying frescos and *trompe l'oeil* paintings, and a sizeable crypt in which sits Juliet's sarcophagus. In theory, Count Paris and Juliet's cousin Tybalt should be here too, but I think we've established that trying to separate fact and fiction is going to break the spell. Whisper to yourself:

For never was a story of more woe
Than this of Juliet and her Romeo.

Then wipe away another tear and leave it at that.

Pinocchio Park, Pescia
Carlo Collodi

pinocchio.it
Open every day March–October; the rest of the year open weekends and holidays
capannori-terraditoscana.org/en/discover/pinocchios-place/the-oak-of-the-witches

Carlo Lorenzini (1826–1890) spent childhood holidays in the province of Lucca, at the Villa Garzoni where his grandparents were employed, and grew up knowing and loving the area. So when he became a writer and wanted a pseudonym, he adopted the name of the local town, Collodi. He then produced the most successful children's book of all time. Estimated to have been translated into about 250 languages, it ranks as the world's third most translated book, beaten only by the Bible and Antoine de Saint-Exupéry's *The Little Prince*.

Perhaps best remembered now from the 1940 Disney film, Collodi's book was a phenomenal success when it first appeared (in serial form from 1881 and as a book two years later), so it's only right that it should be commemorated with its own amusement park.

As you enter, you're greeted with a sign that reminds you (in Italian) of the book's opening lines:

Once upon a time, there was – a king!

No, children, you've got it wrong. Once upon a time there was a piece of wood.

Yes, you've guessed, this is Pinocchio Park, celebrating the tale of the wooden marionette who becomes a real boy only after he has learned to care for others, and stop telling outrageous lies that make his nose grow to a ridiculous length.

Long before Pinocchio was thought of, the seventeenth-century Garzoni Gardens, painstakingly laid out on a steep hillside, were famous across Europe and still should not be missed: a combined ticket admits you to them and to the nearby butterfly house, as well as to Pinocchio Park. This consists of two main sections, each using a different form of art to depict the marionette's adventures. The mosaics of the Mosaic Piazza show everything from Pinocchio's father Geppetto's workshop to the Fox and the Cat who first lead Pinocchio astray and the Serpent with the smoking tail who blocks his path as he is making his way home from one of his many wanderings.

Then there's the Sculpture Trail, with its twenty-one bronze and steel representations of Pinocchio, Geppetto, the Terrible Dog-Fish that swallows them both and the Talking Cricket that acts as Pinocchio's conscience. (You won't find the name Jiminy Cricket here, by the way, nor his trademark blue top hat – those are both Disney embellishments on the original.) There's also a museum full of models of the various characters, and the opportunity to be greeted by actors portraying Pinocchio and the Blue Fairy. Working on the basis that children are more likely to be entertained by a naughty child than by one who has seen the error of his ways, this version of Pinocchio has the long nose that suggests he's still telling lies.

A few miles to the south of the park, on the road to Lucca, you can stop off at Gragnano to marvel at Pinocchio's Oak, also known as the Witches' Oak. It's an impressive 13 feet (4 metres) in girth and 80 feet (24 metres) high, but its branches are strangely flat and wide-spreading. This may be because of the witches who danced and celebrated their rites at the top of the tree, preventing it reaching its natural height. Or it may not.

Either way, local legend has it that Collodi had this tree in mind when he wrote of the Fox and the Cat persuading Pinocchio to plant his four gold coins in the Field of Miracles, with the promise that it would grow into a tree whose branches were laden with money. Funny that Pinocchio, an inveterate liar, should have fallen for something as improbable as this, but the Witches' Oak is the sort of captivating, almost magical tree that makes you happy to believe anything.

Dante's Florence
Dante Alighieri

duomo.firenze.it

Closed on Sundays except for worship

Dante Alighieri (1265–1321) is the greatest figure in Italian literature – as highly regarded as a national treasure as Shakespeare or Cervantes (see pages 190 and 159). He was the first to write in his local language rather than Latin, making his work accessible to a wider, less classically educated audience, and – like Geoffrey Chaucer with English – elevating Italian to the status of a literary language. Born and brought up in Florence, Dante became involved in the political machinations of the day (never any shortage of those in medieval Italy) and spent the last twenty years of his life in exile. It was during that period that he wrote his masterpiece, the epic poem *The Divine Comedy*, divided into three long sections, *Hell* or *Inferno*, *Purgatory* and *Paradise*.

Those section titles give a clue to what the poem is about: the medieval Christian view of the afterlife. So you can't exactly wander around modern Florence following the story. Instead, head for the cathedral and study the fresco by Domenico di Michelino, commissioned in 1465 to mark the bicentenary of Dante's birth. Called 'Comedy Illuminating Florence', it shows the poet presenting his work to the city and gives you an opportunity to 'read' it for yourself. Dante stands front and centre, the laurel wreath on his head designating his achievements as a poet. Holding his book in his hand, he turns slightly towards the walls of Florence. Brunelleschi's famous dome, still a work in progress at the time of the painting, dominates the skyline, and you can pick out other buildings that survive to this day, including Giotto's towering *campanile*. The city gates are noticeably small, particularly in comparison to the gaping gates of Hell opposite. Clearly, although it is scarily easy to get into Hell, it is much harder to gain readmittance to Florence if, like Dante himself,

you have fallen from favour. The anguished faces of the damned don't make the prospect any more attractive.

In the background, the seven tiers of Purgatory are portrayed in lighter colours, their denizens gradually making their way towards the nine spheres of Paradise above. But this is some distance away and a guardian angel decides who is and who isn't allowed in. Like Florence, the more appealing realms of the afterlife aren't available to just anyone.

Oddly enough, a more modern take on the whole business can be found in Dante's old home. He may have been banished from Florence, but the house he lived in has survived and is now the Dante House Museum. Its ground floor is dedicated to his early life as a soldier and to an explanation – no mean achievement – of the political situation that led to his exile. Upstairs, you can see a reproduction of his bedroom and then enter into an immersive experience of *The Divine Comedy*, with video mapping taking you through Dante's journey into the afterlife. The ceiling even turns into a reproduction of the Milky Way: an evocative depiction of the importance of the stars in the poem. Finally, virtual-reality headsets allow you to see Florence as it would have been in Dante's time and compare it with the present day, with an impressive number of thirteenth- and fourteenth-century buildings still standing.

It's noticeable, by the way, that in the early parts of the poem Dante encounters innumerable characters from history and mythology, but doesn't meet a Florentine until well into the lower circles of Hell. The Florentine in question is among the thieves being consumed by a serpent. Dante's reaction?

Rejoice, O Florence, since thou art so great,
That over sea and land thou beatest thy wings,
And throughout Hell thy name is spread abroad!

No love lost between him and his native city, you'd have thought, from these sarcastic lines. But in Domenico's fresco his expression is decidedly melancholy: is he longing to get to Heaven, or merely to be allowed back home?

The Keats–Shelley House, Rome
John Keats and Percy Bysshe Shelley

ksh.roma.it
Closed Sundays
cemeteryrome.it
Closed in the afternoon on Sundays and public holidays

The English Romantic poet John Keats (1795–1821) was living in Hampstead, north London, in 1818–19 – what is often called his 'marvellous year', when he wrote his odes to a Nightingale, to Psyche, on a Grecian Urn and on Melancholy, among others. He was twenty-three, and it was at this tragically young age that it became apparent he was afflicted with the 'family disease' of consumption or tuberculosis. The causes of TB had not yet been properly identified, it had a stigma attached to it (it was associated with weakness and various sorts of sexual problem) and there was no reliable cure. Keats, coughing up blood, recognised what he described as his 'death warrant'.

He moved to Rome for the sake of his health in autumn 1820, accompanied by his friend, the artist Joseph Severn. They lived in the house that is preserved in his memory, on the Piazza di Spagna, adjacent to the Spanish Steps. His doctor, well meaning but ill informed, prescribed exercise, where rest was more likely to have been beneficial, and Keats would at first go out for walks and even short horse rides. Then in December he suffered a haemorrhage and on 23 February, after being bedridden for six weeks, he died.

By his own wish, there is no name on his gravestone in Rome's Non-Catholic Cemetery (an hour's walk away to the south, near the Porta San Paolo);

believing that his work would not live on after his death, Keats asked that the inscription refer to a 'young English poet … whose name was writ in water'. Above these words is the image of a Grecian lyre with four of its eight strings broken, to show, as Severn put it, 'his Classical Genius cut off by death before its maturity'.

The ashes of Percy Bysshe Shelley (1792–1822) are buried in the same cemetery. Like Keats, he had moved to Italy because of his health, but in his case there were also reasons of prudence; his atheism, radical political views and unconventional lifestyle having made him unpopular at home. Keats and Shelley were members of the same social circle but not close friends; nevertheless Shelley's poem *Adonais*, mourning Keats's death, is considered one of his finest works. It begins:

I weep for Adonais – he is dead!
Oh, weep for Adonais! though our tears
Thaw not the frost which binds so dear a head!

As the rest of the poem makes clear, whatever Keats may have thought, Shelley was in no doubt that the younger man's work would live forever.

But let's go back to the house on Piazza di Spagna. Shelley had no connection with it during his lifetime. The Keats–Shelley Memorial Association bought it in the early years of the twentieth century and opened it as a museum and library dedicated to the Romantic poets, particularly those who had spent time in Italy (you'll find mention of Byron and Mary Shelley too). The Piazza di Spagna is as jam-packed as much of the rest of Rome, so the house feels like a place of refuge from the heat and the noise. The museum is small but informative about the Romantic movement and the lives of its various practitioners. It's delightfully cluttered, as if the owners wanted to pack in everything they could, regardless of the lack of space: there's shelf upon shelf of books, and cases full of letters and manuscripts. There are busts, paintings, Mary Shelley's writing desk and even a sculpture of Keats in the form of a bookend. Like anything to do with Keats, it's touching, too, because you visit the room in which he died, only to be told that none of the furniture belonged to him: it all had to be burned to prevent anyone else being contaminated by his disease.

The house is blessed with two terraces, so that from this peaceful spot you can look down on the Spanish Steps and the crowded Piazza and, if the mood takes you, murmur the words Keats spoke to Severn when he was nearing the end:

I shall soon be laid in the quiet grave –
thank God for the quiet grave – O!
I can feel the cold earth upon me – the daisies growing over me –
O for this quiet – it will be my first –

He got his wish. Oscar Wilde, visiting many years later, called Keats's grave 'the holiest spot in Rome', and Shelley, in the preface to *Adonais*, described the cemetery as

... an open space among the ruins, covered in winter with violets and daisies. It might make one in love with death, to think that one should be buried in so sweet a place.

My Brilliant Friend's Naples

Elena Ferrante

The Naples of Elena Ferrante's *My Brilliant Friend* (2011) and its sequels is one of those many cities (compare Donna Leon's Venice, page 143, and Carlos Ruiz Zafón's Barcelona, page 165, to name but two) that play almost as large a role in the novel as the characters themselves. It used to be that you visited Naples for its sheer beauty – 'See Naples and die,' Goethe (see page 99) wrote in 1787, suggesting that nothing else you would ever see could surpass the loveliness of the city's bay. Today you're more likely to go to check out the decidedly less glamorous area to the east of the central station where Ferrante's narrator, Lenù, and her friend, the 'brilliant' but rebellious Lila, grow up, struggling to gain anything beyond an elementary education and with the threat of the Camorra – Naples's Mafia – never far away.

If you take a train to Gianturco station in the Rione Luzzatti area, you'll find that the 'four-storey white apartment buildings' of the 1950s, when the novel is set, are still there. You can get a feel for the boundaries of the girls' childhood world, confined by the railway tracks and the main road: on clear days, Lenù tells us, you can see:

> *... a blue mountain with one low peak and one a little higher, which was called Vesuvius and was a volcano.*

Another of the boundaries that survive to this day is the 'tunnel with three entrances', through which the girls embark on their first adventure away from home. It's exciting to start with, escaping from their parents and heading towards the sea, which they have never seen. But if you intend to follow in their footsteps, take food and drink (they hadn't thought of that) and check the weather forecast first:

> *The sky, which at first had been very high, was as if lowered. Behind us everything was becoming black, large heavy clouds lay over the trees, the light poles. In front of us, the light was still dazzling, but as if pressed on the sides by a purplish greyness that would suffocate it. In the distance thunder could be heard.*

The adventure ends with them tearing home,

> *... blinded by the rain, our clothes soaked, our bare feet in worn sandals that had no purchase on the now muddy ground.*

Of course, they still haven't seen the sea.

Leaving Rione Luzzatti and heading back towards the centre of town, you find narrow lanes crammed with overcrowded dwellings and small businesses that have been in the same family for generations. You can meander down Corso Umberto I, where Lila buys her wedding dress, and explore the bookshops of Port'Alba where, later in the series, the disillusioned Lenù spends her time, rummaging among the used books and 'unwillingly absorbing titles and authors' names', when she skips school. From there, you can continue to the elegant Piazza dei Martiri, with its superb monument to the martyrs of Naples and four lions representing the four uprisings against Bourbon rule between 1799 and 1860. More to the point for Ferrante fans, this is where the untrustworthy, Camorra-connected Solara brothers open their shop, selling the shoes that Lila, the daughter of a shoemaker, has designed.

From here it's a short walk to that incomparable bay, which Lenù finally sees on one unforgettable day in the summer when 'the boundaries of the neighbourhood faded': her father takes her out, to show her, among many other things, 'Vesuvius from close up, and the sea':

> *But what a sea. It was very rough, and loud; the wind took your breath away, pasted your clothes to your body and blew the hair off your forehead ... The waves rolled in like blue metal tubes carrying an egg white of foam on their peaks, then broke in a thousand glittering splinters and came up to the street with an oh of wonder and fear from those watching ... I felt dazed by the powerful gusts, by the noise. I had the impression that, although I was absorbing much of that sight, many things, too many, were scattering around me without letting me grasp them.*

Goethe would surely have agreed with her.

SPAIN & PORTUGAL

H. PISAN

A Don Quixote Tour
Miguel de Cervantes

museocasanataldecervantes.org
Closed Mondays

Alcalá de Henares, twenty miles (thirty-two kilometres) northeast of Madrid, is now widely known for its white stork population: ninety breeding pairs arrive in mid-October and remain until the following August, nesting on almost every tower or historical building. But, ornithological interest apart, this was the first planned university town in the world. The University of Alcalá was founded in 1499 and was instrumental in declaring Spanish a 'language of culture' at a time when most 'cultured' people were reading Latin. The rich facade of the main building – in the flamboyant *plateresco* style that is a Spanish variation on Gothic and translates as 'in the manner of a silversmith' – is the architectural highlight of the town, and you can wander into the courtyard at will; the remaining buildings, notably the magnificent Paraninfo or Great Hall, completed in 1520, can be visited only by guided tour or by cadging an invitation to the presentation ceremony of the annual Miguel de Cervantes Award.

So Alcalá was firmly on the cultural map before Cervantes (1547–1616) was born in a handsome house on the Calle Mayor, but there's no doubt that Spain's most influential author has helped to keep it there. As if welcoming you to his home, bronze versions of Cervantes's great creations, the self-styled knight errant Don Quixote and his faithful squire Sancho Panza, sit on a bench outside what is now the Cervantes Birthplace Museum. Quixote brandishes his lance and gesticulates vigorously, while Sancho keeps his arms patiently folded, wondering what fine mess his master is going to get them into next.

Doubts have been cast over whether the house is actually the one in which Cervantes was born (it's a decent-sized property and his father had fallen on hard times by the time Miguel came along), but it certainly recreates the lifestyle the Cervantes family might have aspired to: there are richly decorated desks and comfortable-looking four-poster beds, as well as a peaceful tiled and galleried courtyard for when the heat of the day gets too oppressive. As for Cervantes Senior, you can get an idea of his job as a barber-surgeon, caring for wounded soldiers, in the fifteenth-century hospital next door.

The Cervantes Award is presented on 23 April, the anniversary of the author's death, but if you are in Alcalá around the date of his baptism on 9 October you can participate in Cervantes Week: this includes theatrical and educational events, a Don Quixote Market, and local restaurants offering dishes inspired by the food mentioned in the novel. Though as Don Quixote's normal diet consisted of 'a stew of rather more beef than mutton, a salad on most nights, scraps on Saturdays, lentils on Fridays, and a pigeon or so extra on Sundays', the restaurants have presumably taken some liberties with the text to produce a gastronomic treat.

The Cervantes family left Alcalá (possibly to escape debt) when Miguel was a small child, and thereafter he lived a rather nomadic life; by the time *Don Quixote* was published he had settled in Madrid. So his unlikely hero doesn't come from his creator's home town. The first line of the novel describes him as living in 'a place in La Mancha, whose name I do not choose to remember'; one scholar suggests that Cervantes chose the arid and rather featureless region of La Mancha as a joke, as the least likely place in Spain to spawn a chivalric hero. Another attraction might have been the region's famous windmills, some of which can still be seen at Campo de Criptana, about one hundred and twenty-five miles (two hundred kilometres) south of Alcalá, and in Consuegra, another thirty miles (fifty kilometres) to the west; bring your own horse and lance if you want to have a go at tilting at them. Or settle for a guided tour.

While you're there, take a detour to El Toboso, home of Dulcinea, the idealised lady of Quixote's dreams; admire the statue that the town has erected to her, and visit more Cervantes-themed museums. There's a Don Quixote Museum in Valladolid, too, and a statue of the knight and his squire in front of the vast Cervantes monument in the Plaza de España in Madrid (which, bizarrely, has a replica in Brussels: the Brussels Remembers website suggests that this may be to commemorate the first non-Iberian edition of the book, published in Brussels in 1607).

This last statue isn't universally admired; the narrator of *Living's the Strange Thing* by one of Spain's most prominent twentieth-century novelists, Carmen Martín Gaite (1925–2000), wasn't impressed by the fact that Don Quixote was so far ahead of Sancho:

> *I always imagine them riding side by side so they could hear each other, because if not, fine company they'd be, and the important thing is what they say, the words that live on.*

Fair point, but this monument is bang in the centre of one of the most frequented squares in Spain and, when it comes to tourist attractions, location beats literary companionship every time.

If, further afield, you find yourself in Golden Gate Park in San Francisco, you may come across Quixote and Sancho kneeling before a bust of Cervantes, created in 1916 for the three-hundredth anniversary of the author's death. *Don Quixote* is often described as the first modern novel and widely regarded as one of the greatest of all works of fiction; it's also in the top ten of the most widely translated works of all time, a list that is headed by the Bible and includes the *Tao Te Ching* and *The Communist Manifesto*. So it's only fitting that there should be memorials, museums and – despite everything – restaurants named after it from Marbella to Manchester, New Hampshire, and from Sydney to Sacramento, California. But the place where it all started is the ancient university city, now a UNESCO World Heritage Site, just outside Madrid. It's intriguing to imagine what fantasy poor deluded Don Quixote would have woven around the big white birds nesting on its rooftops.

Galdós's Madrid
Benito Pérez Galdós

patrimonionacional.es/visita/palacio-real-de-madrid
parroquiadesangines.es
chocolateriasangines.com

Benito Pérez Galdós (1843–1920) has often been described as the Spanish Balzac or the Spanish Dickens. The resemblance to Balzac (see page 31) lies in the vast scope of Galdós's multi-volumed *Contemporary Novels* with its many recurring characters, the central figures in one novel reappearing in minor roles in another. With Dickens (see page 180), the comparison is perhaps more due to the fact that, as with Dickens's London, Galdós's Madrid is a seething, throbbing character in its own right.

A good place to begin investigating Galdós's Madrid is the Royal Palace, official residence of the Spanish Royal Family and home to the Bringas family in *That Bringas Woman*. The novel opens with this cynical overview:

> *It was ... how shall I put it? ... an elegant and highly ornate funereal artefact of great architectural daring and grandiose design. ... It boasted a pyramidal staircase, Greco-Roman plinths, buttresses, pointed arches, pinnacles, gargoyles and canopies. There was a profusion of torches, urns, bats, amphorae, owls, wreaths of everlastings, winged waterclocks, scythes, palm fronds, coiled serpents and other symbols of death and life.*

In fact Galdós is describing the intricate 'hair picture' that the court official Francisco de Bringas is making, but he could equally well be writing about the palace itself. One character, trying to find the Bringas residence, complains

Lope de Vega House Museum

esmadrid.com/en/tourist-information/casa-museo-lope-de-vega

Closed Mondays and public holidays

The great playwright of Spain's Golden Age, Félix Lope de Vega y Carpio (1562–1635) bought a house in Madrid – now a museum – in 1610, and lived there for the rest of his life. Ironically, it's in Calle Cervantes, named after Lope's great contemporary (see page 159).

Much altered and redeveloped during the three centuries after his death, the house was purchased by the Royal Academy of the Spanish Language in the 1930s and restored to resemble what it would have been in Lope's day. Rather surprisingly given his chequered career (which included a period in prison for libelling his former mistress and her family, followed by some years in exile), one of the features of the house is Lope's oratory, a place for private prayer that he had built when he first moved in. It becomes less surprising when you learn that as a young man he had wanted to enter the church and – after all those years of ups and downs – in 1614 was finally ordained as a priest. You can also visit his garden, and the studio containing furniture, paintings and books that once belonged to him. One of his daughters had donated some of them to a convent, but the Academy got them back.

Go in the summer and you can see one of his plays performed. There are plenty of them – around five hundred, by no means all of them masterpieces. With numerous poems and novels to his name, too, he is one of the most prolific authors of all time, in any language. Some of his plays are serious historical dramas, but most are of the 'cloak and dagger' intrigue variety, with complicated love triangles (or even quadrangles)

that you can't come into the palace without a map and a compass. Built in a square overlooking a magnificent courtyard, it has over 3,000 rooms, with only a handful open to the public at any one time. On a good day you can see the breathtaking main staircase, the Throne Hall with a ceiling painted by Tiepolo in the Rococo style, the chapel with a collection of musical instruments made by Stradivarius, and the huge and recently restored kitchens. It's no wonder that Rosalía de Bringas, whose taste already runs to expensive finery, feels she needs to keep up appearances at all costs. On the other hand, if your taste runs to minimalism, this is not the place for you.

driving the plots. Lope's importance really lies in his pioneering of the use of everyday language in literature: he believed – radically for the time – that it was a writer's duty to make himself understood. His old home shows that he appreciated the everyday in his life as well as his art. As he put it in one of his most quoted lines:

> *With a few flowers in my garden, half a dozen pictures and some books,*
> *I live without envy.*

Despite his colourful CV, he seems to have achieved peace towards the end.

To get to the heart of Galdós's Madrid, though, you need to get out on the streets, as he did, eavesdropping on people's conversations so that he could write rich and authentic dialogue. This talent shows best in his masterpiece, *Fortunata and Jacinta*, whose thousand-plus pages sprawl across every possible layer of Madrid society, from working-class but captivating Fortunata to wealthy but barren Jacinta, respectively the mistress and the wife of the playboy Juanito Santa Cruz.

Start at the Plaza Mayor, or rather just off it, in Cava de San Miguel, a picturesque little street once filled with market stalls, taverns and cafés. This is

where Fortunata lives, at number 11, above a shop selling poultry and eggs, with cages of birds everywhere:

> *Juanito took it all in his stride along with those famous granite steps, now black and worn. The effect was that of the approach to a castle or State prison. The wall-facing was plaster on brick and it was covered with marks and inscriptions that were either coarse or stupid. On the side nearer the street, strong iron grilles completed the feudal impression of the building.*

It's here that Juanito first sees Fortunata, eating a raw egg – an incident that Galdós apparently witnessed on one of his rambles.

Head east from the plaza and you'll find the more imposing houses of Calle de Pontejos, overlooking the square of the same name, where Jacinta and Juanito live with his parents:

> *The owners occupied the first floor, which was immense, with twelve balconies over the street and a great deal of space inside ... They had a rather old-fashioned drawing room, with three balconies ... To the right of the drawing room was Juanito's study, so called not because he had anything to study in there, but because there was a table with an inkwell and two beautiful bookcases.*

You can only see these homes from the outside, but you can visit the Church of San Ginés, one of Madrid's oldest, where (again according to what Galdós tells us in *Fortunata and Jacinta*) parishioners brought their early-morning drinking chocolate and had breakfast in the porch. If this sounds a bit primitive, just around the corner, and mentioned in Galdós's collection of historical novels, *National Episodes*, is the Chocolatería San Ginés, founded in 1894 and still furnished with the traditional white marble tables and a blue-tiled counter: you can have chocolate and *churros* here at almost any hour of the day or night. It's warmer than huddling in the porch of a church.

To visit Galdós's birthplace, you need to go to the Canary Islands (there's a museum in Las Palmas de Gran Canaria), but in Madrid there's a plaque outside the house where he died (in Calle Hilarión Eslava, to the north of the palace) and a bustling pedestrianised street named after him a bit further east: here, there are plenty of cafés where you can sit and watch the world go by, and eavesdrop as he did.

One last place to visit: El Retiro, one of Madrid's largest parks. In January 1919, a statue to Galdós was unveiled at its southern end. It shows him as a rather sombre old man, his hands clasped in his lap and his legs covered by a blanket. On that cold winter's day, the elderly author, blind and all but crippled, was lifted up by a crowd of well-wishers so that he could feel the sculpted outlines of his own features. Less than a year later, 30,000 people accompanied his coffin to La Almudena cemetery as a further sign of their respect and affection. Why? As the journalist Carlos Mayoral wrote a century later:

> *... because Galdós had been part of their world. He had engaged with the common folk, the streets, trams, ordinary conversation ... He had kept company with government leaders, shopkeepers, aristocrats and thieves. He had engaged with you and me. Galdós embraced people's ordinariness, regardless of their status or social class.*

Quite an epitaph.

The Cemetery of Forgotten Books, Barcelona
Carlos Ruiz Zafón

If you pass through the arch that leads from Barcelona's well-lit Ramblas into the Calle del Arco del Teatro and the seedier Raval quarter in the early hours of the morning, you may well experience something of what ten-year-old Daniel feels at the start of Carlos Ruiz Zafón's *The Shadow of the Wind* (2001):

> *I followed my father through that narrow lane, more of a scar than a street, until the glimmer of the Ramblas faded behind us. The brightness of dawn filtered down from balconies and cornices in streaks of slanting light that dissolved before touching the ground. At last my father stopped in front of*

a large door of carved wood, blackened by time and humidity. Before us loomed what to my eyes seemed the carcass of a palace, a place of echoes and shadows.

Inside:

A blue-tinted gloom obscured the sinuous contours of a marble staircase and a gallery of frescoes peopled with angels and fabulous creatures ... A labyrinth of passageways and crammed book shelves rose from base to pinnacle like a beehive, woven with tunnels, steps, platforms and bridges that presaged an immense library of seemingly impossible geometry.

Welcome, as Daniel's bookseller father says to his bemused son, to the Cemetery of Forgotten Books.

Sadly, you can explore Raval from dawn till dusk and beyond without finding this building: the Barcelona-born Zafón (1964–2020) was living in Los Angeles when he wrote *The Shadow of the Wind* and is said to have been inspired by the vast hangars full of all sorts of junk he saw on the outskirts of that sprawling city; he simply preferred to fill his version with books and relocate it to his home town. But although the building isn't there in reality, it is in spirit: the arch through which you – and Daniel and his father – pass symbolises the transition from a dependable, intelligible world to the realm of darkness and mystery into which Daniel is lured by virtue of choosing a single book from those crammed shelves.

Back on the lighter side of the arch, you can walk down Calle de Santa Ana, where Daniel's father had his bookshop. A beautifully illustrated mosaic bears the name of the street, and you'll find a shop at the right address, number 27A. It sells gloves and fans rather than books, but it offers you a stylish wooden facade reminiscent of the 1950s, when most of the book is set, and is, as Daniel says, a stone's throw from the Santa Ana church where (spoiler alert) one of the few happy events of the novel takes place. The church boasts an imposing Gothic portal and spectacular cloisters, but perhaps most poignantly – and most significantly, given that part of the story develops against the background of the Spanish Civil War – a fifteenth-century lantern tower that had to be rebuilt after the ravages of that conflict.

Other real buildings appear in among the ones that Zafón imagined: you'll find the café Els Quatre Gats, once frequented by Picasso, Gaudí and other artists, and visited by Daniel and his friend Fermín, just around the corner from the church. Also nearby is the Ateneo library, situated in the former Savassona palace, an eighteenth-century neoclassical building with grand staircases, elaborate galleries and beautiful painted ceilings. As Zafón puts it:

... one of the many places in Barcelona where the nineteenth century has not yet been served its eviction notice ... inventions such as the telephone, the wristwatch, and haste, seemed futuristic anachronisms. The porter, or perhaps it was a statue in uniform, barely noticed my arrival.

To the south of the city centre, Montjuic hill is renowned for giving amazing views over Barcelona, and it's in Montjuic Cemetery that numerous characters in *The Shadow of the Wind* are buried, many of them – thanks to the actions of the vengeful and corrupt police inspector Fumero – tossed without ceremony into unmarked graves. Zafón's own grave is marked, though, and inscribed (in Spanish) with the touching words: 'So long as we are remembered, we remain alive.'

One of the strangest things about Zafón's Barcelona – a city that many tourists visit for its warm and sunny climate – is how much it rains. Visits to the abandoned Aguilar house in particular – on Avenida del Tibidabo (number 32, if you want to go in search) – seem always to take place on dark and stormy nights, and characters frequently turn up on one another's doorsteps in need of warm towels and hot drinks. But the clouds do part at one moment towards the end of the book, when Daniel and Fermín are strolling along the beach at La Barceloneta at dawn on a spring day:

> *Before we knew it, we were walking along the breakwater with the whole city, shining with silence, spread out at our feet in the reflection from the harbour waters, like the greatest mirage in the universe.*

Even then, Zafón gives us a darker view, when the ever-philosophical Fermín observes:

> *This city is a sorceress, you know, Daniel? It gets under your skin and steals your soul without you knowing it.*

This rather spine-tingling description may not be true of the casual visitor's Barcelona, but it certainly is of Zafón's.

Huerta de San Vicente, Granada
Federico García Lorca

huertadesanvicente.com

Closed Mondays and public holidays

I understood they had murdered me.
They searched the cafés and the graveyards
and churches,
they opened the wine casks and wardrobes,
they destroyed three skeletons to pull out
their gold teeth.
Still they couldn't find me.
They couldn't?
No. They couldn't.

Taken from 'The Fable and Round of the Three Friends', published in the anthology *Poet in New York* (1929), this may seem a macabre piece of writing for a man only just turned thirty. But perhaps even then Federico García Lorca (1898–1936) could envisage his own premature death. A poet who rose to fame with a collection of ballads about gypsy culture, who once said that he would 'always be on the side of those who have nothing and who are not even allowed to enjoy the nothing they have in peace'; a homosexual whose plays depict people following their own passions rather than an accepted moral code, and who was an outspoken supporter of socialism when his region had already fallen under fascist control, he ticked quite a lot of the wrong boxes as far as the establishment was concerned.

Lorca's early days had been conventional enough: born into a comfortable middle-class family in a village just outside Granada, he had briefly studied law and the arts at the university in the city. Moving to Madrid, he was introduced to avant-garde circles that included the film director Luis Buñuel, the composer Manuel de Falla and the artist Salvador Dalí. By the late 1920s he had established a reputation as both a poet and a playwright. He travelled, giving readings of his works and lecturing on literary themes, in the United States, Cuba and South America, where the new friends he made included another prominent left-winger, the Chilean poet and future Nobel laureate Pablo Neruda. Yet amid all this high-powered intellectual activity, whenever he could, for Christmas and the summer holidays, he went home to Huerta de San Vicente, the house on the outskirts of Granada that his parents had bought in 1925.

It's this house you can visit today as the García Lorca Museum, and you can see immediately why Lorca loved it. It's situated in what is now the extensive Parque García Lorca, with rose gardens, water features and tree-lined avenues, but in the 1920s and 1930s it would have been surrounded by orchards, some of which remain. Inside you can see manuscripts, drawings, photographs and paintings by, among others, Dalí and another influential contemporary, Manuel Ángeles Ortiz. It's a simple but comfortable farmhouse, designed to protect against extremes of climate: pleasantly cool in summer, surprisingly cosy in winter. Whatever the time of year, it's peaceful: an ideal retreat for someone inextricably caught up in the political and artistic upheavals of the day. It wasn't peaceful enough to take the fire out of his writing, though: it was here, in a sparsely furnished bedroom/study, that, between 1926 and 1936, he composed three of his greatest plays, *Blood Wedding*, *Yerma* and *The House of Bernarda Alba*. All deal with frustrated passion and the bloody consequences of violating family honour; all end with violent death. It seems barely possible in this gentle spot.

In the centre of Granada, the Federico García Lorca Centre is a fine piece of modern architecture that manages to blend happily into its historic surroundings: when you consider that it is just opposite the ornate sixteenth-century cathedral, that is no mean feat. The atrium opens out into a sizeable *plaza*, so that it's hard to know where interior ends and exterior begins; inside there are exhibitions, performances and readings of Lorca's works. Granada is proud of this distinguished son: you can do García Lorca tours around the city and sit next to a bronze version of him on a bench in the Avenida de la Constitución.

The one thing you can't do is visit his grave.

In a time of political unrest all over Spain, Granada was one of the most troubled areas: a right-wing *coup d'état* here on 20 July 1936 marked the start of the Civil War. One of the prominent figures who was arrested on that day was the leftist mayor of Granada, who happened to be Lorca's brother-in-law. Lorca was at Huerta de San Vicente at the time; he was arrested on 16 August, the same day his brother-in-law was executed. It's believed, but has never been definitively proved, that he was shot in a gully outside the nearby village of Víznar three days later. Despite much speculation, much research and a number of expensive excavations, the body of one of Spain's greatest poets and dramatists has never been found.

Seven years earlier, in the poem quoted above, he had predicted precisely that. In another, called 'Farewell', he had written:

If I die,
leave the balcony open.

The little boy is eating oranges.
(From my balcony I can see him.)

The window of his room in Huerta de San Vicente has a little balcony that looks out over the peaceful garden. It's a gentle reminder of a turbulent life.

Luis de Camões Square, Lisbon
Luis de Camões

Most European countries with a long history boast a 'national' poet or author – Shakespeare, Cervantes, Dante and so on – and you can visit their homes to find out more about them. Portugal's equivalent is Luis de Camões (1524–1580), author of the great epic *The Lusiads*. Also known as *The Lusitanians* (from the Latin name for Portugal), it is a celebration of the explorer Vasco da Gama's discovery of a sea route to India, incorporating much of the history of Portugal, particularly the glorious bits. It begins, echoing the opening of Virgil's *Aeneid* but updated to a new, global setting:

Arms and the Heroes, who from Lisbon's shore,
Thro' seas where sail was never spread before,
Beyond where Ceylon lifts her spicy breast,
And waves her woods above the wat'ry waste ...

... and it carries on in that vein, barely pausing for breath for over 1,100 stanzas. So it's epic in both subject and scale.

In addition to all that, the day of Camões's death (10 June) is Portugal's national day, and the most important literary prize for the work of an author in the Portuguese language is named after him. There can't be many writers who so completely dominate their country's literary scene.

Unfortunately Camões's home town of Lisbon was devastated by an earthquake on 1 November 1755 and anything that might have remained of his dwelling places went with it, as did the Convent of Saint Anne in which he was buried. It's unlikely that the French philosopher Voltaire (1694–1778) ever visited Portugal, but he wrote a long poem about the disaster and his 1759 novel *Candide* includes something that reads like an eyewitness account:

Scarcely had they reached the city, lamenting the death of their benefactor, when they felt the earth tremble under their feet. The sea swelled and foamed in the harbour, and beat to pieces the vessels riding at anchor. Whirlwinds of fire and ashes covered the streets and public places; houses fell, roofs were flung upon the pavements, and the pavements were scattered. Thirty thousand inhabitants of all ages and sexes were crushed under the ruins.

Thirty thousand dead is a conservative estimate. The figure may have been as high as fifty thousand.

Anyway, back to Camões. His life seems to have been something of a rollercoaster: the idea that he was his own worst enemy is hard to avoid, though he also suffered more than his share of bad luck. He came from a wealthy background, but his father lost the family fortune (and his own life) in a shipwreck; as a young man he spent time at the Portuguese court, but was banished after an illicit love affair. He became a soldier and later an administrator in various Portuguese colonies, falling from grace in Goa after publishing some satirical verses, then enjoying a period of prosperity in Macao. On a subsequent journey he too suffered a shipwreck that left him with little more than the clothes he stood up in and the manuscript of *The Lusiads*. Returning to Portugal, he was invited back to court with a generous pension, but seems to have fallen foul of a regime change and again lost everything. The huge success of *The Lusiads*, published in 1572, didn't stop him from dying in poverty.

The poem was widely translated and enduringly popular throughout Europe; in the introduction to his eighteenth-century translation, the Scottish poet William Julius Mickle observed that it was the epic poem of commerce in the way that Milton's *Paradise Lost* was the epic poem of religion: big stuff. But it wasn't until a luxury edition was published in Paris in 1817 under the auspices of a Portuguese nobleman that it seems to have occurred to anyone that Camões deserved a memorial.

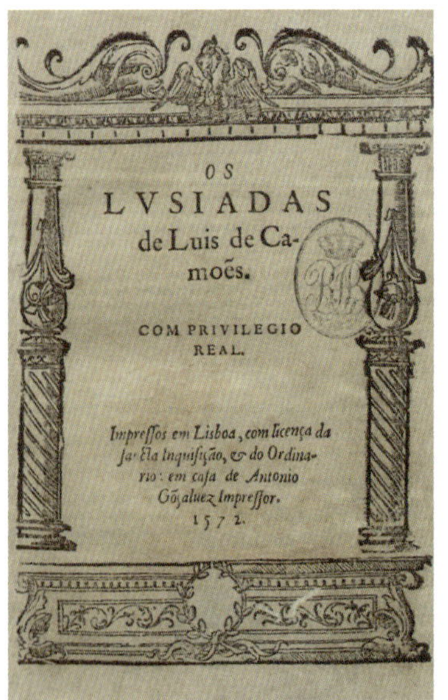

OS
LVSIADAS
de Luis de Camoës.

COM PRIVILEGIO REAL.

Impressos em Lisboa, com licença da sancta Inquisição, & do Ordinario: em casa de Antonio Gõçaluez Impressor.
1572.

Even then, it took half a century to make it happen – but it was worth waiting for. A splendid 13-foot (4-metre) bronze now stands in Luis de Camões Square in central Lisbon, depicting Camões as part soldier, part scholar and courtier: he's elegantly dressed, with his left arm clutching a copy of *The Lusiads* and a pile of books sitting behind his left leg; his right hand holds a sword, a breastplate leans against his right leg, and his head is crowned with laurels in the style of a triumphant Roman general. The pedestal on which he stands is adorned with smaller statues of eight other Portuguese writers and intellectuals of the Renaissance period, including the poets Jerónimo Corte-Real (1533–1588) and Vasco Mouzinho de Quevedo (*c.*1570–*c.*1619).

Luis de Camões Square has become Lisbon's meeting place of choice for visitors and residents alike – the Piccadilly Circus or Spanish Steps of the Portuguese capital. It's busy, full of cafés and fashionable shops, and close to lots of tourist attractions. But it's Camões who dominates. Rightly so: this wasn't a man who did things by halves.

At Large in Lisbon
Fernando Pessoa

abrasileira.pt

If you've been to Luis de Camões Square to check out the statue there (see previous entry), you may choose to stop for a coffee in A Brasileira ('The Brazilian Woman') and notice another statue at one of the pavement tables. This is Fernando Pessoa (1888–1935), the great Portuguese literary figure of his age, who used to do some of his writing – and a considerable amount of drinking – here. Pessoa's posthumously published masterpiece *The Book of Disquiet* has been said to 'give to Lisbon the haunting spell of Joyce's Dublin or Kafka's Prague', which suggests it isn't unreasonable to describe the author as a genius. But there's no denying that he was also a bit of an oddball. He wrote by hand in notebooks or typed on loose sheets of paper, scrawled on the back of envelopes, letters and advertising flyers – poetry, fiction, criticism, philosophy, in Portuguese, French and English – and left a vast jumble of papers to be discovered in a trunk after his death. *The Book of Disquiet* emerged unfinished from these papers: when I say it was published posthumously, I should add that it first appeared in 1982, forty-seven years after the author's death. It had taken that long to come up with a reasonable stab at what he must have intended.

Pessoa not only wrote in a huge variety of genres, he also used over seventy names. He called the more important of these 'heteronyms' (literally 'different names'), a term he preferred to 'pseudonym' ('false name'), because he felt it captured the intellectual independence of each one, and he endowed these alter egos with biographies, physical descriptions, political views and literary tastes of their own. Some of his lesser creations he dubbed 'semi-heteronyms' and in these various guises he wrote everything from a lament for the death of the Emperor Hadrian's lover Antinous to 'Lisbon Revisited', a melancholic study of the sense of alienation he experienced in his native city when he returned there after a childhood spent in South Africa. The supposed author of *The Book of Disquiet* is one of his more important heteronyms, the accountant Bernardo Soares; the book is subtitled 'A factless autobiography' and it's not far from the truth to say that absolutely nothing happens in it. Soares – narrator as well as author – works in the Rua dos Douradores (the 'Street of Goldsmiths'), the same part of town that Pessoa frequented as a freelance journalist and a short walk from Camões Square; he lives in a rented fourth-floor room nearby and writes in his spare time. It's an unexciting part of Lisbon's busy commercial district, but the excitement or otherwise of the city is not Soares/Pessoa's concern. His focus is partly on his own emotions and the meaning of life; partly on the everyday, the tiny details that can be observed in any city by anyone watching the rest of the world going about its business:

> *Today, walking down the Rua Nova do Almada [perhaps heading for A Brasileira – it's in the right direction], I happened to gaze at the back of a man walking ahead of me. It was the ordinary back of an ordinary man, a simple sports coat on the shoulders of an incidental pedestrian ...*
>
> *I suddenly felt something like tenderness for that man. I felt the tenderness one feels for common human banality, for the daily routine of the family breadwinner going to work, for his humble and happy home, for the happy and sad pleasures that necessarily make up his life, for the innocence of living without analysing, for the animal naturalness of that coat-covered back.*

On another occasion, travelling by tram, he becomes absorbed in the embroidered collar of the dress of the woman in front of him, and goes off into a similar form of speculation on the lives of the factory workers who produced it.

On a fine day, as he walks to work:

> *In the baskets along the pavement of the Rua da Prata, the bananas for sale were tremendously yellow in the sunlight.*
>
> *It really takes very little to satisfy me; the rain having stopped, there being a bright sun in this happy South, bananas that are yellower for having black splotches, the voices of the people who sell them, the pavement of the Rua da Prata, the Tagus at the end of it, blue with a green-gold tint, this entire familiar corner of the universe.*

No detail is too small, too trivial for Soares. So it's slightly odd that Pessoa should have frequented A Brasileira, where the details, far from being trivial, are completely in your face. The café dates back to 1905, when the original owner – who had spent time in Brazil, married the daughter of an important coffee producer there and named his establishment in her honour – introduced the virtually unknown concept of drinking coffee to the people of Lisbon. To this day both the facade and the interior are reminiscent of Paris in the heyday of its cafés (see page 23): there are marble surfaces, mosaics, pillars, ornamental friezes and a positively dazzling palette of colours. Perhaps Pessoa, who went to such extraordinary lengths to disguise his own personality and identity, liked the idea of being overwhelmed by a mere coffee shop.

DECUS
IN
LABO
RE

Today, neatly clad in suit and bow tie, one leg crossed over the other, his bronze likeness sits outside A Brasileira, under a sun umbrella, at his usual table. Sadly, his posthumous fame has brought him more attention than he ever had in his lifetime. A Brasileira is one of Lisbon's busiest cafés, not least because of its connection with Pessoa. Tourists sit on his lap all day long and take selfies. The poor man would have been appalled.

Livraria Lello, Porto
J. K. Rowling, José Saramago and others

livrarialello.pt

You may think that the reason to visit Porto is to drink the port. You may well be right, but it would be a shame to go to Portugal's second city and miss out on the country's third most popular tourist attraction, the exuberant Gothic Revival and Art Deco bookshop Livraria Lello. It has been operating from its current location on the smart shopping street of Rua das Carmelitas since 1906, but has a tradition of publishing and bookselling that dates back to 1869. It was then that a young Frenchman called Ernesto Chardron, working as an assistant to his bookseller uncle in Porto and quickly mastering both the language and the local market, won first prize in a lottery and promptly went into business on his own account, founding the Livraria Internacional (International Bookstore). After various changes of management following his early death, it was eventually acquired by another bookseller, José Pinto de Sousa Lello, and moved into its current, purpose-built premises. Its ornate Gothic facade, recently restored to its original glory, stands out from the buildings on either side, as it was always intended to do.

It's hard to exaggerate the contribution that Chardron and Lello's legacy has made to Portuguese letters. In 1862 Chardron's uncle's firm had published *Doomed Love*, which is considered the greatest work of the prolific novelist and playwright Camilo Castelo Branco (1825–1890), the first Portuguese to make a living from his writing. In 1888 the Livraria Internacional published *The Maias* by Eça de Quierós (1845–1900), Portugal's equivalent to Dickens and Balzac. Then in the early part of the twentieth century Livraria Lello was responsible for introducing to the country the works of such foreign greats as Shakespeare, Cervantes, Flaubert and Darwin, many of whom were being translated into Portuguese for the first time. Fast-forward to the 1990s and you find J. K. Rowling (born 1965) teaching English as a foreign language in

Porto while working on the first of the Harry Potter novels; it is strongly rumoured that Livraria Lello helped to inspire her.

Certainly when you walk in you could imagine yourself in the wizarding bookshop in Diagon Alley where, in *Harry Potter and the Philosopher's Stone*, Harry and his mentor Hagrid bought the books Harry needed for his first year at school:

> *... the shelves were stacked to the ceiling with books as large as paving stones bound in leather; books the size of postage stamps in covers of silk; books full of peculiar symbols and a few books with nothing in them at all.*

Livraria Lello's stock may not be as eclectic as that, but it's certainly stacked to the ceiling with books, and almost every inch that isn't covered by books seems to be made of intricately carved wood. The ceiling of the ground floor wouldn't be out of place in an Italian Renaissance church, while the first-floor gallery rivals anything to be seen in an English stately home. On the ground floor, an installation called *The Face of Porto* consists of four hundred clay busts representing famous figures from the city alongside anonymous citizens such as vendors from Porto's iconic Bolhão Market.

The most magical element of the shop is the red staircase, which has been likened to a double helix but which Lonely Planet describes affectionately as 'lolloping'. From the centre of the ground floor it rises to a half landing, then divides and curves around to the upper floor, affording an excellent view of the stained-glass skylight that gives the space a luminosity not always found in old bookshops.

Returning to the Muggle world, you can browse the store's collection of rare books, visit an Enchanted Forest presided over by the Lello Bookshop Fairy or a room dedicated to José Saramago (1922–2010), the first (and so far still the only) Portuguese-language winner of the Nobel Prize in Literature. But there's no denying that it is Harry Potter that has given Livraria Lello its current status, which is first and foremost as a tourist attraction. Be prepared to pay an admission fee (eight euros at the time of writing) and to queue quite a while to get in: the street has sometimes been closed to traffic because of the numbers waiting outside. But once you're inside, be prepared to gasp at the sheer extravagant pizzazz of it all. It's been called the most beautiful bookshop in the world, and also the coolest. It could well be both.

THE UNITED KINGDOM & IRELAND

Dickens's London
Charles Dickens

dickensmuseum.com
Closed Mondays and Tuesdays

The best place to start an exploration of Charles Dickens's London is the museum at 48 Doughty Street, Bloomsbury, where the author (1812–1870) lived for three extraordinarily productive years, from 1837 to the end of 1839. Combining the discipline of a journalist who has deadlines to meet with an inexhaustible supply of energy, he sat in his study for four hours every morning and, in that remarkably short space of time, produced *Nicholas Nickleby*, *Oliver Twist* and the later episodes of *The Pickwick Papers*. Although he didn't start the lucrative public readings that made him a celebrity until after this period, he was already something of a figure in London literary circles and used to invite friends around for dinner, conversation and to listen to him read. In the dining room of the museum is a table set for a lavish meal, while in the corner cabinet a set of silver ladles, used for serving punch, is decorated with characters from *The Pickwick Papers* – a gift from his publisher when he finished the book. On display upstairs are the desk he later took with him on his reading tours of the United States, and the copies of his works that he used as scripts, with significant passages underlined and handwritten notes to himself in the margin.

When you leave the museum, it's easy to take in a number of Dickens 'sites' in an hour or two's walk. A quarter of an hour to the south – past Lincoln's Inn, which plays a role in Bleak House – lies The Old Curiosity Shop, a quaint sixteenth-century building that survived the Great Fire of 1666 to become one of the oldest shops in London. Closed at the time of writing, it's being restored under the auspices of the nearby London School of Economics and may yet reopen. Dickens is known to have visited this shop, and he must surely have had it in mind when he described Little Nell's home in *The Old Curiosity Shop* as:

> *... one of those receptacles for old and curious things which seem to crouch in odd corners of this town and to hide their musty treasures from the public eye in jealousy and distrust.*

Head back north and east towards Saffron Hill, because if by 'Dickensian' you understand 'poor, dirty and squalid', there can't be a more quintessentially Dickensian piece of writing than Oliver Twist's first impressions of this street, where Fagin has his den:

Covered ways and yards, which here and there diverged from the main street, disclosed little knots of houses, where drunken men and women were positively wallowing in the filth; and from several of the door-ways, great ill-looking fellows were cautiously emerging, bound, to all appearance, on no very well-disposed or harmless errands.

Continue south and east to a spot where, if you want to add a touch of cold, damp and fog to the mix, you can revel in the famous opening to *Bleak House*, with its description of 'implacable November weather':

As much mud in the streets, as if the waters had but newly retired from the face of the earth, and it would not be wonderful to meet a Megalosaurus, forty feet long or so, waddling like an elephantine lizard up Holborn Hill. Smoke lowering down from chimney-pots, making a soft black drizzle with flakes of soot in it as big as full-grown snowflakes – gone into mourning, one might imagine, for the death of the sun.

From Holborn, carry on past the former site of Newgate Prison, which Pip discovered when he first came to London in *Great Expectations*:

I found the roadway covered with straw to deaden the noise of passing vehicles; and from this, and from the quantity of people standing about, smelling strongly of spirits and beer, I inferred that the trials were on.

Shudder at the Old Bailey, famous, according to *A Tale of Two Cities* ...

... as a kind of deadly inn-yard, from which pale travellers set out continually, in carts and coaches, on a violent passage into the other world: traversing some two miles and a half [four kilometres] of public street and road [to be hanged at Tyburn, near today's Marble Arch], and shaming few good citizens, if any.

Finally, cross London Bridge to the place where the young David Copperfield, living south of the river, had to wait for the gates of the City of London to open in the morning before he could go to work. Here at last we find a moment of cheerfulness:

> *... my favourite lounging-place in the interval was old London Bridge, where I was wont to sit in one of the stone recesses, watching the people going by, or to look over the balustrades at the sun shining in the water, and lighting up the golden flame on the top of the Monument.*

It's only right to say that you have to use your imagination as you follow this route. A two-bedroom flat in Saffron Hill will fetch close to a million pounds today, so wallowing in filth tends to be frowned upon; the traffic in Holborn would make it difficult for a Megalosaurus to navigate; Newgate Prison is long gone, though some of the old prison cells survive under the nearby Viaduct Tavern; the present main building of the Central Criminal Court, or Old Bailey, dates only from the early twentieth century. Although the sun can still glint off the golden flame at the top of the Monument, David Copperfield's 'old London Bridge' was demolished in 1831 and even its replacement has gone: it can now be seen in Lake Havasu City, Arizona, where it ranks second only to the Grand Canyon on the list of the state's most popular tourist attractions. On the other hand, David wouldn't have to wait for any gates to open before he could cross the Thames: there are no longer walls to keep the drunk and disorderly of Southwark out of the City of London after dark.

It's all change, but it lives on in Dickens's powerful imagery.

In the Footsteps of Jane Austen
Jane Austen

janeausten.co.uk
thepumproombath.co.uk
janeaustens.house
Open daily from mid-June to end September; for other times, check the website
winchester-cathedral.org.uk

Jane Austen (1775–1817) never lived more than about sixty miles (a hundred kilometres) from her birthplace in Hampshire, so a reasonable Austen pilgrimage, covering several places where she lived and one in particular that she wrote about, can be done within that modest distance. Educated largely at home, Austen's first major move came in 1800, when her clergyman father retired and moved the family to Bath. It's not clear whether she had a great

social life there (and therefore had little time to write) or was miserable (and therefore lacked the inclination). Certainly, she gives us conflicting views in the attitudes of two of her heroines: young, eager Catherine Morland in *Northanger Abbey*:

> *I shall never be in want of something to talk of again to Mrs. Allen, or anybody else. I really believe I shall always be talking of Bath, when I am at home again – I do like it so very much ... Oh! Who can ever be tired of Bath?*

... and the more mature Anne Elliot in *Persuasion*, returning to a place where she had previously been unhappy:

> *She persisted in a very determined, though very silent disinclination for Bath; caught the first dim view of the extensive buildings, smoking in rain, without any wish of seeing them better; felt their progress through the streets to be, however disagreeable, yet too rapid.*

Whichever view you take, it's very easy to imagine yourself in Jane Austen's world when you visit Bath today. The Jane Austen Centre in Gay Street, where the Crofts lodged towards the end of *Persuasion*, is in a Georgian townhouse around which you can be guided by actors dressed in appropriate costumes; its Regency tea room will sell you, among other themed treats, a 'Jane Austen blend' of black China teas, popular in her day, before Indian tea was readily available. The Centre also offers Austen-based walks around the city; and every September it hosts a ten-day Jane Austen Festival, which gives you the opportunity to attend talks on her works and/or to dress up in Regency costume to take part in a parade and various balls. Some of the events take place in the Pump Room in Stall Street, where you can still drink the famous waters that may or may not provide a cure for the gout, liver complaints or digestive troubles that were commonplace in hard-drinking Regency society. Today an elegant restaurant, the Pump Room retains many of the original Georgian features, including a marble vase from which the spa water pours.

Other festival events take you to the eighteenth-century Assembly Rooms in Bennett Street, described when they first opened as 'the most noble and elegant of any in the kingdom' and still worth visiting to admire the hundred-foot-long (thirty-metre) ballroom and the Octagon Room, with its four fireplaces, minstrels' gallery and vast chandelier. It's here that Catherine Morland attended her first ball, on the occasion when she had no acquaintance and no one to dance with; sadly, the so-called Lower Rooms, where she met Henry Tilney and had a much better time, were destroyed by fire in 1820.

The Austens lived in Bath for only five years; the Reverend Austen's death in 1805 left his widow and daughters in straitened circumstances and they moved back to Hampshire, to a cottage in Chawton situated on Jane's brother's estate. This is the house you can now visit as Jane Austen's House Museum.

The Austens may have called it a cottage, but it's bigger than that makes it sound: a sizeable red-brick house with a pretty garden whose flowers, herbs, climbers and old roses are all reminiscent of the plants Austen would have known; there's even an oak tree believed to be descended from one she planted herself. It's a very tranquil spot and she enjoyed a tranquil life here, filling her letters with family news, gossip and what was happening in the garden:

> *Our young piony [sic] at the foot of the fir-tree has just blown and looks very handsome, and the whole of the shrubbery border will soon be very gay with pinks and sweet-williams, in addition to the columbines already in bloom.*

Against this background of domestic comfort, Jane embarked on a period of extraordinary literary productivity. She had begun writing stories at an early age and by the time she moved to Chawton had already produced early versions of *Sense and Sensibility*, *Pride and Prejudice* and *Northanger Abbey*.

While living here she revised these, had the first two published, and in quick succession wrote *Mansfield Park*, *Emma* and *Persuasion*. One of the most striking of her personal possessions on display at Chawton is the tiny walnut table at which she did her writing. Austen was a petite woman – her bed would be more suited to a twelve-year-old today – but even so the table is remarkably small for such a prodigious output. Her nephew James Edward Austen-Leigh explained this in a memoir of his aunt published fifty years after her death: anxious to keep her writing secret from anyone beyond the immediate family circle, she always 'wrote upon small sheets of paper which could easily be put away, or covered with a piece of blotting paper'.

Her modesty had its limits, however: she was thrilled to see *Pride and Prejudice* in print and wrote to her sister Cassandra that she had received 'my own darling child' from the publisher in London. She was also happy to pass on the news that her friends Mr and Mrs Cooke 'admire *Mansfield Park* exceedingly':

> *Mr. Cooke says 'it is the most sensible novel he ever read,' and the manner in which I treat the clergy delights them very much.*

Jane's health, never robust, deteriorated in early 1816; just over a year later, in constant pain and largely confined to bed, she moved to Winchester, fifteen miles away (twenty-four kilometres), to be close to medical attention. She died there on 18 July, aged only forty-one, and, apparently thanks to string-pulling by her family's clerical connections (and because she left money to cover the cost), was buried in the cathedral she greatly admired. Her gravestone described her as the daughter of a deceased local minister rather than as a novelist, but referred to 'the benevolence of her heart, the sweetness of her temper, and the extraordinary endowments of her mind', all qualities that admirers of her novels will recognise. As her fame grew in the years following her death, so her memorials in the cathedral increased: in 1870 her nephew invested some of the proceeds from his memoir in a brass plaque beginning with the words 'Jane Austen, known to many by her writings ...'. This is on the wall adjacent to the grave, and in 1900 a commemorative window was installed above it. So visitors now have three memorials for the price of one, and the cathedral ensures that there are always fresh flowers nearby, a thoughtful touch that the nature-loving author would surely have appreciated.

Fantasy Oxford

J. R. R. Tolkien, Philip Pullman and Lewis Carroll

ox.ac.uk/visitors/visiting-oxford/visiting-the-colleges
Check website for times when you can visit the colleges
aliceinwonderlandshop.com
obga.ox.ac.uk

It says great things about Exeter College Oxford that it should be the alma mater of the two most successful fantasy writers of the twentieth century: Philip Pullman (born 1946), author of the *His Dark Materials* trilogy, and John Ronald Reuel Tolkien (1892–1973), creator of *Lord of the Rings*. Established in 1314, Exeter is the romantic ideal of what an Oxford college should be, with a seventeenth-century dining hall and a breathtaking neo-Gothic chapel (where

a bust of Tolkien is on display). From its gardens you look up at the Radcliffe Camera, the iconic dome that dominates the city's skyscape, and it's hard not to feel that there is something otherworldly in this city of 'dreaming spires'. In his parallel universe, Pullman turned Exeter into the fictional Jordan College and imagined it being as amazing underground as it is above, with tunnels, shafts, vaults, cellars and staircases spreading below the surface 'like some enormous fungus whose root-system extended over acres'. Sadly, that part of Exeter/Jordan is not open to visitors, but some of the other colleges are just as alluring.

Having graduated from Exeter, Tolkien became a fellow first at Pembroke College, where he wrote *The Hobbit* and began work on *The Lord of the Rings*, then at Merton, where he completed it. He also spent a certain amount of time in two historic pubs just across the road from each other in the city-centre street called St Giles'. Here he drank with his friend C. S. Lewis (see page 199) and others who formed the writers' group known as the Inklings. The Eagle and Child is currently closed (plans for refurbishing and reopening have stalled, but *nil desperandum*, as the Inklings would probably have said – they may yet get going again). The Lamb and Flag was saved from the same fate by the enthusiasm of a new group of Inklings. With a brief hiatus during the COVID-19 pandemic, the Lamb and Flag has been operating on this site since the seventeenth century, and numbers the novelists Thomas Hardy and Graham Greene (see page 132) among its other literary customers. If you don't mind a fifteen-minute drive out to Headington, you can also have a drink in the Ampleforth Arms, near Lewis's former home, where he and Tolkien used to meet and indulge in conversations that a friend described as 'way above the heads of us locals'.

Back in Oxford itself, there are links with another great fantasy writer: Charles Lutwidge Dodgson, better known as Lewis Carroll (1832–1898), author of *Alice's Adventures in Wonderland* and *Through the Looking-Glass*. At Christ Church, perhaps Oxford's most grandiose college, Carroll was first a student, then for twenty-six years Mathematical Lecturer. For most of that time Henry Liddell was Dean of the college, living in the adjacent deanery; it was for Liddell's daughter Alice that Carroll wrote his famous books.

Christ Church chapel is the cathedral for the diocese of Oxford, so you can imagine that it is pretty impressive, but Alice-hunting is perhaps better done in the sixteenth-century hall. It boasts a series of modern stained-glass windows, one of which celebrates her and her creator. At floor level, the brass andirons in the vast fireplace are moulded into the form of women with enormously long necks, looking remarkably similar to the illustrator John

The Origins of Middle-earth

birminghammuseums.org.uk/sarehole

Open Friday, Saturday and Sunday for guided tours only; and the first Saturday of each month for exploring without a guide

birminghamconservationtrust.org/our-projects/bct-finished/perrotts-folly

Despite J. R. R. Tolkien's long-standing connection with the city, it wasn't Oxford that sowed the seeds of all things hobbit- and ring-related. That happened some sixty miles (a hundred kilometres) north, at an eighteenth-century watermill on the River Cole. It's just five miles (eight kilometres) from the centre of Birmingham, but in the dying years of the nineteenth century, when Tolkien was a small child living opposite, Sarehole Mill was in rural Worcestershire. Unusually for a watermill, it was partially driven by steam; this meant it needed a chimney, which gave it a distinctive silhouette. The young Tolkien was fascinated by this, and by the surrounding countryside, which he later described as 'a kind of lost paradise'. He also recalled that the smoky image of industrial Birmingham on the horizon inspired the hellish depiction of Mordor in *The Lord of the Rings*. Today the mill is a museum with a visitor centre devoted to Tolkien and guided walks entitled 'Origins of Middle-Earth'.

The hamlet of Sarehole itself may have been the inspiration for Hobbiton; it's even been suggested that the local people gave Tolkien the idea for the hobbits, though it's not clear if they all conformed to his own description of how he envisaged his diminutive heroes:

> *... fattish in the stomach, shortish in the leg. A round, jovial face; ears only slightly pointed and 'elvish'.*

A little to the northwest, and still on the fringes of Birmingham, stands something else that fired Tolkien's imagination. Perrott's Folly, overlooking

Tenniel's drawing of Alice as she was 'opening out like the largest telescope that ever was' after eating the cake 'on which the words "EAT ME" were beautifully marked in currants'.

Just up the road from Christ Church, Alice's Shop today describes itself as 'a treasure trove of Alice in Wonderland gifts and memorabilia', but in the nineteenth century it was a grocery on which Carroll based the shop Alice visits in *Through the Looking-Glass*:

Edgbaston Reservoir, and the nearby Edgbaston Waterworks Tower are said to be the models of the 'Two Towers' from which volume two of *The Lord of the Rings* takes its name. The Gothic folly, surrounded now by worn brick walls and an iron gate, would have been the tallest structure for miles around when it was built in 1758, and it is still imposing. There are a number of suggestions as to why Perrott, a local landowner, should have built it; there's no proof that it was to spy on his unfaithful wife, but the folly's ominous and melancholic feel makes that the story you're inclined to believe. Inside, although work has been done to make the tower safe, the narrow winding staircase remains. Each floor boasts a different design of window, and the views would have been an attraction to Perrott's guests, if you take the more mundane attitude that he built the tower as a status symbol to impress the neighbours.

The shop seemed to be full of all manner of curious things – but the oddest part of it all was, that whenever she looked hard at any shelf, to make out exactly what it had on it, that particular shelf was always quite empty: though the others round it were crowded as full as they could hold.

Tenniel's illustration depicts the shop exactly as it was, but with the details in reverse, because we are seeing it in a looking-glass. Even the proprietor was part of Carroll's inspiration: an elderly lady with a bleating voice, she is surely the reason he made his fictional shopkeeper a sheep.

One final stop in Fantasy Oxford brings you back to *His Dark Materials*. When Lyra and Will have to separate at the end of *The Amber Spyglass* (you can't go on shifting between worlds forever, unfortunately), they agree to return to the Oxford Botanic Garden every year at noon on 24 June. Founded in 1621, the garden is the oldest of its kind in Britain, and Pullman's instructions guide you gently 'past a pool with a fountain under a wide-spreading tree' to the right bench, just as Lyra guided Will:

> *There was a massive stone wall with a doorway in it, and in the further part of the garden the trees were younger and the planting less formal. Lyra led him almost to the end of the garden, over a little bridge, to a wooden seat under a spreading low-branched tree.*

It's likely to be busy at Midsummer, with Pullman fans hoping to catch up with Lyra and Will, but for the other 364 days of the year it's ... well, it's truly magical.

Shakespeare's Stratford
William Shakespeare

shakespeare.org.uk

Shakespeare's Birthplace is open year round; Anne Hathaway's Cottage and New Place open from late March to early November

The life of England's – probably the world's – greatest-ever playwright is full of mystery. Did he really spend those missing years in Italy, picking up the stories for *Romeo and Juliet* (see page 145), *Othello*, *The Merchant of Venice* and the rest? How did his young son Hamnet die? Why did he leave his wife Anne Hathaway only his *second*-best bed in his will? We simply don't know, though Maggie O'Farrell's multi-award-winning 2020 novel *Hamnet* gives a plausible answer to the second and third of these questions, and it surely can't be long before some novelist or filmmaker tackles the first.

But we do know some things, and many of them are centred on the Midlands town where William Shakespeare (1564–1616) was born and died, and whose name is now completely inseparable from his: Stratford-upon-Avon.

To begin at the beginning, the Shakespeare Centre, in Henley Street in the centre of town, may be a twentieth-century complex, but Shakespeare's Birthplace, which forms part of it, is the real deal: the sixteenth-century

half-timbered cottage where he was born. It was purchased by what is now the Shakespeare Birthplace Trust in the mid-nineteenth century and much restored and renovated, but the uneven floor is the very one he first toddled over and the rooms you visit are the ones in which he grew up, furnished as they might have been in his childhood.

In the café area of the Shakespeare Centre you'll find the first of two fine statues: a 10-foot (3-metre) bronze of the Bard, dating from the 1960s. If the café seems a strange place to put such an imposing piece of art, that's because it was originally commissioned for the entrance hall. But it weighs over a ton and a half, so when the building was reconfigured it seemed sensible to leave the bronze where it was and to work around it.

The second statue, just along the street, is called The Jester and portrays a jester in traditional dress, with bells on his shoes and cap; he's balanced precariously on one foot, looking as if the slightest wobble would send him tumbling off his plinth. The inscription at the front, 'O noble fool! A worthy fool!', is from *As You Like It*, but other quotations on the base include the famous 'Alas, poor Yorick!' from *Hamlet* and a great line spoken by the clown Feste in *Twelfth Night*:

Foolery, sir, does walk about the orb like the sun; it shines everywhere.

So the statue doesn't depict a specific character; rather it's a representation of all the wonderful wise fools that Shakespeare scattered through his plays.

Back past the birthplace towards the Royal Shakespeare Theatre (where you should definitely try to take in a performance), New Place, the home that Shakespeare bought in 1597, was at the time the largest house in the borough and the only one with a courtyard; it had five gables, a long gallery and a grand medieval hall, a sure sign that his career had taken off and he was earning good money. Sadly, this fine residence is long gone; what you visit today is an exhibition in the house next door, casting new light, its promoters say, 'on Shakespeare as a father, husband, writer and citizen of Stratford-upon-Avon'.

The real joy of New Place is the garden, created on the site where the house once stood, and including a knot garden based on designs that Shakespeare would have recognised; specially commissioned artworks include a bronze with an ass's head, inspired by *A Midsummer Night's Dream*, and a gleaming silvery globe depicting the world as it was known in Shakespeare's time.

The third home you should visit is a mile or so (one and a half kilometres) out of town. Anne Hathaway's Cottage was Shakespeare's wife's home before she was married. Her family were prosperous farmers and had lived here for several generations before Anne was born; the surviving kitchen and parlour were part of the original house, dating from the mid-fifteenth century. You can also see the so-called Hathaway bed, an impressive four-poster with ornately carved oak. As at New Place, the gardens are delightful, with a tree garden planted with species Shakespeare mentions and more sculptures inspired by his works. A woven willow circle includes a seat that definitely invites you to linger, and perhaps seek inspiration ...

Back in town, at Holy Trinity Church, you'll find Shakespeare's grave, along with those of other members of his family. It's inscribed with these surprising words, said to have been written by Shakespeare himself:

Good friend for Jesus sake forbear,
To dig the dust enclosed here.
Blessed be the man that spares these stones,
And cursed be he that moves my bones.

The question as to why he should have chosen this epitaph when he had 'Our little life is rounded with a sleep' (from *The Tempest*) or 'Out, out, brief candle' (*Macbeth*) at his fingertips has puzzled scholars for many years. But it became particularly newsworthy in 2016, the four-hundredth anniversary of Shakespeare's death, when ground-penetrating scans of the grave found no trace of a skull. Had his bones indeed been moved at some point? Or his grave desecrated? If so, how on earth had he predicted it? We'll probably never know, but it's surely no bad thing that the world's greatest dramatist should have the power to surprise us four centuries after his death.

The Brontë Parsonage Museum, Haworth
Charlotte, Emily and Anne Brontë

bronte.org.uk
Closed Mondays and Tuesdays
haworthchurch.co.uk

'Wuthering', according to the opening chapter of *Wuthering Heights*, is:

... a significant provincial adjective, descriptive of the atmospheric tumult to which its station is exposed in stormy weather. Pure, bracing ventilation they must have up there at all times, indeed: one may guess the power of the north wind, blowing over the edge, by the excessive slant of a few stunted firs at the end of the house; and by a range of gaunt thorns all stretching their limbs one way, as if craving alms of the sun.

Wuthering Heights is the only novel published by Emily Brontë (1818–1848); she was also a prolific and deeply moving poet. Much of her work is spiritual, reflecting on life, illness and death, but she did sometimes write as if she were just sitting, staring out the window over the Yorkshire moors beyond her father's parsonage in Haworth. 'High Waving Heather' begins:

High waving heather, 'neath stormy blasts bending

and includes the lines:

All down the mountain sides, wild forest lending
One mighty voice to the life-giving wind.

Consider also the famous beginning to Jane Eyre, written by Emily's elder sister Charlotte (1816–1855):

There was no possibility of taking a walk that day ... the cold winter wind had brought with it clouds so sombre, and a rain so penetrating, that further out-door exercise was now out of the question.

The weather, and protecting yourself against it, played a key role in the Brontës' lives.

Charlotte, Emily and Anne (1820–1849), also a novelist and poet, were three of the six children of the Reverend Patrick Brontë, and Haworth Parsonage, where they moved in 1820 and lived for most of the rest of their short lives, is now a museum dedicated to them. A visit there gives quite an insight into why the sisters wrote the way they did, particularly if you opt for a grey and windy day, when little light penetrates into the smaller rooms. It must have been incredibly cramped: there were two servants to be accommodated, in addition to the large family. The Reverend Patrick's wife Maria died not long after they moved here, but her sister remained with the family as nanny and housekeeper. Everyone seems to have moved frequently between the few bedrooms, as their various ages and needs changed.

Inseparable from any study of the Brontës is the extent to which they were beset by tragedy. Tuberculosis claimed the two eldest daughters as schoolgirls, then the only son, Branwell, when he was thirty-one, swiftly followed by Emily and Anne at thirty and twenty-nine respectively. Charlotte, left alone with her father, carried on the ritual she had established with her sisters: they had done most of their writing together, in the dining room in the evening, walking around the table, reading and discussing work in progress. After the others had died, one of the servants recorded that 'My heart aches to hear Miss Brontë walking, walking on alone.'

Charlotte lived long enough to see herself established as a successful novelist; she married her father's curate and remained at the Parsonage for the few months that were left of her life. Even so she died before her thirty-ninth birthday. The Reverend Patrick outlived them all and conducted the funeral services for all but the youngest. Anne died at Scarborough, where she had gone to see if sea air would improve her health; her grave is there, in the churchyard of St Mary's. This seems to have been Charlotte's decision, relieving her father of some small part of the pain of burying three of his children within the space of eight months.

Just a few steps away from the Parsonage, there's a Brontë Memorial Chapel in the church of St Michael and All Angels; it's built over the family vault, near where the family pew used to be. Apart from the eighteenth-century tower, this isn't the church the Brontës knew: it's a late-nineteenth-century replacement which includes a stained-glass window dedicated to Charlotte, donated by an American admirer.

If the weather isn't too wuthering, you can extend your Brontë experience by heading out across the moors, following signs along the Brontë Way and passing the pretty little Brontë Waterfall. An hour or so's walk brings you to Top Withens, a ruined farmhouse sometimes said to be the inspiration for the Earnshaws' home in *Wuthering Heights* – the place where Catherine Earnshaw meets Heathcliff and the whole doomed business begins. There's no compelling evidence for this, but that hardly matters: the location must be very much what Emily had in mind and it makes up in atmosphere anything it may lack in literary authenticity. If you're there on a fine day (they do crop up sometimes), you can consider the dreams of Catherine's daughter Cathy and her friend Linton, Heathcliff's son:

> *He said the pleasantest manner of spending a hot July day was lying from morning till evening on a bank of heath in the middle of the moors, with the bees humming dreamily about among the bloom, and the larks singing high up overhead, and the blue sky and bright sun shining steadily and cloudlessly. That was his most perfect idea of heaven's happiness: mine was rocking in a rustling green tree, with a west wind blowing, and bright white clouds flitting rapidly above; and not only larks, but throstles, and*

blackbirds, and linnets, and cuckoos pouring out music on every side, and the moors seen at a distance, broken into cool dusky dells; but close by great swells of long grass undulating in waves to the breeze; and woods and sounding water, and the whole world awake and wild with joy.

They come close to quarrelling over these differing views but, as Cathy continues:

At last, we agreed to try both, as soon as the right weather came; and then we kissed each other and were friends.

It's good to know that it wasn't entirely doom and gloom.

Literary Edinburgh
Sir Walter Scott and others

edinburghmuseums.org.uk/venue/scott-monument
edinburghmuseums.org.uk/venue/writers-museum

If you walk along Princes Street in the heart of Edinburgh, it's difficult to miss the vast Victorian Gothic monument between the Princes Street Gardens and Waverley Station. It's dedicated to Sir Walter Scott (1771–1832) and if you know anything about him and his work, you're likely to think, 'What's he doing here?' Because Scott is much more closely associated with the Scottish Borders than he is with the capital: he's often said to have 'invented' the Borders, in the sense that his historical novels created a romantic heritage associated with them and even in his lifetime drew visitors to the area. Certainly, the home he created for himself at Abbotsford, on the banks of the Tweed, is as romantic a spot as you could hope for: Scott's great artistic contemporary, J. M. W. Turner, thought so, and painted it more than once.

But, to answer your original question, Scott was born in Edinburgh, studied at Edinburgh University and began his literary career here. He's entitled to a monument.

At the base is a statue of the man himself, carved by the sculptor John

Steell from a single 30-ton piece of Carrara marble. Once you've admired that and embarked on the monument's 287 steps, you may be grateful to find the Museum Room on the first floor and have a break. It will tell you lots about Scott himself, and also has four fine stained-glass windows, depicting saints Andrew and Giles (patron saints of Scotland and Edinburgh respectively), and the coats of arms of the city and the country. If you then plough on to the higher viewing platform, you'll be rewarded with views that have inspired many writers, some of them more gifted than others: the twentieth-century Scottish poet Norman MacCaig (1910–1996) vividly described Edinburgh as 'sprawling like seven cats on its seven hills', while the famously appalling doggerel of William Topaz McGonagall (1825–1902) includes – in his poem *Beautiful Edinburgh* – such immortal lines as:

The Prince Albert Consort Statue looks very grand,
Especially the granite blocks whereon it doth stand,

and ends:

Of all the cities in the world, Edinburgh for me;
For no matter where I look, some lovely spot I see;
And for picturesque scenery unrivalled you do stand.
Therefore I pronounce you to be the Pride of Fair Scotland.

You can probably see the Albert Memorial from where you are standing: it's about half a mile away (eight hundred metres), in Charlotte Square Gardens. It is indeed quite grand and stands on a substantial base of Peterhead granite.

As you climb back down Scott's monument, take the time to look at the statues of various characters from his novels that adorn it: they include Louise, the Glee Maiden, playing a mandolin (from *The Fair Maid of Perth*), Julia Mannering (the hero's daughter in *Guy Mannering*) and even Bonnie Prince Charlie and Queen Elizabeth I, who feature in *Waverley* and *Kenilworth* respectively. There are also sculpted heads of Scottish writers including Lord Byron (1788–1824, whose mother was Scottish), Robert Burns (1759–1796) and James Thomson (1700–1748), who wrote the words to 'Rule, Britannia'.

One Edinburgh-born writer who came along too late to feature on Scott's monument (completed in 1846) is Robert Louis Stevenson (1850–1894), but there's no doubt that the city inspired one of his most famous stories, *The Strange Tale of Dr Jekyll and Mr Hyde*. Indeed, some say that Edinburgh is a Jekyll and Hyde city, the elegantly laid out New Town being Dr Jekyll to the higgledy-piggledy Mr Hyde of the Old Town, which is dominated by the castle, perched high on a rocky crag at the top of the Royal Mile. Although set in London, *Dr Jekyll and Mr Hyde* was based on the true story of Deacon William Brodie, a skilled Edinburgh cabinet-maker by day who by night turned to crime in order to finance his gambling habit. On the northwest corner of St Giles Cathedral you can still see the site of the Old Tolbooth, where he was publicly hanged in 1788. Just a minute's walk away you can drink in the tavern named after him: its walls are covered with images referring to his double life, and outside there are two pub signs, one showing the solid citizen, the other a masked and furtive-looking man carrying a bag of what is obviously swag.

Speaking of pubs, it's hard to do a literary tour of Edinburgh without including Ian Rankin's hard-drinking detective John Rebus. His watering hole of choice is the Oxford Bar in the New Town. 'The Ox' is half an hour's walk from Rebus's home in the Marchmont area to the south, but on one occasion (in *Black and Blue*, 1997) it's described as:

> *... a long detour, always worthwhile. The gantry and the optics had a quietly hypnotic effect, the only possible explanation as to why the regulars could stand and stare at them for hours at a stretch.*

Ian Rankin (born 1960) isn't the only writer attracted by the Oxford; the pub itself tells a story about another regular (and another poet with a fine middle name), Sydney Goodsir Smith (1915–1975). Nursing a hangover one morning, he wandered into what looked like a pub – it had brass fittings; what else could it be? When he ordered a restorative drink, however, the bank teller behind the counter was obliged to tell him he had made a mistake.

For more sober literary treasures, drop in at the Writers' Museum, just off Lawnmarket – you'll have passed it if you walked from the Deacon Brodie to the Oxford. It's primarily a celebration of Stevenson, Burns and Scott and contains a real cornucopia of 'stuff'. To mention a rocking horse Scott played with as a child, a cast of Burns's skull and a wardrobe belonging to the Stevenson family made by none other than Deacon Brodie, is no more than to scratch the surface of this wonderfully eclectic collection. It's sad to think that two of these three great Edinburgh writers died before they were forty-five, and that the other (Walter Scott) spent his life staggering from one financial crisis to another. But they've left us some fine mementos for all that.

C. S. Lewis Square, Belfast
C. S. Lewis

visitbelfast.com/partners/cs-lewis-square

Clive Staples Lewis (1898–1963) is so closely associated with Oxford – where he studied and taught from 1917 until the end of his life and was famously friendly with fellow academic J. R. R. Tolkien (see page 186) – that it may come as a surprise to learn that he was born in Belfast. Indeed, according to his 1955 memoir *Surprised by Joy*, the twenty-year-old Lewis took one look at the place that was to become his home and decided he loathed everything about it, from the landscape to the unfamiliar accents that seemed like 'the voices of demons'.

England has long since forgiven the author of *The Chronicles of Narnia* for this early lapse in taste. The Narnia Window in his local church, Holy Trinity Headington Quarry, is one of the most beautiful pieces of stained glass to be found anywhere: it's mostly white, as befits Narnia's permanent snow-covered winter, and dominated by a majestic image of the lion Aslan in one panel and in another the flying horse Fledge soaring elegantly over the deserted citadel of Cair Paravel. It's worth a trip to Oxford just to see it.

But the author's birthplace has also recently laid artistic claim to him, with a magnificent collection of public art. C. S. Lewis Square, in Belfast's EastSide, across the River Lagan from the city centre, opened in 2016 and is host to outdoor concert and theatre performances, markets and more. It also features more than three hundred native trees, so it covers a large area, but the highlights are the bronze statues scattered around and about the site, representing characters from the *Narnia* books: the White Witch, Mr and Mrs Tumnus, Maugrim, the Beavers, the Robin and, at a distance, surveying everything that goes on around him, a 10-foot-high (3-metre) Aslan.

He's a bit fierce-looking, this Aslan: his mane and whiskers are – well, bronze, obviously, so they're hard and spiky, and his mouth is just slightly open, as if he were considering taking a bite out of you but hadn't quite made up his mind. This is not an Aslan you feel tempted to stroke. The same is true of Maugrim, the Wolf, but then if you've read the books you'll know you don't want to go anywhere near him, with his flaming eyes and his mouth wide open in a howl of rage (on that occasion, being so angry that he has to howl is the only reason he doesn't grab Peter by the throat). Let's just repeat that: you'd be better off not stroking Maugrim.

The White Witch is cool and aloof-looking; Mr Tumnus the faun is smiling, his arms outstretched as if to invite you into his woodland retreat. The Beavers look suitably hospitable too, just the sort of creatures who would welcome you into their home and feed you (as they fed the children in *The Lion, the Witch and the Wardrobe*) tea and freshly caught fish and 'a great and gloriously sticky marmalade roll, steaming hot', just out of the oven.

Of all the statues, the representation of the Stone Table is perhaps the most faithful to Lewis's description:

> *It was a great grim slab of grey stone supported on four upright stones. It looked very old; and it was cut all over with strange lines and figures that might be the letters of an unknown language. They gave you a curious feeling when you looked at them.*

'Yep,' you'll think when you study the one in C. S. Lewis Square. 'That's what I always thought the Stone Table would look like.'

Everything, indeed, is as the Narnia lover would expect, except ... At the far eastern side of the square, a full-grown (bronze) man – Lewis himself, perhaps? – stands reaching out his hand to open a wardrobe the same size as he is. The door is very slightly ajar, as if Lucy had just gone inside, 'leaving the door open, of course, because she knew that it is very foolish to shut oneself into any wardrobe', and was about to discover Narnia. Or possibly it's an invitation to the rest of us. When he was commissioned to produce these statues, the sculptor Maurice Harron said:

> *I want to recreate the emotions within Lewis's world, so that – like Lucy, Edmund, Peter and Susan – you never quite know what's around the corner.*

Perhaps he was thinking that we too could venture through the wardrobe, beyond the rows of fur coats that attracted Lucy and into the magic of 'the middle of a wood at night-time with snow under her feet and snowflakes falling through the air'.

A Dublin Highlight

visittrinity.ie/book-of-kells

Trinity College Dublin is the Irish capital's oldest and most distinguished academic institution. It's the alma mater of any number of Irish literary figures, from the eighteenth-century satirist Jonathan Swift (see page 203) to contemporary bestselling novelist Sally Rooney (born 1991) via Bram Stoker (1847–1912), author of *Dracula*, Nobel Prize-winning playwright Samuel Beckett (1906–1989) and many more.

Going back a bit further than any of these distinguished alumni, in the magnificent Old Library you can see Trinity's greatest treasure. *The Book of Kells* is a twelve-hundred-year-old manuscript of the four New Testament gospels, so beautifully decorated that it's often referred to as 'the work of angels'. In addition to the gloriously illuminated lettering you expect from medieval manuscripts, there are innumerable portraits adorned with symbolic animals such as serpents, lions and peacocks, and the whole is embellished with intricate Celtic knots. It's likely that it was produced by monks on the Scottish island of Iona and brought to Ireland for safekeeping when the island was raided by Vikings, so it's survived not only twelve centuries, but potential pillage and a hazardous long-distance voyage as well.

Once you've finished boggling at the effect *The Book of Kells* must have had on its original ninth-century audience, to whom colour illustrations would have been a novelty, move on to the library's Long Room. Dating back to the early eighteenth century, it earns its name by virtue of being 213 feet/65 metres long and contains some 200,000 of Trinity's oldest books, including a Shakespeare First Folio and a first edition of the Book of Mormon. For two centuries this was Trinity's only library, so this is the space where Swift, Stoker and Beckett did their studying. In addition to apparently endless rows of bookshelves, the room is lined with a collection of marble busts, notably one of Swift and four recent commissions of distinguished women, including Lady Gregory (see page 209) and the feminist writer Mary Wollstonecraft (1759–97).

The Irish Literary Revival

abbeytheatre.ie

Check the website for times of backstage tours

Situated just across the River Liffey from Trinity College, the Abbey Theatre was co-founded as a national theatre for Ireland in 1904 by W. B. Yeats, Lady Gregory (see page 209) and others. To this day it makes it its mission to tell the whole Irish story to all of Irish society. A backstage tour covers not only how plays are staged today but much of the Abbey's history, which includes a great tale about one of the theatre's earliest productions, *The Playboy of the Western World*. Written by another of the Abbey's founders, John Millington Synge (see page 213), its portrayal of the Irish peasantry was deemed so insulting that audiences rioted. The play's American tour in 1912 went one step further: the whole cast was arrested in Philadelphia for performing an 'immoral or indecent work'. *The Playboy of the Western World* is now much praised for its evocative language, drawn from a poetic Irish vernacular, but clearly the good people of Philadelphia didn't appreciate that.

Two Dublin Satirists
Oscar Wilde and Jonathan Swift

oscarwildehouse.com
stpatrickscathedral.ie

Dublin ranks high on any list of European literary capitals and you can follow any number of literary trails there, either pre-ordained or of your own making. One of the most fun pays tribute to two of the most biting wits the city has produced.

Begin about ten minutes' walk away from Trinity College (see page 201), in elegant Merrion Square, where you'll find the childhood home of one of that college's many famous alumni, Oscar Wilde (1854–1900). The house is now the headquarters of American College Dublin, so you can visit only at weekends; guided tours give you an insight into the stimulating ambience in which Oscar was raised. His mother was the radical poet known as Speranza, his father William a distinguished eye and ear surgeon and amateur archaeologist and folklorist. Their Saturday afternoon parties – at which the young Oscar and his brother and sister were often present – were renowned for the writers, academics, politicians and actors they attracted; the artist John B. Yeats, father of the poet W. B. Yeats (see page 209), Bram Stoker, and another Gothic horror writer, Joseph Sheridan Le Fanu, were among their regulars. A portrait of the adult Oscar now presides over the first-floor salon where the gatherings took place. The current furniture didn't belong to the Wildes, but the 250-year-old oak floorboards are genuine, and the imposing Georgian stairwell, the stained glass of the front door, and the cabinets in William's consulting room all give an impression of what the house must have been like when the budding author was picking up what he described as 'the best of his education in boyhood' from this association with his parents and their talented friends.

Across the street from the house is the Oscar Wilde Memorial Sculpture, showing Wilde, his characteristic smoking jacket carved from green jade with a pink thulite collar, reclining against a huge quartz boulder. At first glance the expression on his face is – well, odd, frankly. But according to the sculptor Danny Osborne the left side is happy while the right side is sad, reflecting the deeply divided nature of Wilde's personality.

From Merrion Square, a pleasant stroll across St Stephen's Green will take you to St Patrick's Cathedral, where – more than a century before Wilde was born – Jonathan Swift (1667–1745) was dean for over thirty years. Dublin born, Swift divided his adult life between London and Ireland, becoming ordained as a priest in the Church of Ireland as well as establishing himself as a writer of satires and political pamphlets. Although he's now chiefly remembered for *Gulliver's Travels*, he gained notoriety with *A Tale of a Tub*, a satire on the various branches of Western Christianity, and *A Modest Proposal*, which suggested that Ireland's economic problems could be alleviated if the poor, who were frequently burdened with a large number of children, sold their spare offspring as delicacies to be eaten by the rich.

Nearly three centuries after his death, Swift's footprint is to be found all over the cathedral he served for so long. A roll of honour of past deans obviously contains his name; there's also an elegant marble bust, and the north pulpit displays his portrait, death mask, writing table and chair. His grave is marked by an ornate brass plaque in the mosaic floor and a scroll nearby quotes the poem he wrote as his own epitaph. Towards the end of his life, worried about his mental health, he gave money to establish one of the world's first asylums for the insane, and subsequently chose to be remembered by the lines:

He gave the little wealth he had,
To build a house for fools and mad
And show'd by one satiric touch,
No nation wanted it so much.

Long before W. B. Yeats and his contemporaries (see page 209) took up the literary cudgel on behalf of Ireland, the Irish people and Irish culture, Swift was a fervent supporter. He just had his own unique way of expressing it.

Leopold Bloom's Dublin
James Joyce

jamesjoyce.ie
Closed Sundays and Mondays
gardinerstparish.ie
davybyrnes.com
sweny.ie

£5 reward, lost, stolen or strayed from his residence 7 Eccles street, missing gent about 40, answering to the name of Bloom, Leopold (Poldy), height 5 ft 9½ inches [176 cm], full build, olive complexion, may have since grown a beard, when last seen was wearing a black suit. Above sum will be paid for information leading to his discovery.

This advertisement is pure speculation in the mind of Leopold Bloom, hero – if you can call him that – of James Joyce's *Ulysses*; he's wondering 'what public advertisement would divulge the occultation of the departed'. Unfortunately, there's no point in heading to Eccles Street to see if he has turned up; the house was demolished half a century ago. The doorway was rescued, though, and can be seen, shabby and in need of a coat of paint, at the elegant eighteenth-century house in North Great George's Street that is now the James Joyce Centre. Joyce (1882–1941) knew the room on the ground floor when it was used as a dancing academy, run by a Mr Denis J. Maginni, who flits through the pages of *Ulysses*, noted both for his 'grave deportment' and for being 'gaily apparelled':

> *... silk hat, slate frockcoat with silk facings, white kerchief tie, tight lavender trousers, canary gloves and pointed patent boots ...*

In real life, the dancing master was an Irishman called Maginn, who had added an i to his surname to make it sound Italian and thus more appropriate for his profession. The walls of the Maginni Room still display medallions showing elegant dancing figures that might have inspired Denis's pupils.

The action of *Ulysses* takes place over a single day – 16 June 1904. Today 'Bloomsday' is celebrated annually throughout the world, but nowhere as exuberantly as in Dublin. For a few days around the middle of June, the city comes alive with readings, performances, pub crawls and walks that follow the path that Bloom takes as he goes about his daily routine of selling advertising space for the *Freeman's Journal*.

There are plenty of guided walks, but if you want to do it yourself (or go at another time of year), you can dip into the novel more or less at random and find locations that feature in the course of its rambling thousand-plus pages. To pick just a few – also at random – there's the former red-light district, close to the now-defunct Great Northern Railway terminus in Amiens Street, where Bloom perceives 'miscellaneous effects of female personal wearing apparel':

> *A pair of new inodorous halfsilk black ladies' hose, a pair of new violet garters, a pair of outsize ladies' drawers of India mull, cut on generous lines, redolent of opoponax, jessamine and Muratti's Turkish cigarettes ...*

There's the Jesuit church of St Francis Xavier in Gardiner Street, where he contemplates music, confessing to himself that Wagner is a bit too heavy for his taste:

> *He also yielded to none in his admiration of Rossini's Stabat Mater, a work simply abounding in immortal numbers, in which his wife, Madam Marion*

Tweedy, made a hit, a veritable sensation, he might safely say, greatly adding to her other laurels and putting the others totally in the shade.

A neoclassical building dating from the 1830s, once described as the most elegant church of the period in Dublin, St Francis Xavier still prides itself on its music.

At Sweny's Pharmacy in Lincoln Place, Bloom wants to replenish his wife's supply of the soap that had made her skin 'so delicate white like wax', and asks the pharmacist to check in his book to make sure he buys the right thing:

The chemist turned back page after page. Sandy shrivelled smell he seems to have. Shrunken skull. And old. Quest for the philosopher's stone. The alchemists. Drugs age you after mental excitement. Lethargy then. Why? Reaction. A lifetime in a night. Gradually changes your character. Living all the day among herbs, ointments, disinfectants. All his alabaster lilypots.

Sweny's is no longer a pharmacy, but it retains the Victorian interior; today it hosts Joyce-related readings and gatherings in a potpourri of a shop that sells second-hand books, Joyce-themed t-shirts – and that distinctive lemon soap.

There's no shortage of *Ulysses*-related places to stop for refreshment ('Good puzzle would be cross Dublin without passing a pub,' Bloom muses as he passes Larry O'Rourke's on the corner of Eccles and Dorset streets, today the Eccles Townhouse), but your odyssey should definitely begin or end at Davy Byrnes in

Duke Street. There's been a hostelry on this site since 1798, though Davy Byrne himself was the landlord in Joyce's day and the pub has borne his name only since 1889. Joyce was a regular, as is Leopold Bloom: he refers to it as a 'moral pub' where the landlord doesn't chat, but stands a drink now and then. Here Bloom – having rejected the possibility of Dignam's potted meat as something cannibals might eat with lemon and rice – has a Gorgonzola sandwich and a glass of Burgundy, both of which are on offer to customers today. Whether the current owners would thank you for repeating Bloom's reaction of 'relish of disgust, pungent mustard, the feety savour of green cheese' is another matter.

While you eat and drink you can also admire the pub's unexpected art collection, which includes murals depicting Joyce's Dublin and portraits and sculptures of the author himself. Admire the architecture, too, as Bloom did:

> *Nice quiet bar. Nice piece of wood in that counter. Nicely planed. Like the way it curves there.*

And perhaps treat yourself to another glass of something. Bloom would have done.

Raglan Road, Dublin
Patrick Kavanagh

Today, Raglan Road is one of Dublin's most expensive pieces of real estate. Set back from its tree-lined pavements, luxurious residences vie for position with the embassies of Morocco, Mexico and Turkiye, to name but three. So it's surprising that a penniless poet should have moved here because he couldn't afford the rent just around the corner in Pembroke Road; and surprising, too, that he should have immortalised the street in verse when his earlier work had largely been about Ireland's impoverished peasants.

Patrick Kavanagh (1904–1967) was born into a farming community in County Monaghan and moved to Dublin in 1931 in an attempt to further his literary career. This was at a time when the literature of a newly independent Ireland was trying to establish its own identity, distinct from its British counterpart, by celebrating things that were uniquely Irish, including the poverty of its rural population. Kavanagh's background meant that, after early struggles, he was able to establish himself as an authentic voice. Indeed, later in his career, as his confidence and alcohol consumption increased, he would express considerable contempt for the effete literary types who were faking sympathies and experiences that came naturally to him.

So why 'On Raglan Road', in which an older man reflects on his unrequited love for a much younger woman? The story goes that Kavanagh, aged forty and anxious to impress a young medical student named Hilda Moriarty, asked her to read his work; she enquired whether he could not write about 'anything other than stony grey soil and bogs'. 'I will immortalise you in poetry, Hilda,' was his reply. (Not strictly true, as her name isn't mentioned, but he did write a number of other poems about her.) In 'On Raglan Road', the narrator, walking years later along 'a quiet street where old ghosts meet', recalls how he had loved not wisely but too well, as another poet put it, and had neglected his higher calling – writing poetry, presumably – because of his love for 'a creature made of clay'.

If any of this sounds familiar, it may be because Kavanagh's words were subsequently set to music – to a seventeenth-century tune that makes them sound like a traditional Irish folk ballad – and have been performed by Irish artists as varied as The Dubliners, Sinead O'Connor and Van Morrison.

Kavanagh himself was voted Ireland's second most popular poet – after W. B. Yeats (see next entry) – in a 2000 *Irish Times* poll, and you can see a rather po-faced wax likeness in the National Wax Museum in Temple Bar. More appealing, perhaps, is the bronze of him on a bench by the Grand Canal, a place where he often sat and, according to the sculptor John Coll, 'contemplated his life'. From the look on his bronze face, his thoughts can't have been happy ones. But he would surely have been pleased with the result: in his poem 'Lines written on a Seat on the Grand Canal, Dublin', he asks to be commemorated where there is water, 'canal water, preferably' and ends with the heartfelt prayer:

> *O commemorate me with no hero-courageous*
> *Tomb – just a canal-bank seat for the passer-by.*

He has got his wish.

Thoor Ballylee Castle, Galway

W. B. Yeats

yeatsthoorballylee.org/home

Open April–September, but can be viewed from outside all year round

ladygregoryyeatstrail.com

Any well-preserved fourteenth-century Hiberno-Norman tower is likely to be a tourist attraction, but Thoor Ballylee, near the market town of Gort in County Galway, draws visitors from all around the globe because of its connection with one of the key literary figures of the twentieth century, William Butler Yeats (1865–1939). Generally regarded as the greatest of all Irish poets and a devotee of Irish folklore, he spearheaded the Irish Literary Revival (see page 202) and co-founded – with fellow playwrights Lady Gregory (1852–1932), John Millington Synge (see page 213) and Edward Martyn (1859–1923) – the Irish National Theatre Society, later based at the Abbey Theatre in Dublin. But he drew much of his poetic inspiration from the building that has become known as the Yeats Tower and from the countryside around it. Another great Irish poet, Seamus Heaney (1939–2013), described it as 'the most important building in Ireland'.

Under Ben Bulben

drumcliffechurch.ie

Two hours' drive north from Thoor Ballylee (see page 207), some five miles (eight kilometres) beyond of the town of Sligo on the picturesquely named Wild Atlantic Way, you'll find the village of Drumcliffe (sometimes spelled Drumcliff) and a church dedicated to St Columba, the sixth-century abbot who founded the famous monastery on the Scottish island of Iona. Today's church stands on the site of a monastery that dates back to Columba's time.

What's left of that monastery is worth visiting for itself alone: there are the ruins of a round tower and several well-preserved and ornate high crosses in the ancient burial ground. But most people come to Drumcliffe to visit the more modern part of the graveyard, adjacent to the church, to see the grave of W. B. Yeats.

Yeats was born near Dublin, but his mother came from County Sligo and the family moved back there when he was a child. Despite his attachment to Thoor Ballylee, Sligo remained his spiritual home, what he

described as his 'country of the heart'. Towards the end of his life, staying in the South of France because of his failing health, he asked his wife Georgie to have him buried, when the time came, in the local cemetery and 'then in a year's time when the newspapers have forgotten me, dig me up and plant me in Sligo'.

A modest time span, you might have thought, for any Nobel Prize-winner, and in fact, with the Second World War intervening, it took Georgie ten years to carry out Yeats's wish. By then there was some dispute over whether or not the remains that were transferred to Drumcliffe were complete or even authentic. But the numerous visitors to St Columba's are undeterred.

Yeats did more than specify where he wanted to be buried: he wrote his own epitaph, in a poem meant as an inspiration to future generations of Irish poets. Called 'Under Ben Bulben', referring to the remarkable flat-topped rock formation that can be seen from the church, it was written when he was confronting his own imminent death. Its last verse goes:

Under bare Ben Bulben's head
In Drumcliff churchyard Yeats is laid,
An ancestor was rector there
Long years ago; a church stands near,

By the road an ancient Cross.
No marble, no conventional phrase,
On limestone quarried near the spot
By his command these words are cut:

Cast a cold Eye
On Life, On Death.
Horseman pass by!

Georgie, who is buried in the same grave, obeyed this wish too: those last lines are engraved on the tombstone.

It's a special place, Drumcliffe Monastery, with 1,500 years of spirituality at its back and Ireland's greatest poet looking ahead to the 'indomitable Irishry' whom he hopes will pick up his literary baton. On a less elevated plane, as with anywhere in this part of Ireland, the weather is unpredictable, but the views over lush green countryside and the rocky outcrop of Ben Bulben more than make up for that. You can see why a local boy – however well travelled or acclaimed – would want to be buried in its shadow.

In the early twentieth century, Coole Park, the estate on which the tower stood, was owned by the wealthy Lady Gregory, to whom Yeats had been introduced in 1896. An important patron of the arts as well as an established playwright herself, Lady Gregory welcomed Yeats, his brother the painter Jack Yeats, the playwright George Bernard Shaw and many others to her home, and Yeats soon fell in love with Coole and all that surrounded it. He describes Thoor Ballylee in an essay published in the collection *The Celtic Twilight* in 1902:

> *There is the old square castle, Ballylee, inhabited by a farmer and his wife, and a cottage where their daughter and their son-in-law live, and a little mill with an old miller, and old ash-trees throwing green shadows upon a little river and great stepping-stones. I went there two or three times last year to talk to the miller about Biddy Early, a wise woman that lived in Clare some years ago, and about her saying, 'There is a cure for all evil between the two mill-wheels of Ballylee.'*

It was that rundown tower and cottage that he purchased in 1916 or 1917 for the token sum of £35. He promptly set about restoring it to turn it into a summer home for his family, and from 1919 to 1929 spent most of his summers there. The Tower, as it was generally known, features in many of his best-known poems. 'In Memory of Major Robert Gregory', written as a tribute to Lady Gregory's son, killed during the First World War, begins:

> *Now that we're almost settled in our house*
> *I'll name the friends that cannot sup with us*
> *Beside a fire of turf in th' ancient tower,*
> *And having talked to some late hour*
> *Climb up the narrow winding stair to bed.*

'A Prayer for My Daughter', written shortly after the birth of his first child in 1919, is clearly set in the same place:

> *I have walked and prayed for this young child an hour*
> *And heard the sea-wind scream upon the tower,*
> *And under the arches of the bridge, and scream*
> *In the elms above the flooded stream.*

Other works refer to the battlements, the surrounding trees and the impressive views, all of which are available to the twenty-first-century visitor. You approach by crossing the river via a narrow bridge and the stepping stones, after which you can stroll in the gardens, admiring Yeats's beloved pear trees, follow the stream up to the old mill and back, then venture into the

Tower and up that famous – and narrow – winding stair. 'I declare this tower is my symbol,' Yeats wrote in 'Blood and the Moon', and you can see why.

If you have the car with you (and you probably do – it would be hard to get here otherwise), you might choose to take in other local sites, including Coole Park itself, where the names of Lady Gregory's famous guests are carved into the 'autograph tree', and the lake which Yeats loved is now a sanctuary for wintering swans, whose ancestors had inspired one of his greatest poems, 'The Wild Swans at Coole'. Then there's a walled garden at Woodville, once owned by Lady Gregory's brother; and the fine Celtic Revival cathedral of St Brendan at Loughrea, with its unparalleled collection of works from the Arts and Crafts movement, including stained glass commissioned by Edward Martyn, and banners embroidered by Lily and Lolly Yeats, W. B.'s sisters. Along with Thoor Ballylee, these sites are promoted under the guise of the Lady Gregory–Yeats Heritage Trail and are within about twenty-five miles (forty kilometres) of each other.

Seamus Heaney's remark about Thoor Ballylee's importance may provoke debate, but it's hard to cavil with Yeats's own view: 'To leave this place,' he wrote to a friend, 'is to leave beauty behind.'

Aran Islands, Galway
John Millington Synge

visitgalway.ie/explore/heritage-and-history/historic-buildings/teach-synge

Born and educated near Dublin, John Millington Synge (1871–1909) might never have become a successful playwright if he hadn't met W. B. Yeats (see previous entry) in Paris when he was twenty-three and just starting out as a writer. It was on Yeats's advice that Synge first visited the sparsely populated Aran Islands in Galway Bay, off the west coast of Ireland. He subsequently spent several summers there, immersing himself in the people, the language and the culture, and finding the inspiration for his best-known plays, including the riot-provoking *Playboy of the Western World* (see page 202) and the tragic *Riders to the Sea*. Having rejected the Christian faith in which he was reared, Synge was fascinated by what he saw as the pagan beliefs prevalent among the nominally Catholic islanders – the holy well that was famous for cures of blindness and epilepsy; the house that lay in ruins because its owner had been 'driven away by the fairy host'.

These examples are related in his journal, *The Aran Islands*, as are his first impressions of the home on Inishmaan (the 'middle island') in which he stayed. Now known as Teach Synge (Synge's House) and turned into a museum devoted to his life and works, it's a thatched limestone cottage, dating from around 1800 and refurbished to reflect how it would have felt when he wrote these words in 1898:

> *The kitchen itself, where I will spend most of my time, is full of beauty and distinction. The red dresses of the women who cluster round the fire on their stools give a glow of almost Eastern richness, and the walls have been toned by the turf-smoke to a soft brown that blends with the grey earth-colour of the floor. Many sorts of fishing-tackle, and the nets and oil-skins of the men, are hung upon the walls or among the open rafters; and right overhead, under the thatch, there is a whole cowskin from which they make pampooties [the local rawhide shoes].*
>
> *Every article on these islands has an almost personal character, which gives this simple life, where all art is unknown, something of the artistic beauty of medieval life. The curaghs and spinning-wheels, the tiny wooden barrels that are still much used in the place of earthenware, the home-made cradles, churns, and baskets, are all full of individuality, and being made from materials that are common here, yet to some extent peculiar to the island,*

they seem to exist as a natural link between the people and the world that is about them.

The house is close to the centre of the island, but a five-minute drive west will take you to Cathaoir Synge (Synge's Chair), his favourite viewpoint, used for centuries as a place from which to watch for shipwrecks. Looking out over those rolling North Atlantic waters, watching them crash against the neighbouring island of Inishmore and imagining the tiny canoe-like *currachs* in which the locals still put to sea makes it easy to conjure up the Aran islanders' true god. The real protagonist of *Riders to the Sea* is not the elderly widow Maurya, who has lost so many of her menfolk to the ocean, but the ocean itself, the implacable force against which they wage a constant but ultimately unavailing battle. As Maurya recalls poignantly to one of her daughters:

There was Sheamus and his father, and his own father again, were lost in a dark night, and not a stick or sign was seen of them when the sun went up. There was Patch after was drowned out of a curagh that turned over. I was sitting here with Bartley, and he a baby, lying on my two knees, and I seen two women, and three women, and four women coming in, and they crossing themselves, and not saying a word. I looked out then, and there were men coming after them, and they holding a thing in the half of a red sail, and water dripping out of it – it was a dry day, Nora – and leaving a track to the door.

'It was a dry day, Nora' – what a simple, haunting way of saying that the dripping water could have come only from that all too familiar sight, the body of a drowned man.

Synge was visiting the Arans when he was in his twenties; he divided most of the rest of his short life between London and Dublin, involving himself in politics as well as the theatre, and never far from controversy. But reading his work today suggests that a large part of his heart remained in these isolated islands, with their tragic, stoical people, forever buffeted by the unforgiving ocean and, possibly, just possibly, visited by fairies.

List of Illustrations

Index

First published in 2024 by
The British Library,
96 Euston Road,
London NW1 2DB

ISBN 978 0 7123 5494 3

Designed and typeset by
Nicola Bailey

Printed in the Czech Republic by
Finidr.